NEW MODEL ARMY

Also by Adam Roberts from Gollancz:

Salt

Stone

On

The Snow

Polystom

Gradisil

Land of the Headless

Swiftly

Yellow Blue Tibia

NEW MODEL ARMY

ADAM ROBERTS

GOLLANCZ

LONDON

The right of Adam Roberts to be identified as the author of this work
has been asserted by him in accordance with the Copyright,
Designs and Patents Act 1988.

First published in Great Britain in 2010 by Gollancz
An imprint of the Orion Publishing Group
Orion House, 5 Upper St Martin's Lane, London WC2H 9EA
An Hachette UK Company

A CIP catalogue record for this book is available
from the British Library.

ISBN 978 0 575 08360 8 (Cased)
ISBN 978 0 575 08361 5 (Trade Paperback)

1 3 5 7 9 10 8 6 4 2

Typeset at The Spartan Press Ltd,
Lymington, Hants

Printed in Great Britain by CPI Mackays,
Chatham, Kent

The Orion Publishing Group's policy is to use papers that
are natural, renewable and recyclable products and made
from wood grown in sustainable forests. The logging and
manufacturing processes are expected to conform to the
environmental regulations of the country of origin.

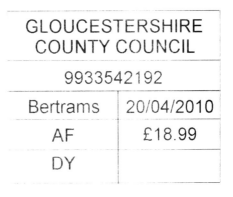
www.adamroberts.com
www.orionbooks.co.uk

As the classes of an aristocratic people are strongly marked and permanent, each of them is regarded by its own members as a sort of lesser country, more tangible and more cherished than the country at large. As in aristocratic communities all the citizens occupy fixed positions, one above the other, the result is that each of them always sees a man above himself whose patronage is necessary to him and below himself another man whose cooperation he may claim. Men living in aristocratic ages are therefore almost always closely attached to something placed out of their own sphere, and they are often disposed to forget themselves. Amongst democratic nations new families are constantly springing up, others are constantly falling away, and all that remain change their condition; the woof of time is every instant broken, and the track of generations effaced. Aristocracy had made a chain of all the members of the community, from the peasant to the king: democracy breaks that chain, and severs every link of it.

De Tocqueville, *Democracy in America*, II:2:2

It's too late, it's too soon, or is it—

The Hives, 'Tick Tick Boom'

PART 1

PANTEGRAL

1

I am not the hero of this story. Because I am narrating it, and because it relates events mostly from my point of view, you may conclude it is somehow about me. I ask that you remember, throughout, that it is not. The hero of the story – in the old style of these things, according to the way novels have traditionally been made – is that New Model Army of which I was formerly a component.

Transparency is one of those necessities for the proper operation of any democracy. Indeed, a democracy can be gauged as successful insofar as it approaches the asymptote of complete Zamiatin transparency. You find that thought distasteful. You want to preserve your privacy. I understand, although it necessarily means that you are not properly committed to the idea of democracy. It's hard for you, I appreciate; given that you've been conditioned from an early age to pay lip service to the idea of democracy. All I'm saying is that you don't accept the fullest consequences of that allegiance. I hardly need to add, besides, none of the so-called democracies in the world today are properly democratic. They are, rather, rigid hierarchies, whose oligarchs consent, every few years, to punctuate their routine with a single mass reality-TV-show-style plebiscite. That's not what democracy means.

If the ideological commitment doesn't persuade, then perhaps you'll at least concede that NMAs are a much cheaper way of putting an army together than the traditional mode. It is cheaper because we avoid the redundancy inherent in the older feudal military structures. Each soldier in our army sorts themselves for food, obviating the need for a specialized catering corps. We all have access – a simple credit chip – to the army's bank savings, and so can buy our own kit, and arrange for our own travel. It is in our interests to buy good kit, and to look after it; a soldier who bought cheap kit and pocketed the difference would suffer on the battlefield. And a soldier who simply stole money would swiftly be discovered by his colleagues and as swiftly dealt with.

There are dangers, of course, associated with having army funds pooled centrally. Thirty years ago this would have been a mortal weakness; for we would probably have banked with a national bank, and left ourselves vulnerable to that nation's government seizing our assets, should they at any stage become hostile to us, as they might well. But global and non-national banking saves us from that risk. Medical corps: we tend to ourselves and to our friends. Technical support, we attend to ourselves. It is much easier to do this, in the interconnected age of knowledge, than you might think – some little training, most of it arranged by the soldiers for themselves, augmented by immediate access to all the world's databases, wikis and resources covers most eventualities. As to staff officers, we have none. We monitor one another. It is, again, in our interests to do this. As to an officer corps: we repudiate so archaic-aristocratical a notion as *commanding officer*. We have no need for that sort of thing.

In those paragraphs you have the whole logic of the NMA.

I fought in a German NMA for a year; one of the three NMAs that fought at the Battle of Rawalpindi. That was a debacle, and the best thing I can say is that it was a greater debacle for the conventional forces than for us. After that I got out. I decided civilian life was for me. I could do this without letting my comrades down because, by the end of the week of

fighting, the three NMAs had only enough personnel to con-
stitute one NMA and, as it recoalesced, people had the
opportunity to leave without inconveniencing anybody else.
So I left.

I came home. Had you asked me then, as an individual, 'what
is home, to you?' I would have said UK-EU. Nowadays, of
course, I have a different answer. You'll see why. Back then,
though, I thought in national terms. After a year of floating from
one job to another it occurred to me that I was poorly cut out for
civilian life. I was, you will note, very far from the first soldier to
leave an army and spend months uncovering that obvious fact.

I decided I ought to go back in the army. One does not,
however, become part of an NMA by walking into a recruitment office. Were any NMAs so foolish as to establish such
offices, national governments would close them down. The
legal situation of NMAs, under national and under UN law is
– I need hardly tell you this – awkward, to say the least.

It came to me that I could serve a spell in a conventional
army, so I joined up with the British Regulars. But the New
Model Army had spoiled me for conventional army work –
officers peacocking around, giving me orders, and me *having to
follow the orders* no matter how idiotic they were. In retrospect
it was foolish of me to think I could stick it. But I am not
inclined to judge myself too harshly. I was thinking as a soldier
thinks – thinking what am I good for, really, if not being a
soldier? Setting me to work as a chef, or in a shop, or tailoring
marketing emails all day in a swEtshop, was like using a
scimitar to plough the soil.

So for a while I was in the regular army, and sixty per cent of
the energy in a regular army is expended in keeping the soldiers
locked in the hierarchy called, variously, 'rank', 'King's
Regulations', 'orders', 'the glorious traditions of the King's
Own South Downers'. This is the feudal model along which

armies have been organized since the earliest wars: you have a place, and you stay in it. You do whatever you're told by the people above you in the hierarchy, because they, effectively, *own* you – they may dispose of you, send you to your death, no matter how futilely, or idiotically. Some people say that the death throes of this system came with the First World War, when the officers exercised their deadly seigneur-droit via an unprecedented prodigality of deaths amongst the lower orders. I've never been persuaded by that argument myself. It is true that the British officers wasted their men's lives: yes, but they *won*. In those times, with those weapons and that terrain, and most of all with that feudal organization, there really wasn't another way *to* win.

The change happened later. It was this: democracy colonized new technology.

Consider the Second World War. History tells us that war was a fight to see whether a democratic system could beat an authoritarian one. The axis-fascists argued that democracy must be defeated, because it is in the nature of democracy to be riddled with internal contradiction, dissension, bickering and faction – that for instance no democracy could focus the *will* to stay in a long, destructive and expensive war – that the mob would grow tired of the hardships, losses and deaths long before an iron-willed fuehrer would give up. But then the democracy-allies won, and that victory was taken by many precisely to signal the inherent strength of democracy as against authoritarianism. So in the period after that war, 'democracy', or its slogan 'freedom', was boss. And many people took it to be a virtue so plain as to be self-evident.

So one of the shaping ideological forces of the second half of the twentieth century is that democracy is not just ethically better than dictatorship, it is *practically* superior. Hey, people said: look at the number of wars fought between the two regimes and always won by the former. This era was ushered in, and ideologically validated, by the fact that armies from democratic nations fought armies from authoritarian nations and won. But although that was the case, nobody suggested that *the armies themselves should be run on democratic lines.* There has never been in the history of humankind a properly democratic army. There were mental incapacities in place that made it hard for people even to think the possibility; but they boiled down to – release ordinary soldiers from their feudal bonds and they'd all run away from battle, like cowards! This is a version of the older anti-democracy complaint: give people the power to run their own countries and they'll do nothing but vote themselves bread and circuses! Or in more up-to-date form: they'll vote to cut taxes and to raise welfare!

That's not what happens, though, actually.

This is the way the story begins: in 500 BC, or thereabouts, Athens invented democracy. It's hard to believe that nobody had thought of running a country that way before, since it seems so natural and right – but so it was. At about the same time Athens got lucky; for only a few years after inventing democracy they discovered silver in southern Attica and were able to open a network of mines that made them, very quickly, very rich. Because they were a democracy this meant that the *state* was rich. So they called an assembly to decide what to do with all the money. Some proposed distributing it amongst the citizens to make them all, individually, wealthy. Others said, no: spend it, rather, constructing a navy, building and equipping ships, training our people to sail them. Everybody voted, and the democracy chose the latter option. In other words: right at the start democracy showed itself able to make the harder, not the softer, choice. Democracy, since then, has shown itself consistently able to prioritize harder, collective goals over shorter-term individual gratifications.

And it was fortunate the Athenians made the choice they did. It meant that when the autocratic Persians invaded Greece in 480, the Athenians were equipped to be able to defeat them at Salamis. And it meant that the democracy of Athens, more adaptable and flexible than the autocratic city-states that surrounded it, and gifted with more motivated population, went on within a century to overrun the whole of Greece and the eastern Mediterranean. Because of democracy they became the top dog in the area. An army of free men is always going to have higher morale than an army of slaves. That's common sense. But we didn't realize how true that was until the NMAs, because until the NMAs every army had been an army of slaves.

So: the important change did not begin to happen with the First World War, nor with the Second – for in those wars both ideological blocs were served by feudal authoritarian-model armies. It started to happen with the wikipedics of the end of that century (this new vogue was: the wisdom of crowds, infotopia, wikinomics). The new e-democracy utopianism is fuelled by new technologies that make it much simpler to canvas everybody's opinion quickly and efficiently. Then came the establishment of the first two New Modelled strike forces, and their extraordinary success.

Modern democracy is a watery affair compared with the Athenian original. In Athens every citizen ran the state; only slaves and women were exempted (unjustifiable exclusions by modern eyes, of course). Everybody assembled in the ecclesia and discussed affairs of state. Everybody got involved. Nowadays people abdicate their democratic responsibilities: elect representatives to rule on their behalf. Once they're elected they have years and years when they can do whatever they like; that's the nature of representative democracy. We don't have democracy, in the world of politics today; we have oligarchy punctuated by occasional contests to determine who has the most effective control of the media.

The received wisdom is that we can't run countries nowadays like Athens was run, because there are too many people – seventy million in the UK alone – to fit into a single assembly and vote on every issue. Maybe that's true; maybe not – seventy million can vote online easily enough. But there is inertia in the logic that determines how countries are governed. That inertia is so important a principle that it even has a specific political name and affiliation: conservatism.

That's by the by, because my concern is with the NMAs. I suppose it is true that the huge size of contemporary populations means modern democracy lacks *fit* to the Athenian original. But an army of good size – I mean, one large enough to be effective in proper battle, but small enough to retain manoeuvrability, logistic manageability, flexibility – is exactly the size of an antique Mediterranean city-state. This is one of the mistakes made by those generals who have gone to war against New Model Armies. They think they are fighting a corps of men and women. They are not. They are fighting a *polis*. That is why they lose.

2

There was a boy with a key embedded in his forehead.

Stop.

The British Army is 100,000 bodies strong or so, and can call, in times of greater need, upon 50,000-or-so reserves. Of course, were times to get direr still it could mobilize many more, for it has a large population base on which to draw. The British Army enjoys a fierce reputation around the planet. It is divided into a certain number of corps, divisions, brigades, all arranged according to internal hierarchical logics and distributed meta-hierarchically. It is centuries old.

Our NMA, 'Pantegral' as it is now known, consists of a shade fewer than ten thousand people – many of them British, of course, though not all. It is four years old – a mere toddler. It has no truck with internal hierarchies of any kind, and as an entity it related on similar meta-principles of equality with other NMAs.

150,000 troops against 10,000. There is no question which army had more, and more advanced, and most of all *bigger*, ordnance. I know the British Army: for although my service lasted only a few months, I did serve in it.

As far as my Regular Army military service goes: it became clear to me quickly that I had stumbled into a stiflingly feudal machine. I was like a twenty-first-century man tricked into the eleventh century and startled by how primitive and brutal existence is. So, when I realized this, I applied for discharge. It was declined. Accordingly, I went absent without leave. This

outraged the authorities, although it did not bother my immediate colleagues, men (exclusively) who had never taken a
liking to me. Since they were not bothered I had no qualms
about going, although it necessitated a good deal of skulking
about the country whilst Military Police – another costly and
burdensome paramilitary organization for which NMAs have
no truck – chased me here and there. I was saved, in effect, by
the Succession War. Since this war also destroyed me, as you
will see, my statement may look paradoxical: but you'll see it is
true. And as for the key, intersecting the bone of the skull –
what is it? It is the seed. And what does it seed? Let us
say, thought: or consciousness; or awareness. Awareness is,
perhaps, the best way of putting it.

3

Let's deal with the key. I must of course find the best way of dealing with this object. What I will do is put it in its context: the Battle of Basingstoke.

The first thing we saw when we went in at the front door was a child's body lying in the entrance hall on its back.

Not to get ahead of myself.

There is a particular way that masonry gets sheared and snapped by war. You realize in such moments that houses are in essence structures built from dust that has been compacted to an extraordinary degree, such that they unpack into clouds the size of counties. Spent cartridges littered the ground like cigarette butts. They gleamed when the sun put its head through the clouds, like a kind of treasure. There had been a firefight, here, upon this spot, and not long since. The houses all around were covered in the new-drilled rivet holes of bullets.

The bombardment had stopped, and we three darted out from our cache and hurried down the street, through all the metal confetti and the stony litter. The warrior knows. Take this house, here: its front messed and fractured, but the whole still standing and solid. Chunks of brick and concrete like icing littering the path.

Three of us went into that house to assess its strategic capability – three storeys tall, with a good corner view down two long straight roads. A bomb had detonated out front of it, and this detonation had instantly milled the windows to glass powder and pushed the grindings into the front rooms. But the main door still stood, and the plaster was only a little fragmented.

We came into that house and checked the hall, and there we saw a child's corpse lying on its back in the entrance hall. The child had a key embedded in its forehead. The key was an old-style piece of ironmongery: a metal ring and shaft at the end of which was fused an abbreviated row of metal tetris blocks. I suppose it had been in the keyhole, and that the blast outside had shot it out like a bullet straight into the head of that poor kid.

It was not pleasant to see that dead child.

The door, though, had held: a great windowless slab of black-painted wood, like the monolith in 2001, locked and steady on large nineteenth-century brass hinges.

We stepped through the empty window frames of the front room and came through to the hall that way. And there he was, that poor wee kid.

'What's he doing in the hall, on his lonesome?' asked Simic.

'He won't be here by himself,' I said. 'His parents are still in. I'd say they all decided to dash out the front door until a detonation persuaded them otherwise.'

We went all the way through the ground floor, our rifles like dalek-eyes, room by room. The kitchen was at the back, and it was in a state. It's easy enough to distinguish the sort of mess made by careless living – unwashed dishes, an open margarine container on the side, a pellet of milk souring at the bottom of a glass – from the mess made by people desperate to grab some provisions before fleeing. The fridge was open, humming to itself to pass the time. Pasta squirls littered the floor. Tins had been yanked from a cupboard and strewn. A bottle of wine lay Humpty-Dumptied upon the floor, contents on the lino in a red-mirror puddle.

The back doors were double glazed, the glass still intact although pierced at one place and marked as if by a spiderweb. A corresponding bullethole on the floor puckered lino into an 'oo!' The garden was a wedge of lawn that didn't lead anywhere.

There was an annexe off the kitchen, and inside this a sumo-squat washing machine had committed ritual suicide: its door open, its guts spilling out in sodden tangles of denim and cotton onto the floor.

I was first up the stairs, step by step, and came out onto a spacious landing. The carpet looked brand new. There was a fleur-de-lys pattern on the wallpaper. At the front was the master bedroom, the windows all powdered and scattered across the duvet and sown like seeds into the thick pile. Other rooms at the side and the back of the house were quiet and neat and untouched. At the back was a room with a piano in it. It was still turned on, its screen reading KRAFTWERK HARP-SICHORD YES/NO? Had they really been right in the middle of playing the keyboard, and unloading the washing, as troops scurried and exchanged small-arms fire all around them? Had they only interrupted their routines when the bombardment began literally knocking at their door? Civilians do indeed act in unpredictable ways in the middle of battle.

'They should have gotten out days ago,' said Simic.

'Hindsight's easy,' was Tucker's laconic opinion.

That poor little kid. Death by key.

All around us, in that town, such civilians as had elected, for whatever reason, not to become refugees were lurking in cellars and under stairways and wherever they could lock a door and pile mattresses. Thousands of them, probably. And this family had been in the middle of tinkling on their electric piano.

A narrower spiral stair rose from the back of the first-floor landing, curling tightly up into the second, top floor. As I put my foot on the bottom step the bombardment began again outside. It was the usual sound: the big drums, trailing their beats through the muddy noise of echo and structural collapse. Whooomph and whoah. Grumble, tumble, rumble,

There was some rapid wifi. '[This one's aerial,]' said Durcan, who was part of a squad down by the river. Three or four others duploed this assessment.

'[They're making passes from the east,]' said a trooper called Patel whom I'd never met in person, although I knew him well enough. '[We're on the library hill, and you can see them coming in, settling into attack flightpaths. They're aiming at the ring road.]'

'[They've got four cars coming in, down here,]' interrupted Capa, on priority. Cars, meaning tanks. He had two dozen comrades with him, and every one of them duploed this. The consensus was that our cars were the targets.

'[We're moving them,]' said Capa, the sounds of the detonations around him scuzzing his transmission.

'[What were they in the fucking *open* for?]' prioritized a trooper called Thirlwell. This was poor form. He was immediately blanked by twenty men for misusing priority: cut from the wiki for ten minutes: his contribution not being constructive, a ten-minute sinbinning was the usual sanction.

Four priorities jammed the wiki, and the system ranked them and rattled through them: three from soldiers in the west and one from Patel on library hill:

'[They're sending in shock troops.]'

'[Eighty runners, give or take, crossing the ring road now.]'

'Riders?' Tucker put in.

'[All runners no riders. Wait a mo.]'

'[They are bringing up their own cars.]'

'[Why *yes* they are.]'

'[Helicopters, behind the planes.]' This last from Patel.

'[I propose we group in Mall plaza,]' said Moffett. '[Good terrain for defensive combat.]'

'[I counterpropose,]' said a breathless sounding trooper whose tag flickered before resolving – presumably a symptom of electromagnetic interference attendant upon rapid arms fire near his position. Crowley, his tag said; and he was in the west. '[We divide by location, west to fight the western incursion, those near library hill counter the helicopter drop troops.]'

A trooper would have to have an outstandingly brilliant third notion, or to have had something pretty deadly urgent to report, to insert a third proposal at this point. It sometimes happened, but rarely. So we all voted. I was halfway up the second, winding stair when I keyed in my vote. It was pretty clear, on this occasion, which way to cast. Simic and Tucker were standing beside me, voting.

The decision went with Crowley's counterprop. It was the better proposal, in the circumstances, after all.

We got on with it. The rest of the communication was all orientation chatter: updates on where the enemy was massing, or moving. The three of us got into the top floor. The rooms up here more poky, and more cluttered with everyday junk. And here we found the rest of the family: a mother holding another kid, no more than ten years old, clutching very tightly to her mam; a father doing the same thing with a rucksack full of food. They had packed themselves neatly enough into the corner of the top room.

I kept a rifle on them as Simic went through the rucksack; but it was all food, no weapons.

'Why didn't you get out?' he asked.

The man stared at him like he had a tonguedectomy; but the woman said, 'We were going, but, but, but there was there a lot of sudden, a lot of sudden *noise*.'

'Noise?'

'Outside – it was all the sound of guns and it was other sounds. We got, we got spooked.'

'Try to get unspooked, now,' Tucker told them. 'For your own benefit.'

I checked the windows. The ones in the front room gave excellent defilades down the two roads on which the house stood. Along the western one I could see all the way to the large glass corporate building positioned, I knew, on the ring road. Now that I had a vantage point there was a reason to googlemap the area. I checked what I could see against what the map told me, and annotated it hurriedly with a few salient details, uploading to my comrades on the battle's wiki.

The man found his voice. 'Don't kill us,' he said.

'Hssh now,' said Tucker, taking up a firing position at a side window and also updating his googlemap. He had seen my update, so he must have had something else to add.

'Please don't kill us.'

'I tell you what, though,' said Simic, prodding at a hatch in the ceiling with his rifle butt, and apparently in a more talkative mood than we other two. 'The top floor's not the best place to hide yourselves. You got a cellar? You should go down into the cellar.'

'We couldn't get into the garden, because there was shooting, somebody was shooting,' said the woman, her voice high and warbly. 'And when we went to the front door there was an explosion and somebody shot Pierce.' At this the man began to cry like a child, ungainly gulping sobs. He clutched his rucksack close to his torso. The woman did not cry, though she looked stunned and unhappy.

The girl, holding spider-monkey tight to the torso of her parent, watched us with very large eyes.

It was really pretty upsetting. That is to say: I was aware it was going to *be* upsetting, at that point in the future when I would have time to think about it properly. It wasn't upsetting there and then. I was too busy to be upset, there and then. You understand.

'Hssh,' said Tucker again, to the civvies. And then, to me: 'That car?'

I could see all the way down the long perspective of the western road: a few parked civilian vehicles, a few vehicles smashed or overturned, a great spoor of debris all the way along. Worthy of a 1st January morning before the cleanup. Trash everywhere, the bins toppled and scattered. Water poured from a jag in the concrete where the main had been fractured, fountaining from stone like a magic source. One crazy civilian whizzed along the pavement on a pushbike. I checked the scene over a second time.

'See it?' Tucker prompted.

He was right. At the far end, the gun-limb of a small tank was visible poking out from a side street. His googlemap update had been spot-on.

I balanced my weapon, taking the best and most careful advantage of its aiming software, whilst Tucker pinged the whole troop's attention to his map update. Then we waited, and listened to the sound of the sobbing man in the room with us, and the distant accompanying cacophony of battle to the west. Listened to the distant scraping sound of jets in the sky. From time to time there was a ping as one trooper or another added details to the collective understanding of the situation. Simic went through to the back, checking all the remaining top floor rooms. It doesn't pay to be careless about that kind of thing.

But we didn't have to wait long. Once we'd reported the car's position, some comrades took it on themselves to flush it out. Far up along the street a shell's impact turned the side of one building into fizzing popcorn. The ground shook. The car rushed forward and both Tucker and I fired at the same time.

We drew, as if we were artists, perspective lines in smoke all the way from our building to the body of the car. Our projectiles hit its front turret and the whole component flew away, kicked clear from the chassis. The turret span whole in the air and clattered against the tarmac – it made, even at that distance, an audible clang. The recoil massaged my shoulder.

That moondust smell of gunpowder. The noise of our weapons-fire had shocked the sobbing man into silence.

Naturally I felt sorry for them, that civilian family. But by the same token, of course, that *feeling sorry* thing couldn't happen in that time at that place. Fighting, for a soldier, is all about emotional deferral. The ability to postpone those sorts of reactions, to take them and bundle them through the inward time portal into the future, is what separates the good soldier from the bad. That's not as hard to do as you might think.

I switched over my rifle's feed and directed thirty seconds of smallfire into the body of the car. There was a familiar and intense satisfaction in doing this. It was the sense of precision, I think, as much as the sense of power. The decapitated car lurched forward, turned, and whined with acceleration, speeding up the road directly towards us, its one remaining gun swivelling to orient a fix. Simic was at my window now, and followed my tracer line to aim his own punch-shell. The thing had covered half the distance when we stopped it properly, with a bloom of hard yellow flame and spreading anemone tentacles of smoke. It skidded and juddered, tipped up. It held for a moment, and then it went over on to its side. Nobody got out.

Ground troops were making doorway-to-doorway dashes in the distance. They were enemy soldiers. They didn't look that different to our own people, and might easily have been

mistaken for them, except that they hadn't identified themselves on the wiki. I would have liked to take some shots at
them, but Tucker pointed out one of the jets turning in the
sky. 'It's locking,' he said. He meant: let's go.

The problem jets have in modern warfare is, ironically
enough, precisely the reason feudal generals love them so much
– their speed. But of course speed is not an unalloyed good.
Good for dogfighting, clumsy for ground assault. It takes a pilot
an age and an age to turn his machine around and acquire a new
target, and it's too obvious to ground troops what he's doing as
he does it. Cities are too compact for jets to fight in, except
when it comes to long straights of preplanned strafing or
bombing. And when you are facing an army that doesn't bother
to put its own planes in the sky, so that there's nobody to
dogfight, then your planes, your outrageously expensive and
vulnerable planes, find themselves somewhat at a loss. They
could drop a big bomb, of course, and wipe out the whole town.
But let's consider that possibility for a moment. It would kill
large numbers of civilians, and a number of your own troops, as
well as killing us, which probably isn't what you want to do.
And besides, given the nature of modern weaponry, it's just as
easy to do that nowadays with a €10,000 suitcase missile as with
a billion euro plane. I don't doubt that feudal generals sit in
their regimental palaces just craving a good clean old-fashioned
war – where the enemy waste their money and resources on their
own jets, so as to provide dogfights, or at the very least where
the enemy lurk in Torah Borah caves and can be pounded from
the air. But no NMA would be so foolish as to condense all its
forces in that way. Modern wars are fought in densely populated
areas, and in the age of global media – news TV and the web –
which makes it harder and harder for generals to order actions
that will kill large numbers of civilians. So the old saw *air
superiority wins wars* no longer obtains. Why else, if not a

symptom of the sluggish inertia of hierarchical armed forces, have you not yet realized this?

Still, this particular jet was on its way to us.

'Downstairs,' yelled Simic, at the cowering civvies. 'I *strongly* recommend.'

Tucker took hold of the woman's arm and pulled her and her child along. Her complexion was white as summer clouds, and her eyes kept jittering left to right, but she held tight to her remaining child and stumbled down the stairs after Tucker. I held my hand out to the man, but he started wailing 'don't kill me, don't *kill* me' and quailed away. There was no time to loiter, so I left him. I told myself; these people aren't my problem. Or perhaps I didn't have time even to think that. I just left.

Their lad was on his back in the ground-floor hallway with a key embedded in the bone of his forehead. Nothing I could do about that.

And indeed as I thudded down the second set of stairs I heard the father coming after us, so presumably his fear was not so overwhelming as to prevent the thought *perhaps I'd better move* to intrude.

We clattered all the way downstairs and the three of us made it out into the back garden, as the plane lion-roared through the sky directly over our heads. Man, but that is a *loud* sound. The roof of the house exploded behind us. There was the whumph, and for a moment my shadow stood out against the lawn at bright noon. And then I was on my face in the grass and the soil and debris was clattering all around, and – it seemed – the jet was screaming in my ears right on the back of my head. But it passed. As the philosopher once said: everything passes. Wise, that. Death blew up the roof, and it knocked me down, and it yelled in my ear, but then it passed on. It was dragging its pterodactyl fingernails down a blackboard in hell. But it moved on quick enough.

We couldn't stay there.

Up we hopped, yea, and on we jogged. The jet was circling, its turning arc wide as a supertanker's and almost as slow. I daresay it was planning to come back and drop a scattering load of sycamore ordnance to mop up any footsoldiers; but we would be gone by the time it returned. I kicked down a garden fence panel. 'Which is closer?' shouted Simic. He meant: where are we needed?

'Library hill,' Tucker said. He was checking his arm to see where everybody else was, working out where we might be needed. 'Is that Dr Indulge?' he asked the arm.

A fxx and a fzz. We ran down a diagonal gravel path, past nodding red-pink flowerheads, twin beds of barbed and wiry rose bushes. My blood whooped and laughed inside me. There is no other thing that makes you feel so alive. We passed marmalade-coloured bricks, and a high narrow roof like hands at prayer, and then we jinked down the side passage. Simic hauled a tangle of pushbikes away to clear the way. 'Fucking *bikes*,' he said. They came away all in one tangle, as if they were right then in the middle of a pushbike orgy from which even war couldn't distract them.

'[Terence?]' This was the Dr's voice. Terence was his personal nickname for Tucker. Don't ask me why.

'Is this a direct patch?'

'[Direct.]'

We came out at the front of the house, and starting jogging down the road, past a VW Bonus, parked and immaculate. I had once contemplated buying exactly that model of car. The car next to it, a Ford, had all its windscreens smashed and a chunk of concrete sitting in a dent in its roof.

'Three of us,' said Tucker; 'coming up towards the hill from – what's this?'

'It's either Kaye Drive or the start of Kaye Avenue.'

'Where do you need us?' Tucker asked.

'[There's sixty or so enemy,]' said the good doctor. '[You'll come up behind them in two minutes if you come up the avenue. Distract them, would be good.']'

The jet roared again overhead, fifty metres to our right and a hundred metres up, and as it passed another house disassembled with monstrously exaggerated Brownian motion. Bits and chunks rattled on the tarmac all around us, and on our helmets and shoulders, like hail.

It was one minute's running, keeping our posture hunched and making as much use as we could of parked cover, to clear the residential area. Almost at once we saw where the sixty – fifty, I'd have said; but maybe there had been sixty a little while before – enemy combatants were positioned. Walmart Local was offering three-for-two on all bathroom products. I knew this because a cartoon figure on the storefront's screen was obsessive-compulsively repeating the same simple movements with his arms, and widening his eyes over and over, his mouth blowing out a speech bubble containing that information. He blew that bubble and popped it over and over again.

Beyond that the road continued its gradient upwards, and I could see the library itself: its broad window-curtain frontage chopped to icicles and stalactites of glass.

Somebody put in a general request; but this came from the other side of town from where we were, so we couldn't help. Half a dozen people closer chimed in.

We stopped behind an adshell – a bus shelter, it was. Poor cover, but it kept us out of sight. As I tried out a couple of aims, we were pinged.

'[We see you,]' said a gleeful Trooper Hesleff. I knew her from a chess tournament we'd both participated in, though I'd never met her face to face.

'In which case please don't shoot us,' I said, looking around. 'Where?'

'[We're seventy yards, north-north-east. What's your defilade?]'

The combatants were arranged in a large mass. Sloppy tactics, that. They had taken their cover partly behind parked vehicles, and partly behind the bulk of one of their own armoured cars. They were working towards concentrating their fire uphill, away from us.

'Good.'

'[Ours also. Count of three.]'

We counted it together, and then opened fire. The enemy, at first, did not know where the new assault was coming from. All bunched together like that – it was just asking for trouble. To be fair to them, when you have been receiving fire from the front, and you start to receive fire from the back *and* the side as well, there can be a natural sluggishness that prevents you understanding that the enemy is not all located in the same place. Half a dozen dropped before they could gather themselves to return fire; and another half dozen followed as they looked frantically from place to place. The quicker-witted amongst them withdrew into the doorway of the Walmart – although that, under its awning of glass, was hardly a safe spot. Others stood and tried to pick out targets down the slope, aiming at cars, buildings, anything. Most clustered more closely about their armoured car, as the solidest cover in the vicinity.

The car itself wasn't idle, of course: it span its turret about and sneezed fire promiscuously downhill. One of its barrages broke up the plastic of our adshell and forced us to flatten ourselves against the ground. But they weren't shooting *at us*, specifically. They were just shooting. The barrage swept away and we were able to get back up again and resume firing. Debris gravelled the pavement.

Then one of the Doc's threesome managed to squeeze a detonator-shell in between the cladding of the turret and the chassis. I'll give you this tip: no matter how effective its armour, any car that has moving parts – let's say, a revolving turret – has an unarmoured *seam*. And with modern weapons, and modern aiming technologies, that's all you need. Doc, or one of his fellows, put a shatter-shell in exactly the right spot first go, which is good shooting. Not that we wouldn't have squeezed one in there sooner or later, if we had persevered.

The turret snapped up like a Pringles' lid and flipped right over in the air before hitting the ground with a prodigious clatter. The second time I'd seen such a thing in half an hour. There was a flare of smoke and many tinkles as shards of metal rained through the glass front of the Walmart Local.

Then, comically enough, somebody from the innards of the car poked his head up through the hole. He did not look scared or angry so much as *bewildered*. Don't you think bewilderment is one of the most human of all expressions? After all, it is one of the most unselfconscious things we do with our faces. It always strikes me as an especially intimate thing. A soldier in combat ought to be guarded, and seeing one so evidently *unguarded* was like seeing him nude.

This fellow blinked, blinked, looked around. Then Simic aimed his weapon and put a bindi-mark in the middle of his forehead, and the fellow sat down again.

We had culled the fifty enemy combatants to thirty, or to a number, at any rate, in that ballpark, before they properly got their bearings on us. After that, things got hotter and considerably less pleasant. A dozen of them located us precisely with their aims, and began pooling their fire. That's one of the cornerstone tactics of the old-style feudal army: you need to *get a whole bunch of soldiers together*, and *focus all their firepower upon a certain point*. It's a strategy that has its uses, although it is also solidly arthritic, because it needs a whole bunch of soldiers to stand together, and it works best if the target stays where it was. We didn't.

Instead we extracted ourselves and made a run, behind a parked 4by4 and into a doorway. As we dashed we got pinged again: two more squads of our people had found their way to us, and started shooting at the shooters from different positions. I didn't look behind; but I can imagine that their confusion was pitiable. '[Down to ten]' reported a trooper called Jiggs (I didn't know him personally, though I'd spoken to him on the wiki several tines) and his words were swaddled, before he spoke and then again immediately afterwards, by bursts of avant-garde symphonics, all rattle and smash and white noise.

'[I thank you, sir,]' said the Doctor.

A jet roared overhead, loud, then *much too* loud, then going off. Its swollen sound faded, and then the noise of an approaching helicopter could be heard, creeping up behind. It was surprising that this machine was still airborne after an hour of combat. Of all aerial devices helicopters are most vulnerable to small-arms fire; and that it was still flying meant it had been lucky, or we had been careless.

The three of us jinked from our doorway to the end of the block, which is where Simic got shot. He was on my right, and he was running with his daft knees-high gait, and then, exactly as if he had tripped on a loose pavingstone, he was down on his front. I skidded to a stop and in doing so, stupidly, overbalanced such that I fell down myself. I hit the ground with my face and cut something in my mouth: tooth against tongue-tip.

Like: ouch.

I could see Tucker stopping in *his* tracks too, and probably he was thinking that we were both shot, so I scrabbled up to my feet again and waved him on.

I gobbed blood, and shouldered my rifle. The cymbal crash of a detonation, somewhere off to the left. Simic wasn't moving, which was not an encouraging sign. If I had stopped to think about the possible implications of this, I might have felt genuine terror, for I loved Simic more than any other human being. But it can be the case that the momentum of battle sweeps you along through even the profoundest fear. I didn't think about it. I grabbed a shoulder strap and hauled him, main force, across the pavement. The ground was covered with a layer of those transparent beads generated by the shattering of an automobile's windshield, and that made transport rather easier than it would otherwise have been. Like moving a menhir on ballbearings. Simic, you see, was not a thin man.

The air was full of gunfire's slow sizzle.

Round the corner, and Tucker took the other of Simic's arms. We pulled him faster now. My mouth was full of that unpleasant black-pudding flavour of blood. I spat, and spat again. Out came my saliva, Bovril-coloured.

We found some cover, and took a moment, laying him down. 'He's OK,' said Tucker, rolling Simic on his back. This meant: he's not dead yet. It did not exclude the possibility that he would be dead soon.

'Can you hear me, Sim?' I yelled, in the fellow's face. Or, more precisely, I tried to yell that, but the words came out all rubbery and peculiar, and as I spoke I dribbled blood on to his front.

Tucker pulled Simic's medical supplies from his pack and pressed an analgesic ampoule against his neck. Simic's eyes were open. 'Don't der,' he said. 'Don't der.' These seemed all the words he could get out. 'Der, der. Don't der.'

'I bit my tongue,' I wailed, the words smearing as I spoke them.

'Don't der-*dribble*,' Simic gasped, 'on my lovely clean jacket.'

'*You're* OK,' said Tucker.

'My legs have,' he panted, 'gone numb.'

This didn't sound good. We were all of us, as NMA soldiers, medics as well as fighters; in the same way that we were all engineers, and staff officers, and logistics and supply, and cooks and laundrymen. Which is to say, we were all these things with the help of google, and as much self-training as we could fit in to our otherwise busy lives. I spat, and spat, and called up the appropriate wiki. Tucker rolled Simic on his side and took a look at the wound. 'It's low, but to the side,' he said.

'Is it?' Simic gasped. 'Is it?' I've seen a lot of people shot; and I've been shot myself; and I'll tell you – the main thing about a bullet wound is that it knocks the *puff* out of you. It's a bodyblow punch in the first instance, and a sword-stab only subsequently. 'Is it spinal?'

'No way.'

'Kidney?'

'No kidney.'

'No kidding?' Simic wailed. 'Who's kidding?'

'With a *begging your pardon*,' Tucker asked his arm, putting out a localised ping. 'A little help? It's Simic, and he's shot in the back.'

'[Who's it?]' came an immediate reply. The speaker's tag didn't register at first. The air crackled. Overhead, a hundred metres or so away to our left, a helicopter thrummed past. That deep-resonant lawnmower sound, *as the sun beat down and I lay on the grass I could almost hear* – I glanced across at it. The fireworks package slung under its belly was dispensing, with insolent little puffs, packages of sycamore bullets; but it was firing away to our left, not at us.

'You're tag is stalling,' said Tucker, to this pinger.

If the fellow had said anything like 'where are you?' or 'what's your location?' or tried to give us *his* details verbally, we would have known something was wrong, and snapped the connection. But he did the right thing. He said: '[It's a firefight here, there's cracklefire, I'll try again]' and he repinged us. This time his tag came through fine: it was a man called Todd, somebody I knew a little. '[Who's down?]'

'Simic.'

'[I know Simic. He's a *Chelsea* fan,]' said Todd, disdainfully. Behind his voice there was a shower of battle noises on the line.

'The intersection of Hill Street and Silkmarket,' I cried. But my mouth was slimy with blood and my words didn't come out well.

'[I don't speak bloody *gibberish*,]' said Todd. '[Again in English, which is the global lingua franco after all, too-ra-loo.]'

'Franca,' said Simic, from the ground. He was a pedant, even when shot in the back.

Tucker gave him our location again, and we waited for thirty seconds or so. If Todd and his comrades could get to us to help they would, even for a Chelsea fan; if they could not then we'd have to try and sort Simic ourselves. I darted my head round the corner and pulled it back: a dozen or so enemy combatants were approaching. They were keeping a neat line, a discipline particularly prized, incomprehensibly enough, in feudal armies. They were not coming forcefully; but advancing hesitantly, and looking over their shoulders, so I deduced that they were in retreat, rather than advancing.

I took aim.

At that very moment the sun chose to wipe a great cloth of brightness over the pavement and the road, and let off its silent white fireworks in the glass frontage of the office block opposite. I looked up. The clouds gaped like a widescreen special effect: a beam of light broad as a football pitch. There was a cathedral-like aspect to this ceiling of grey and white and this sculptural, massy shaft of sun slanting down. I could see, far away and to the west, two helicopters; and I was able, as thought slowed, to connect what I saw with the drowsy bee-buzz somewhere else in my sensorium. Sudden light refreshed the whole city. The up-billows and reaches of smoke were there to link earth to grey sky. A dark line was tracing itself, etch-a-sketch, upon the white ground of the western cloud cover, and this line joined dots: rooftop dot; helicopter dot. The right-hand copter jiggled and bloomed into a chrysanthemum shaped tangle of fire and smoke. The sound of the explosion arrived seconds later.

Cloud sieving light.

Then the effect passed. I dropped my sightline as the clouds closed and the brightness departed from the stone and the tarmac. I began firing.

A target went over.

A dog appeared from nowhere and dashed hard across the road. That squeezebox way dogs run: compressing their whole bodies to tuck all four legs together beneath them, and then stretching themselves out *wide*. The beast went right through the middle of the troop and out the other side. Christ knows where it came from, or what it thought it was doing.

I shot again. Another target went down.

It's always at the back of your mind: if they get *to* me, they will *kill* me. Sometimes it comes into sharper focus and adrenaline spikes in your bloodstream and does its caffeiney work. Mostly that thought stays in the background somewhere, grinding along. But this keeps your focus. Then the memory of that boy came back to me, on his back in his own house with a key stuck in his forehead. Projectile. I aimed, and loosed another round. Another.

The enemy combatants were looking about themselves. Several skidded to a stop and tried skittishly to aim their weapons. But it took them seconds to work out where the firing was coming from. Others carried on their running, several in blind panic.

Tucker was on one knee beside me, shooting. Another target dropped. Another target dropped. The easiest ones to hit were the ones running blindly.

The others, getting more of a handle of their composure, were jinking, and trying to keep low, and going for cover. There were several parked automobiles nearby. There was a sports car. There were a couple of 4by4s. I tend to disapprove of 4by4s on principle, on environmental grounds. They can have a terrible effect on the environment.

I fired my weapon. Another target dropped. More than a dozen remained.

I was pinged. '[There's a push, a large group trying to break out, westward.]'

'[A good sign,]' put in somebody else: there was a delay on his tag, then it said McGinley. I'd never met him face to face.

I fired again, and this time my bullet went harmlessly into my target's body armour. It didn't, I could see, penetrate; but the force of it caused the man, whilst running, to put his leg out to the side and hop on the other foot once, twice. He regained his balance.

He turned his head in my direction.

The next ping was Todd. '[Can you handle your man Simic by yourselves?]'

'Sure,' I said. I fired again. Missed.

'[We'd come help, but we're bogged.]'

My target had, as the phrase goes, acquired me. I like that idiom. It comes from the vocabulary of *possession*, and that's the right way to talk about the selection of a target in battle. You take it; you *collect* it; it's yours; you take the pride of ownership in it. You don't want to let it go.

He levelled his weapon in my direction.

I pulled my head from round the corner at exactly the moment his weapon discharged, rapid fire. There was a ferocious clatter, and a steam-kettle spume of masonry dust and fragments from the edge of the wall. 'Let's,' I yelled, to Tucker. 'Let's.'

He had already shouldered his weapon and the two of us grabbed Simic and hauled. This was not ideal. If the enemy had figured that they were facing only three people they would come straight round the corner and we would be facile targets. But perhaps they thought we were a whole squad, because we were able to cover sixty metres or more without being fired upon. We hauled Simic into the lobby of a building – marble floors, a mosaic on one wall of a carp the size of a cow, all orange and tomato-red with olive-black eyes against a blue backdrop. Our footsteps echoed chunkily.

There was nobody at reception.

Behind the desk a tic-tac-toe grid of television screens showed varied perspectives of empty office rooms.

The lifts were working, which made life a little easier. We hauled Simic into one of the aluminium rooms and punched the button marked 2. And up we went, to the muted sound of Carole King telling us that we made her feel, that *we made her feel*, like a nat-u-ral woman – and the lift bell chimed. So we dragged Simic out and into a small hallway. Past a monolithic snack-dispenser machine. Through some double doors and into an open plan office. Our charge was gasping with discomfort a little now – which, if it meant he was getting feeling back in his legs, was a good thing.

Cluttered desks, and forty screen savers all rolling the same corporate logo across forty screens – the carp again. We propped Simic near the window, so he could keep an eye on things and possibly contribute, upending a metal desk between him and the glass.

Tucker rolled him on his front and pulled his clothes up to be able to examine his wound. Examining, here, meant peering at the gash and comparing it to some google images on his armscreen. Then I squirted in some stem-cream on the red crater, and applied a fat plaster. Simic had his own analgesics, if he needed them, but he didn't seem to be in much pain. Which was either a good, or a terribly bad, thing.

Back in the little hallway I was all for shooting through the Perspex of the snack machine to get at the contents, but Tucker disagreed. 'You'll just make holes in it and smash up the candy,' he said. So instead we pulled the thing from the wall and actually *unscrewed* the back – Tucker, characteristically, brought his tool stick straight out, whilst I fished for mine in amongst the detritus of my pockets. Then we went back through into the office and piled a heap of stuff into Simic's lap, all those bright coloured bars and packages, all those silvers and golds and sapphires and emeralds, all that crinkly foil wrapping. It felt more like treasure, more like *wealth*, than actual money. There's a childish element to it as well, of course. I know *that*.

'OK?'

'My legs are still pretty numb,' said Simic, checking the screen on his arm to see how the battle was getting on.

'It's a good vantage,' Tucker said. Below us several roads and a wide paved square were in plain view, bodies lain out irregularly like litter and many other signs of damage.

'When you say numb, you mean you can't feel them *at all*?'

'Just bugger off the both of you,' said Simic. 'Sooner we wrap up the town the sooner you can come back for me.'

We went down the stairs, chewing Snickers and slurping Diet Rand as we went. Risking a lift was one thing when we had a body to haul up; but of course a staircase is safer than a liftshaft. Battle is risky enough as it is, without adding unnecessarily to the danger.

4

Let's say there was another hour or so of hard fighting. After that we had most of the enemy concentrated, in a defensive knot, in a square of buildings in the south of the town. The planes had gone – not, according to the wiki, shot down; just flown away – and both helicopters had crashed to earth. I passed one as I made my way to the last stand: its cracked canopy like a whale's sorrowing head, its rotorblades twisted into dreadlocks, the metal of its body wrung like a cloth.

To summarize, then. Let's say our eight thousand men, coordinating themselves via their wikis, voting on a dozen on-the-hoof strategic propositions, utilizing their collective clever-ness and experience (instead of suppressing it under the lid of feudal command) – that our eight thousand, because they had drawn on all eight thousand as a tactical resource as well as a fighting force – had thoroughly defeated an army three times our size. Let's say they had a dozen armoured- and tank-cars; and air support; and bigger guns, and better and more weapons. But let's say they were all trained only to do what they were told, and their whole system depending upon the military feudalism of a traditional army, made them markedly less flexible; and that each soldier could only do one thing where we could do many things.

Anyway, we beat them.

Here's something else: they couldn't believe we had beaten them, even long after we had done it. I don't mean 'they couldn't *believe* it!' as a periphrasis for general astonishment. I mean they literally could not believe it. It did not seem real to them. Something was wrong somewhere, and the wrongness must be somewhere else than the feudal logic of old-style military thinking (they outnumbered us by so much! They were better armed by so much! They were a professional experienced army! And so on). But we beat them for all that.

There were three hours, give or take, of further fighting, although it was intermittent and we neither killed nor were killed in large numbers. They held out that long, I suppose, hoping that reinforcements could be sent up from Deepcut, where another Regular Army corps was fighting another NMA. But neither that force, nor the much larger body of men and machine to the north, was free to come to their aid. After it became apparent that nobody was coming the battle wound itself up smartly. We selected a dozen negotiators – some NMAs like to decide on negotiators before battle, but I've always thought that a short-sighted thing to do (what if they get killed or wounded in combat? It takes no time to have the wiki randomly identify a dozen troopers, and we're all, more or less, equally capable when it comes to such negotiations). Our negotiators went in and talked to the surviving ranking officers, and terms were agreed. We confiscated their remaining cars, and took some civilian automobiles as well; and then we loaded up the weapons we had seized into those and took them away.

We had a quick wiki debate about what to do with these two thousand unarmed men, some wounded (some wounded badly) and some not. If our enemy had been like us, their well men would have tended their unwell and everything would have gone better for them; but since it was a feudal force it depended upon specialized medics to look after the sick. Of course it is in the nature of such specialists that there are always too many of them, with not enough to do, in peacetime; and always too few, with too much to handle, in battle. The ranking medical officer insisted to us that his men be given hospital care. There was a hospital on the outskirts of town, but it wasn't a very secure space – wide-sprawling, low fences and hedges, lots of opportunity to get out. So that was not an option. Generally it is a good idea to put your defeated and disarmed enemy prisoners in entertainment locations: football or other sports stadia, large theatres or cinemas, where the exits are few and easily guarded. But this town had no football stadium, and its cinemas were too small to take thousands of men; so we voted and agreed to march them out to the outskirts to a commercial mall.

This took several hours, with the healthy ones carrying the wounded, and the officers carrying nobody at all – which, in a nutshell, is everything that is wrong with old style feudal armies. The officers busied themselves with complaining about the violation of military rights, which helped nobody, least of all their own men. Then we gathered them all in two car parks, and set a guard about them, whilst our own wounded received treatment. Of course we gave our own people priority.

Let's say the army we faced, regular troops, was twenty thousand strong. I would say we killed two thousand – killed outright, or wounded so severely they could not fallback with their colleagues. Another fourteen or fifteen thousand men had retreated from the battle in reasonable order and gone into countryside, whither we know not. Possibly to try and link up with their other divisions at Deepcut or elsewhere. A thousand more deserted, in ones and twos, when the balance of the battle shifted decisively in favour of us. The remainder were prisoners.

Let's say our New Model Army consisted of eight thousand men and women. We lost seven hundred dead, and two hundred wounded so badly they could not fight for us again. There were also a number of civilian deaths. The boy with a key in his forehead was one of those. Once the adrenaline diffused and dissipated I found myself thinking a good deal about him. The force of an explosion, which is the breath of death, blowing hard through the locks.

That was the battle for Basingstoke.

5

I don't want to fill this narrative with detailed accounts of fighting; because it would become tedious. And, more to the point, it's not the street-to-street stuff that is the theme of my narrative. Awareness is the theme. On the other hand, as I understand it, when putting a novel together you ought to include, near the beginning, a scene in which the hero goes about his business. That is what I have done: shown you our ungentle giant at work. As for Simic, we picked him up after the fighting stopped, and he was fine, with chocolate lipstick messily on his face like a chubby little child. We took him to a private clinic – a drive of a hundred miles, well out of the war zone. I personally admitted him to a small Med@End surgery. His spine was uninjured, which was good for him; although contusion and tissue damage in the muscles of his lower back, combined with damage to the bone in his hip, had compressed his spinal cord, which resulted in a temporary paralysis.

After that we proposed ransom for the soldiers we had captured. This sometimes goes over, and sometimes does not. On the occasions when it doesn't go over it will usually be because an NMA encounters old-school feudal officers who consider ransom demands outrageous and so flat reject them. That leaves us with the logistical problem of carrying several thousand people along with us – since, clearly, we do not have the facilities to incarcerate them in a standing gaol, any more than we have people spare to stand guard over them, or territory secure enough for such an antiquated arrangement.

Personally I think the advantages of bringing prisoners generally outweighs the inconvenience – for in what does the inconvenience reside, except in applying a large number of handcuffs and requisitioning many secure trucks? The advantages, on the other hand, are that these prisoners provide us with cover from aerial obliteration in areas where civilians are few. The better case, of course, is where feudal officers agree to the ransom demand, and here the advantages (I am stating the obvious and you will have to forgive me) are that we disencumber ourselves of a logistical burden and the army accounts receive a sum of money. We were not, at that stage, short of money; but money, like numbers, is always receptive to addition.

You will have heard stories of NMAs executing their prisoners, sometimes in the many thousands, so as to be rid of them before going to battle. I will not deny that such things have happened, although I tell you, and I expect you to believe me, that our NMA has never done it. There are dangers in the rhetoric here. Saying 'awful things happen during war' is to speak truthfully but unpersuasively. Alternately, to say: 'if our enemies established smoothly operating structures of ransom and reclaim these things would never happen' – although also true – strikes even me as unhelpfully coldblooded. My NMA hasn't executed prisoners en masse because we have never needed to. And naturally enough you want to know what would happen if we *did* need to? Let's say, if our enemies refused to ransom after a number of consecutive battles and the numbers of prisoners became unmanageable?

Well, what would happen in those circumstances is that we would take a vote on what to do. That is what democracy means.

You want more details. I must move into hypotheticals. I presume that different proposals would be put before the army:

as it might be, 'I say we shoot them all', and 'I say: we leave them all behind – find some warehouses, lock them all in and piss off out of it.' Then there would be a debate, with any and every soldier entitled to put his case. Some would say 'if we leave them and walk away, then the enemy will learn that they do not need to pay a ransom to get their troops back, and we'll never collect a ransom again.' And others: 'war is one thing, but mass-murder is a crime against humanity.' And then we would vote, and act on the result. The result might be: lock them up. Or it might be: execute them all, to make the point that we're serious about ransom. Or maybe it would be some clever compromise, or third way. It is the vote that is the important thing.

But it has never happened. Not in my experience. You may want to counter with the case of that Croatian NMA, the one the media call Don Quickshot. I heard about what happened after the Fighting in Zagreb. But that's not my personal experience. This is a personal account. Pantegral has never done that.

At any rate, after the battle for Basingstoke, we prepared for the transport of many enemy prisoners whilst waiting to hear from the British Army high command on the subject of ransom. Our ordnance had fared pretty well in the battle, and with the materiel we had seized we needed little by way of resupply, although half a dozen of us were delegated to take a plane to Turkey and bring back small-arms ammunition. This was a day trip: leaving before dawn and returning late in the afternoon. This trip was not without danger, given that we were at war; but much safer with one small plane than with a convoy of larger transports, something which was sometimes required. The trick is slipping through the crowded skies without being noticed. That's easier than you might think.

On the ground we prepared to ship out.

We are at our weakest when it comes to mass transit of this sort. It's not what we are best at doing. Moving in swarm, thousands of individuals making their own myriad ways, is our natural mode of transport. Moving en masse puts us at danger. But I do not offer this to you as a tip, since if pressured tactically at such a moment – should you, in plain language, seek to take advantage of that situation – we can easily eliminate the problem by killing our prisoners and dispersing ourselves. We would prefer not to, but it is an option available to us: and in that case the problem is removed. The only difficulty would be in killing such a large body of people quickly enough not to be disadvantaged tactically; but here the nature of NMA combat structures – the fluid and rhizomatic nature – was on our side. A feudal army would, I suppose, select a number of men as an execution detail, and work methodically through the mass of prisoners. But we were all armed, and there were more of us than the prisoners; so once the vote was taken it would be a simple matter for each member of the NMA to pick a prisoner, dispatch him, such that it would all be over with a single boomingly multi-tracked gunshot. We are all equally capable, and responsible.

At any rate, on that particular day we moved on.

What happened next was that we discovered our negotiatory delegation of six had been taken prisoner. This was short-sighted by the commander in question, a British Army officer, feudal old school. I could imagine his justifications to the others in his hierarchy. They would be: 'I will not treat these criminals as if they are soldiers.' But it was a foolish play. We, after all, were the ones who had won the battle. Negotiations would have given the British Army the chance to get two thousand of its men back, and perhaps to have arranged a cessation in the fighting. But this, of course, was not what our anonymous feudal officer wanted. He did not want peace. He wanted another battle, because he wanted to smash us. He could not believe that twenty thousand men at Basingstoke had failed utterly to destroy eight thousand (as he saw it) irregulars, rebels, mercenaries and amateurs. He was a stubborn-minded individual, I'd guess.

What this meant is that he – the giant who is the hero of our tale – shrugged his shoulders. We moved out and we trailed two thousand men in several dozen trucks, arranged in a convoy only in the sense that all the drivers were linked in the wiki, but otherwise travelling at different times along different roads.

I'll say something now about surveillance.

The British Army has access to satellite reconnaissance – billions of euros of money spent in launching and maintaining these devices – and this gives them a good sense of where our NMA is. Part of that technology involves them fighting (as it were) on multiple fronts with people who resist the culture of secrecy involved in blocking access to such imagery. Google Earth doesn't derive from military satellites, but since the Goog has now started updating their images quarter-hourly it's almost as good. Military attempts to block access to it run up against fierce civilian opposition. How could the media have covered the battle of Basingstoke otherwise? Those blocky knots of His Majesty's troops, in various sticky situations; the rapid ant-scuttle from all sides of our troops.

We also had toy planes. You would be surprised just how much recon you can get from a €50 toy plane fitted with a €70 digital camera – in many respects more than you can get from a satellite. We set a bunch of these planes buzzing about, and processed the info, and discussed things on the wiki, drawing on the expertise of people who knew the area and people who had escorted prisoners before. As a result we went through the countryside like coffee through grinds. We moved quickly and in a coordinated manner. There were localized regular army formations in villages and farms in the sweet British country-side, and a mass of troops was gathered at Reading, presumably for a counter attack. But it takes time to assemble tens of thousands of troops; or at least it takes time to do this according to the exacting structural logic of the old army. We could move much more quickly. We picked a path through half a dozen defended farms and villages. In each case we noosed an advance completely around the redoubt. I fought personally at an industrial farm called Honeysuckle, the main memory of which for me is the intense stink of the pig sheds – big metal hangers swarming with writhing pink bodies. This resulted in us suffering rather more casualties than was ideal, since the men we were fighting, lacking a route of escape, had no option but to uncover within themselves reserves of ferocity and determination. But we took all the targets, nonetheless. Had the positions been reversed the Regulars would either have fought, or else would have obliterated the farm and everything in it (men, pigs, all) from the air, so in that respect the feudal troops were luckier. But we took few prisoners, and vacated the sites as soon as we had prevailed.

This took a day and a half; and we debated – on the move – whether to rest and recuperate, or to push straight on for Reading. We were all exhausted, which was a powerful argument on the side of the former proposition, but the strategic advantage was with the latter.

The feudal enemy expected us to rest, because that is what they would have done. But we pressed directly into Reading, and fought rapidly through to the shopping centre and railway station in the town centre. The middle of Reading is littered with oversized cubes and boxes of brick and concrete, big edifices of glass. A little ordnance makes a big crash and bash in such an environment. Sheared stumps of concrete: the strands of iron cable poking up from the point of fracture like hairs from a wart.

To spare you the tedium, I will not give a street-by-street account of the battle for Reading. We ignored the suburbs and cut straight to the middle, and most of the fighting was by the river. It is larger than Basingstoke but is basically the same place – tight, antique centre, larger modern sprawl, a motorway running to the south. Motorways, by the way, are ridiculously easy to clog. Civilians are so habituated to travelling along them, and by no other route, that they continue to try to make their way even when a barricade of vehicles has blocked the route.

After Reading we rested in shifts, and reopened negotiations. A necessary preliminary was the release of our previous negotiators, and this was achieved by lunchtime the following day. I don't know what happened to the feudal officer who had ordered their arrest, for it is in the nature of the traditional hierarchies by which these armies are run that a metaphorical *losing face* can be as dangerous as an actual wound.

We had a long drawn-out, slightly ragged debate (because some of us were asleep, or else were waking up as others slept) about this. It went on for several hours. One upshot of it was that we appointed a new team of negotiators, and my name was put forward. This happened on the reasonable grounds that I had served in the British Army; although, since about a third of our force could claim the same distinction, I am not sure it explains my personal distinction. Indeed I put the point that, since I had absented myself from the British Army without leave, there was a risk that they would use that as a pretext to detain me. Several debaters thought the British 'wouldn't be so stupid as to try that trick twice', although my view was that saying so showed them ignorant of the conceptual inertia of the organization in question. But the vote was passed, and that was that.

6

The usual number is six emissaries, but given our previous experience with the British Army we sent only three this time, myself, and two women: Sol Barber, a soldier I had pinged several times in the previous two battles but never before met, and a sureshot called Theodora, last name unknown, whom I knew very well. We serviced our weapons – of course we took our weapons with us – and drove a vehicle through the outskirts of Reading. Most of the houses were more or less untouched; a little pockmarked in places: just a little work for the glazier and plasterer. There were some enemy corpses that had not yet been cleared from the thoroughfare, and many automobiles lay slumberous on their sides or backs.

Our vehicle's tyres hissed disapproval at being required to roll over the granulated glass littering the road. The wiki buzzed with all sorts of traffic: tactical speculation, and facts plucked from the internet, patches and apps to further enhance our wire-security wormed into the weave of connectivity.

Further out of town we passed a shopping mall that was in some disarray, and further still a cement works that had been hit several times by high detonation shells. It was everywhere covered with heaps and piles and grey snowdrifts of cement powder, like the aftermath at Pompeii.

We were emailing the British Army informing them of our route and our mode of transportation, but there was nevertheless always the risk that we would be targeted and killed as we travelled. That, indeed, would have been a safer way for a feudal army commander to vent his fury at defeat than *arresting* us, as had happened with our predecessors. Murdering us could always be passed off as accidental fire, or a misunderstanding, where locking up half a dozen accredited negotiators clearly could not. But we made our way out of town just fine, despite knowing full well that the enemy had a satellite tracking us, cannons adjusting their elevation incrementally as we moved, and planes ready at a single word to swoop down and burst us to bloody fragments.

I tried not to think about all that.

It was, actually, a pleasant drive. The countryside was starting to fizz with early spring. Blossom was all over the trees like the stuffing spilling from upholstery. There were very many varieties of green. You think of spring green as a single colour – but take a look and you'll see it's more than twenty: darker, lighter, sea-tinted and saltlike, or olive green, or bright young green, or green mixed with a dose of steadying black.

'Nice day,' said Sol Barber.

'That cloud?' said Theodora, not pointing. 'It's bruised. Means rain.'

'Pessimist,' I said, with excessive sibilance.

'Rain is not a *bad* thing,' Theodora elaborated, blithely. 'Nice refreshing spring rain.'

We drove along the high-banked road for ten minutes or more, and then we were compelled to stop by a herd of moo-cows: prodigiously massy and logjamming the way. The brainless *heft* and solidity of cows is a striking thing, when you encounter it up close – I know that saying so, of course, marks me a city boy. Anyway, the fact that these beasts had spilled from their field and now milled about untended suggested that their farmer had vacated his smallholding. Which was sensible of him, given the intensity of fighting in that area.

It was hard to get past the cows. They're too heavy to shove, and they greet attempts to persuade them with the blank walls of their eyes, and the saliva-tasselled motion of their enormous jaws. Theodora tried discharging her weapon into the turf-bank to our right, and it made a right old noise, but although several of the beasts stiffened and stopped chewing, a shiver going through their slow bovine souls – the Ghost of Abattoirs Future shouting to them across time – it did not clear them out of the way. In the end we inched forward in our vehicle, regretting that we had not commandeered a 4by4, nudging here a flank and there an arse until eventually, after twenty minutes or more, squeezing a way through, we came out the other side. It left our front bumper well and *truly* dented, I don't mind telling you.

By the time we got going again properly the light had dimmed and Theodora's bruised portion of cloud had swollen, as bruises tend to do. Then a thin drizzle began, raindrops as tiny and persistent as midges. Then the rainfall gathered pace, and the windshield wipers flapped ineffectually. Rain's glass acne across the view, constantly wiped away and constantly returning.

'Bravo,' said Sol, sarcastically. 'Brav-*oh*.'

We drove on to the sound of Nature's applause.

Theodora was chatting in a loud voice, to Sol I thought at first, until I realized that it was somebody on the wire. 'But these new software patches are not just inert,' she was saying, brightly. 'They're *adaptive*.' Pause. 'No, no, not given the stress our firewall is under, we need roaming antiviral. We really couldn't do without a roaming antiviral. The sorts of risks you're talking about are pure science fiction. The benefits outweigh any – I said, fiction. Science *fiction*, I said.' Pause. 'It's raining pretty hard here, so I'm finding it hard hearing what you – I said raining pretty hard here. The new antivirals are quasi-AI, so they can respond adaptively to – no, I said, *raining.*'

We drove on. The rain died away.

Soon enough we reached a checkpoint. These things, I can tell you, are another fetish of the old feudal army. They are not necessary things, because in this day and age it's possible with a wiTag to locate any and every element in an army, to know exactly where they are and where they are going; and that is a much more useful thing than counting people through temporary barricades. But this is how the Regular army had always done things, so this is how they continued to do things. A clutch of squaddies sang out 'halt!' and aimed their rifles at us, and we had to go through the rigmarole of stopping and getting out and surrendering our weapons and boarding a British Army truck to be shipped up the temporary command centre to meet the officers.

Sol Barber did a sudoko on her armscreen. Theodora watched the countryside go by, and made vocal notes as to the expressions on the faces of the soldiers we passed. There were a great number of these last, standing or sitting, smoking or talking, and none of them looked happy. 'Sucking a wasp,' Theodora said, of one. 'Face like a ballbag,' of another. 'Smacked in the gob with the glumstick,' of a third. They did all look pretty sorry for themselves, too. The technical term for this (if you'll indulge me) is *morale*, and maintaining morale is one of the major burdens placed upon commanders in the old feudal-style armies. It is a very major issue because a serf has naturally very *low* morale. What is more demoralizing than being a slave? So morale must be artificially inflated and maintained, and that takes colossal effort and application; and the slightest thing punctures it. These men were conscious of having lost three battles one after the other, each time to a much smaller and more primitively equipped force, and their morale had consequently fallen upon the bedrock of their own servitude.

We don't have this problem, and I'll tell you why not. Because we are not slaves.

Field Command was on a small hill, and ringed around with many large-scale thorn-crowns of barbed wire. We were greeted by a lieutenant and were requested politely to wait. This annoyed my companions, although it was what I expected. Hierarchical structures of power have their own little rituals and crotchets, and this business of forcing people to waste their time cooling their heels before granting them access to the VIP higher up the pecking order was one of them. It was supposed, I guess, to convey the sense that simply being in the presence of the VIP was a valuable thing, purchased with hours of tedium and inconvenience. To a mind inculcated into the logic of the hierarchy this all seems natural and normal. To a mind used to properly democratic interaction it is one of the oddest of cultural eccentricities.

The lieutenant attended us, like a servant (which, of course, is what he was) during this period of waiting. He took off his helmet, revealing unruly stuck-up hair. That, combined with the roundness and relative flatness of his face, rather gave him the look of a spork. His job was to chaperone the three of us until the Top Brass were ready. It was an easy enough matter to engage him in conversation, for he was constitutionally bored.

'I don't know how much you know about the British Army . . .' he said, at one point.

I told him I had served in his army for several months. This bewildered his poor young spork-face.

'I don't understand that at all,' he said. 'You fought *for* us? And now you've joined the marauders – pardon me, the mercenary group?'

'You've not been detailed to us on account of your diplomatic skills,' I noted.

His attitude was one of radical noncomprehension. We met these sorts of soldiers all the time. A man with pips on his shoulder like silver boils would march up to a group of us and say: 'Right, who's *in charge* here?' Such a person would fume at our blank looks. But when you're faced with somebody who plain does not *get* it, what can you do but look blankly? Who's *in charge?*

I mean: really.

My spork-face soldier had the grace to dip his head a little. 'I apologize,' he said. 'It's a little hard for me to understand. How can you call yourselves an army when you have no chain of command?'

'Perhaps,' I suggested, in return, 'you mean: how can we keep beating you in battle, given that we lack the chain? Do you really consider this chain essential to military success?'

He went pink, and put his helmet back on. The rosé-tint was anger, not embarrassment. Reminding a soldier that you have beaten him will, naturally, enrage him.

'Don't bait him,' advised Sol Barber.

'It's my turn to apologize,' I said, quickly. 'I don't mean to gloat.'

'You *have* been lucky,' he said, through lips set like a letter slot. 'Battlefield lucky.'

'Lucky would be one explanation. Or perhaps we've better tactics.'

This loosened him, and his cheeks turned back from rosé to chardonnay – their natural tint. 'That's what I don't get. How could you evolve these tactics? You're – forgive me, but you *are* – a rabble.'

'Your definition of rabble?' I asked.

'I mean that you don't really have any discipline. Not as I understand it.'

'I disagree.'

'No order, no drill, no chain of command!'

'But these things are not at all the same as discipline.'

'And another matter,' he went on. 'I don't see what's *in it for you*.'

This was an unusual question, and it gave me pause. 'How do you mean?'

'Well, it's not as if there haven't been groups of bandits before,' he said. 'Look through the history books. Bandits get together, they don't much bother with military discipline, grab what loot they can and then – you know. They disband to enjoy their gains, or else hole up somewhere safe – in the mountains, say. But that's not what *your* bandits do.'

'Indeed not,' I said, drily.

'Why do you exist?'

'Why do *you*?'

He looked puzzled at this, perhaps because he had intended his 'you' to refer to the whole of my NMA whilst assuming *my* 'you' referred to him alone. Rather than tangle with the existential anxiety implicit in trying to answer such a question, he said: 'What?'

'Your army,' I said, 'What's it for?'

'To defend the country,' he said.

'By?'

He peered at me. 'What?'

'How do you defend your country?'

'We fight our enemies.'

'Exactly. In point of fact, *that's* what you're for. Fighting.'

'Of course. But for a *cause*.'

'It's the same for us. What we are *for* is fighting. The present cause is defending ourselves, since the British Army is trying to follow through their declared aim of eradicating us. That in turn is because we were appointed by the anti-successionists to . . .'

'Nonsense, nonsense,' he said, waving his hand, evidently prepared for this last reference. 'Never mind that. All that Celtic fringe nonsense. That's just politics. I mean, what's in it for *you*?'

'I don't mean to be facetious,' I said, 'but I could again turn that question round on you.'

'You're asking why am I in the British Army? Because I take pride in serving, in defending my country. Because I'm a professional. '

'Because,' I said, 'you belong here.'

He didn't contradict this.

'That's the bottom line,' I said. 'I fight because that's what I do. And I fight for my army because that's where I belong. From *my* point of view, it's hard for me to imagine why a smart guy like you can feel so at home in a feudal organization like the British Army. Why fight as a slave when you can fight as a free man?'

He puffed at this. Again, it was, I concede, insulting of me to call this young officer's spade a spade. People installed in the feudal logic of their army don't like to be reminded of their true condition.

I was spared the need to apologize because that was the moment we finally received the summons into the presence of the officer in command, the Major-General himself. Through we went, accompanied by two red-capped military policemen, into the tent of the M-G. He (of course, *he*) was sitting straight up in his chair like a fairground target: stiff spine, wide shoulders. He was a young man; good-looking: evenly brown hair cut short and intense, algae-green eyes. He was wearing combat fatigues.

The Major-General's coffee was sitting, untested, on the desk beside his open laptop. Threads of steam fine as dental floss floated up from it. We had not been offered coffee. A snub, I don't doubt.

'Sit down,' he said. 'Sit down.' He nodded at the three folding chairs positioned before his folding desk.

According to the logic of the hierarchy there are two things to do: either to do as the Authority Figure says, or else to make some token resistance, insofar as the feudal world permits such a thing, by saying (for instance) 'I prefer to stand, sir', and then standing awkwardly with yours hands behind your back. We did neither. Sol Barber and I walked around the tent having a good old look at everything inside it. Theodora took a folded chair from a stack by the tent's entrance, unfolded it and sat down there.

The Major-General was not happy. You might think that, since he was near the top of the hierarchy, his morale would be higher than the grunts lower down, with the whole weight of the irrational do-as-you're-told army on top of them. But it was not so.

'Shall we begin?' he barked. 'I take it you *are* here to discuss terms?'

'How do you like to be addressed?' I asked him. 'I know you feudal army types are very particular when it comes to modes of address.'

His young face pinked at my insolence. 'I am Major-General Crawford-Smith,' he said.

'Well, Major-General Crawford-Smith,' said Theodora. 'Let's neg. Oh!' She opened her eyes very wide, like a clown.

'She,' I said.

'*Ate*,' Theodora finished.

The young Major-General looked from one to the other, and then stretched out his gangly longs legs under his table so that the boots poked through the other side. 'The time,' he said, 'is most fucking *undeniably* out of joint.' He spoke this modified Shakespeare with a sort of furious gloominess.

Theodora laughed.

We negotiated. There were two main matters of business: ransoms and the parameters of the ceasefire. We spent much longer time on the former than on the latter: the question of ransoming back to the British Army the several thousand of their men for a sum not in excess of eight hundred thousand euros. We haggled on a per man basis, rather than on the flat fee basis of some other NMAs. It was our view that a larger group of prisoners should cost more to ransom back than a smaller: since getting their men back in good health provided the army with a more valuable resource to then put back into the field.

I'm aware, of course, that this business of *ransoms* is a thing that excites very great animus against the NMAs. But I am honestly not sure why. To be precise, I can see why people are unhappy at their tax money being disbursed in this manner, but given that our business is, you know, *killing* people for a living, it seems to me low on the list of ethical outrages associated with our trade. Ransoming is an efficient trans-action: it speaks to our market share. People contract New Model Armies to fight their wars because we are much cheaper than regular armies, and the strategies we employ to keep client costs down is crucial to our activity. Scotland had once sold oil on the world market but was now reduced to that international dole, tourist income, supplemented by sales of a type of sulfur-coloured alcohol. She did not have enough money to compete, militarily, with England. That was why they hired us.

There are, it goes without saying, certain baseline costs associated with the business of waging war – a certain spec and amount of core ordnance, a supply of ammunition, per diems for soldiers in terms of food, healthcare and accommodation. We keep these to a minimum, and so we stay in business. Ransoms are a necessary augmentation of our income.

Nevertheless Major-General Crawford-Smith was deeply unhappy at having to pay *anything* to get his serfs back – he had the belief that the conquering army should luxuriously barrack prisoners during the war and afterwards give them back for free. But I believe he had not fully understood what is involved in serfdom. A feudal logic is such that serfs are there to be bought and sold, transferred from owner to owner. Ransoming was, by this logic, one of the least New Model things we did. He hadn't read *Dead Souls*, I suppose.

Then we discussed the ceasefire. Major-General Crawford-Smith wanted us to withdraw from Reading and to concentrate our force in Basingstoke, which town, graciously, he conceded to us. We, obviously, had no intention of doing anything so foolish, on either score. You could see, as he discussed the matter, he was desperate to dismiss us entirely – to hurl us from his tent, to bawl us out. He could not *believe* we had beaten his army three times in succession. Some part of his mind was saying: let's have it out one more time: for surely we'll beat them *this* time. But good sense overcame impulse. That's a pretty fair definition of military discipline, right there.

We came to an end of our negotiations, and everything was agreed. It left Major-General Crawford-Smith in a state of near bursting.

'I'll tell you what I think,' he said, his fury bulging palpably with his words. He jabbed at his laptop, presumably turning off whatever machinery was recording our encounter. 'And I'll *thank* you to pay heed. I think your New Model Armies are a *plague*. Do you understand?' His young, fruity vowels.

'Plague,' said Sol Barber, testing the word.

'Human communities have constituted armies to protect them for as long as humans have walked upright,' he said. 'And those armies have always *served* the communities. Service is the essence of the military life. That is what makes it a worthwhile occupation for a man. There is nothing nobler than service, and service in which you are prepared to risk your life to protect your community is the highest of all. But these *New Model* types of force serve no community but themselves.'

'I can't speak for any other NMAs you may have been fighting,' I said. 'But we were contracted by the Scottish Parliament.'

'That's not what I mean! You know *very well indeed*, that is not the point! Don't pretend otherwise! You are not a territorial army. You serve no territory.'

'He's right about that,' said Theodora, in an insolent voice.

'You're like locusts, passing over the land and consuming it. You have no *home*.'

'I shall interrupt you to correct you, Major-General Crawford-Smith,' I said. 'We *are* our home.'

But he wasn't to be distracted. 'You, sir, and you madams, and your entire force of armed irregulars – are an abomination. I don't use the word lightly, believe me. We have treated with one another here today, and as I am an officer in the British Army and my word is my bond. But you and I, we can look further than this particular treaty I hope.'

'By all means.'

'You *will* be eradicated. Your kind will be eradicated. That will, once the hiccoughs of the succession business are disposed of, that will be the great project of the times. Augustus Caesar's first claim to eminence was that he rid the Mediterranean of pirates. Some commander will perform the same purging activity upon these islands, to rid them of New Model Armies.'

'We're an army, just as you are,' said Sol Barber.

'Except that we're better at fighting than you are,' added Theodora.

'Pirates is an inexact comparison, I think,' I said. 'Pirates existed to steal money and make themselves rich. We're not interested in theft, or riches—'

'The ransom we have *just negotiated*!' he spluttered.

'Oh, sure, we need *money*. So does your army, Major-General Crawford-Smith. But we need this money for supplies, not for enriching ourselves. Otherwise we exist to fight, because we are soldiers and that's what we do. And we fight for our army because it's our home.'

And in the end, after so much bluster and feudal-gobbledy-gook, Major-General Crawford-Smith finally said something perceptive. 'But that is *exactly* what is so monstrous! You're a *closed loop*, the lot of you! You don't *have* the usual motivations or human habits. Your whole army is a self-sufficient organism that exists just *to keep itself alive*. It's a dragon, feeding on England, and roaming from town to town. But one day you'll encounter a Saint George. You mark my words. One day a Saint George will arise, and mankind will begin the business of wiping you and all your brethren from the face of the earth!'

The three of us looked at one another. 'I like that,' said Sol. 'Dragon. That's well put.'

The Major-General made polo-mint eyes at each of us in turn. His eyebrows made a dash for his hairline.

'*You* have the knack of talking to him,' Theodora said to me. 'Make him see the future belongs to the dragons. Tell him, the name of this fucking dragon is democracy, and if he doesn't like democracy he'd better learn to lump it. Feudalism's a dead end, tell him that.'

'Piracy,' muttered the young Major-General, his face pinking further, 'is nothing new. Mercenaries are *not the future.*'

One trick I have picked up: if you are in negotiations with a feudal officer – or, indeed, with a soldier lower down the rankings – then let them have the last word. It doesn't mean anything, in concrete terms; but you'd be amazed how malleable it renders them. It is another one of the peculiar features of the psychological distortion of the feudal mindset.

7

What was this war about?

The war began when the Scottish Parliament voted to contract us. Our experience (we are a giant, after all, and a warrior) begins with that action. But there are *casus belli* in any conflict, and it's good to be informed about them because they speak to, for instance, the morale and application of your enemy, the disposition of civilians and so on. The danger — here's me offering you advice, again — is that looking too deeply into the causes of war may encourage you to try and tease out right and wrong. That's a mistake, not because right and wrong aren't crucial and real in-the-world (of course they are), but because if the rights and wrongs could be easily sorted out then people wouldn't have gone to war over them in the first place. That's not an infallible description of human inter-action, I might add; but it is one that obtains in the vast majority of cases. War is painful and costly and nations or groups indulge in it only when less painful and less costly alternatives are unavailable. War is precisely the index of incompatible notions of right and wrong.

So, what can I tell you about the *causes* of the Succession War? Those causes trail a very long way back in time, into the historical relations between the Celtic portions and the English portions of these islands of Britain. There have been many wars between those two tribes. I wouldn't have space, in this document, to detail the half of them. Take the long view, and it's been mostly war, actually, occasionally interspersed with uneasy periods of truce. But a clutch of centuries ago the Saxon south-east got the upper hand and imposed an 'Act of Union'. The twentieth and twenty-first centuries have been, amongst other things, the story of a slow Celtic unpicking of that union. The first to do so were the Irish, fighting an old school war against the English. They took advantage, cannily, of the First World War to begin the process – an advantage not because the English soldiery were otherwise engaged (that war finished a few years after the Irish began their rising) but because it had been so devastating a conflict that the immediate aftermath was characterized, in England, as elsewhere, by weariness and war-satiety. So the Irish used that as leverage and fought their way to freedom, though their army was smaller and less well equipped. So began a century in which the Napoleonic logic of war – the logic that war is won by the Grand Army of the Republic and by throwing *all* of that Grand Army *wholly* into war-making – began to be corroded. This Total War philo-sophy was not demolished altogether in one go, of course. Indeed, the twentieth century saw some of the greatest achievements of the Grand Army philosophy. Most notably, perhaps, the Soviets repelled what ought, by all lights, to have been an unstoppable German invasion by simply throwing all their adult males at the invaders. That worked in 1940; and it might work in 2030 too, except that the terrain has changed – the social terrain, the cultural terrain, the technological terrain. And for those who could see, the nature of war had changed too. Mao took a small band and conquered the enormous military of the old Chinese regime. The wasp of the Viet Cong beat the American tarantula. First the Soviets, and then the Americans and British, poured trillions of euros and hundreds of thousands of men and all the most expensive ordnance into Afghanistan and could not eliminate a small group of hairy, poorly-armed men. Then there was that business in the Indian subcontinent – although by then, of course, NMAs had leapt, fully armed, from the forehead of History.

This is to digress. Why did the Scottish Gaels hire us?

Again, this is to speak to the twentieth-century history of the island, which was governed in large part by Saxon-versus-Celt tensions in the four other portions of the former UK that had yet to declare independence. Some Celtic forces in Northern Ireland attempted to replicate the military success of the South, making sporadic, often amateur assaults upon English soldiers and English targets, in Northern Ireland and in mainland Britain. With, as the historians note, their bombs, and their guns, and their guns, and their bombs. This assault was prolonged over decades, an in-its-way impressive piece of determined application. But in the end it failed. They failed, history says, because they were fighting a guerilla but otherwise conventional war against a superior force, and – beginning in the late 1960s and fighting through to the 1990s – they could not capitalize on war-weariness the way the South had done. Perhaps that's true; but I'd tend to believe that they fought in too feudal a manner, and put too much of their energy into such feudal goals as 'holding territory' and 'status' and 'national identity.'

Some elements in Cornwall were also eager to free themselves from the English, but they were swamped by economic rather than military inundation. The fact that Cornwall is amongst the most attractive portions of the British Isles, in terms of landscape and climate, combined with its relative proximity to the English heartlands, meant that a great many English bought property and established lives there. As in Northern Ireland, a divided home population – some of whom wanted to fight the English, some of whom *considered* themselves English – vitiated the effectiveness of belligerency.

But in Wales and to an even greater degree in Scotland the situation was forced by an increasing concentration of wealth in the south-east. There was a temporary amelioration of this towards the end of the last century when the Scots capitalized on the oil discovered off their coastline. And a general UK prosperity meant that the English could make funding subventions to poorer areas of the kingdom and thereby buy out a degree of dissatisfaction. But the great crash of o8, and the emptying of Scottish oil wells by the mid teens, took away the money that enabled that strategy of financial pacification. Perhaps, indeed, people had even forgotten why nations imperialize in the first place – money, of course. Why else go to the bother and danger of building an empire if not for money?

As the twenty-teens ground on, life in the Celtic portions of the country became less and less agreeable. Recession deepened. The Scottish Parliament made a number of legislative gestures towards administrative independence. But the English asserted their control over the remaining natural resources. Then immigration – a classical source of national wealth, and one that had been previously spread around the whole country – dried up; indeed, it reversed in many areas. Such immigration into the island as still occurred (for historical reasons this was mostly from south-central Asia and Eastern Europe) tended to concentrate in the south-east, because that was where most of the wealth was still pooled.

Perhaps it seems that I am saying the root causes of this war are economic. Isn't such a statement merely tautological? We can do better than that.

The proximate causes are easy to identify. The UK monarchy, boasting an unbroken succession since William the Conqueror, but actually dating from the importation from Germany of a nineteenth-century Queen, had long since given up active political decision-making. But they represent, even in our century, a considerable political reality for all that, compounded of symbolic and semiotic potency and a degree of popular-cultural 'celebrity' acuity. And in the twenty-first century being a certain kind of celebrity was as important a feature of the political landscape as being an elected official.

By this light the seed for war was sown when Prince William, first son and heir of the King, died in a helicopter accident. He was a soldier in the feudal army at the time, although not on active service – the copter had been taking him, ironically enough, to a Scottish holiday retreat. Grouse, startled by the machine's passage, leapt into the air in large numbers. The rotors diced and minced birdflesh. According to the accident report some of the rivets in the cockpit's perspex dome were faulty. A weight of grouse smashed into the windshield, the perspex broke and the inadvertent missile disabled the pilot. The machine crashed into a Scottish mountain top killing six of the eleven on board, the prince amongst them.

You will remember – you can hardly have forgotten – the orgy of national grief that attended that one man's funeral. I was living in the south-east at that time, and *for months* it was egregiously a feature of day-to-day life.

According to the arcane Gormenghast rules that govern royal inheritance, the status of 'heir to the throne' passed over to the King's second and last remaining son. There were those who put forward the properly democratic argument at this – namely that power inheres in the people, not in one particular aristocrat; and that a nation cannot escape servility whilst still observing these antiquated traditions and making this antiquated obeisance. Who could deny the reasonableness of such a case? But the national mood in England was heightened and indeed hystericized by the first prince's death, as it had been by the early death of his mother in a car accident. Rational debate was impossible.

Opponents therefore took a different course. After a compacted and hurried portion of internal national debate the Welsh Parliament passed a motion that it would not recognize Harry's investiture as (again, according to the Gormenghast logic of the office's title) Prince of Wales. They refused this, they said, pending a DNA test to determine whether Harry was indeed genetically descended from the King.

Of course, it seems to me, and perhaps it seems to you too, that this sort of strategy ought to be deprecated, as precisely inhabiting the same archaic logic as the royalists. What do *bloodlines*, of all things, matter in the twenty-first century? The Welsh Parliament, though, viewed matters from another angle, and arguably it was a strategically canny approach. There were rumours that Harry, a man physically rather unlike his father, was the result of an extramarital liaison, long publicly suspected, in which his mother had indulged before his birth. The supposed father was still alive, and was not a King. The Welsh non-successionists insisted upon a paternity test not because they believed that would block the accession of a new Prince of Wales (even if the case had been proved and Henry disbarred – prodigiously unlikely outcome – there was a long queue of other members of the family who would have taken the position) but precisely because they knew the King would refuse any test outright.

So he did, and angrily. So did the UK government. Royalist supporters, particularly concentrated in the south-east, gave expression to the destructive nature of their anger. There were riots, and incidents of violent crime against Celts. The tabloid newspapers – dying a slow death, as newsprint passed out of economic viability, and desperate to regain their markets – showed quite extraordinary intemperateness. The Welsh reiterated their refusal, and when Harry was invested anyway (at

Windsor, not in Wales) their Parliament refused to acknowledge his authority.

The Scots were not far behind. An Act of Scottish Parliament declared, grandly and rather unrealistically, the dissolution of the Union. Although this Act was postdated, and would not officially become legislation until the death of King Charlie, the mere fact of passing it brought matters very quickly to a steamhead. Some said that the Scots Parliament did not possess the legal power to pass such an Act without a prior referendum – and as I understand this was indeed a detail of the Parliament's charter, although the idea of a democracy being bound by the legal particularities imposed upon them by an occupying power seems strange to me. But we have already established that I ascribe to a more radical notion of democracy than some.

The UK put troops on show in Edinburgh and Glasgow; armed patrols through the main streets, helicopters in the sky and so on. The central administration in London had, though it had permitted the Scots their own assembly, never been so foolish as to give this Parliament an army of its own – and indeed had continued posting fairly large concentrations of its own troops in those cities. During this crisis, these troops were brought out of barracks. British Army soldiers drove up and down the streets of the big Scottish cities in armed cars and small tanks, and marched ostentatiously and conducted drills and training exercises in the cities' parks. The talk was of 'calming the situation'. Other people talked precisely of *inflaming* the situation. Successionists, who believed in the virtue of continuity and the preservation of the older hierarchical and quasi-feudal orders, stressed the necessity of *preserving the line of succession* – which meant, on the surface, recognizing that Harry was heir to the throne, and beneath the surface meant preserving the old feudal, conservative traditions and structures of power. Anti-successionists, on the other hand, declared the virtue of democracy (not my kind of democracy, of course; not real *democracy*) and asserted the desirability of Scotland becoming an independent Republic. A Scottish populace that had been largely indifferent to these questions during the prosperous 80s and 90s were motivated to pick sides by the severity of economy hardship. And where these sorts of tribal affiliations are concerned rational self-interest is often subordinated to something more primal and vigorous.

Of course, it would not be thorough of me if I did not identify my kind – the New Model Armies – as another cause of the conflict. What I mean when I say this is that had the Scottish Parliament not had access to an effective army, they would not have been able to enforce their decision to split. By 'have access to' I mean, of course, *afford*. Scotland, never especially rich, was now markedly poor, and made poorer by what amounted to financial sanctions put in place by the English. Fifty years earlier they would have grumbled and put up with things. Now they had an alternative.

Representatives of the Scottish administration entered into negotiations with our NMA and with two others. We three tendered various contracts, and ours won.

If armies are generally speaking complex and very expensive assault weapons, NMAs are the AK-47s of statecraft; for we are cheap and easily available and reliable. This has changed the way states deal with states.

We signed the contract as Pantegral.

8

Have I already told you about the crazy academic?

You'd be in the middle of fighting a battle, fierce and very dangerous, and you might occasionally see a journalist. Most were canny enough not to risk their souls to get a story, but some would brave it, wearing two flakjackets at once and helmets that looked three sizes too big for them, scuttling from firing position to firing position in Quasimodo postures to interview us *in situ*. They got a battlefront by-line, which I suppose made their stories easier to sell. But this crazy academic was a different matter. He came from the University of London, and was doing research on *neural networks*, of all things. This was when we were fighting in Reading, and the battle was pretty fierce. Rounds were biting deeply into the masonry. The air itself was snapping and buckling with detonations. Then, in amongst the useful and tactical information, the wiki started to note this fellow – wearing a brown suit, they said, and carrying a *laptop* computer. You can't miss him, somebody posted; he has a real child-in-sweetshop expression on his face. And then I saw him with my own eyes, toddling along, asking various questions of various NM-soldiers, sometimes whilst they were in process of actually fighting, moving on again. He seemed to take rebuffs and abuse blithely.

He came upon me as we – myself and five comrades – were targeting a knot of enemy combatants trying to break out from a burning hi-fi shop. It was ticklish work, because they (I suppose there were something like forty people inside the building) didn't all come out at once, but darted out in ones and twos at irregular intervals, and ran pell-mell in all directions across and along the street. Accordingly we needed to concentrate and keep our concentration, whilst, of course, also checking and feeding the wiki, and keeping part of our attention on the general wire.

'Hello, I'm Professor Such-and-such,' he said brightly (I really can't remember his name). He had popped round the corner without warning, and without caution. It's a miracle somebody didn't shoot him dead there and then. 'I'm doing research on neural networks. Would you mind answering a few questions?'

'You answer one first,' said Tucker, with whom I was fighting at that moment. 'Are you a crazy man?'

'Ha! That's very good!' He was wearing a brown suit; his shirt was a *Watchman* design: a black ground and the sunlike yellow disc of a smiley, but with the red splatter minute hand showing four minutes past instead of four minutes to. 'I'll explain what my research is about, by way of,' he said, and his burbling was drowned out by an explosion, and a prolonged series of high-hat smashing noises. Then a dozen enemy combatants ran from the shop all together, several of them with their packs or uniforms actually on fire. We concentrated our shots and knocked all of them over. When the sound of rifle fire cleared, and my nostrils were twitching to the stink of cordite and propellant and the background whiff of something much, much less tolerable, there was his voice carrying on in its same burbly way, as if there had been no interruption. '. . . the applications in specifically *computational* terms. So, what I'm really interested in is the spontaneous generation of meaning nodes – you'll pardon my jargon – in horizontal networks. Like your battlefield wiki. Your battlefield wiki is an absolutely fascinating case study, in fact'

'Are you for real?' I asked, in my *Blade Runner* snake-dancer voice.

'I would certainly appreciate your help,' he said, fixing his gaze on me. There was no madness in his eyes; just a sort of childish enthusiasm. He twitched, when something very loud sounded, just as anyone would. But he genuinely did seem oblivious to the very real risk of death.

'AI?' I said.

'That's right,' he said. And there he was, opening up his antique laptop – it had keys, and everything! – right there in the middle of the battlefield. 'I'm not fond of that phrase, actually' he went on, 'because scientifiction has loaded it with so many distracting connotations. But that is more-or-less what I do. The moment where computation tips over a complexity threshold into something that approaches AI. My wrinkle, in terms of research, because,' and he snickered, as if he really were actually saying something funny, 'because everybody is researching AI at the moment! Really, everybody! So my wrinkle is the way *actual* systems work. Not lab-systems, or world-web systems, but systems that are designed to operate in hostile environments. And this is a pretty hostile, a pretty hostile, environment! I think we can agree!'

'You, mister,' said Tucker, leaning across, 'are plain surreal, mister.'

'A few questions then,' said Professor Such-and-such, tapping at keys on his laptop with his accusing finger. 'Do you find that your interpersonal connection, the link from soldier to soldier—'

'The wire,' I said, and three more enemy combatants came out of the shop. They were not in a good way, flaming and smoking. I don't really want to describe them, actually.

Describing them would bring them before my mind's eye with a little too much precision. So all I will say is that gunning them down was a kindness.

I recognize the irony in me saying that. Or perhaps you'd prefer some other term? Kismet? Karma? One k-word or other.

'I understand,' the academic gentleman was saying, speaking more loudly to be heard over the background noise, 'that you employ a cradle of ADAP firewall patches? Is that so? I'm particularly interested in the question of how quasi-AI, re-sponsive and adaptive software patches like those interact with the complex of your wiki networks.'

The roof of the building opposite was starting to roar like a lion, which meant that the rafters were giving way and air was being sucked inside at a greater rate. The whole expanse was a field of spiky yellow flame: a hologram of Bart's haircut on a Brobdingnagian scale.

'So let me be specific,' the university fellow was saying. 'The combination of ADAP patches and general interpersonal wiki communication. Do you find the wire more or less reactive after a battle, when compared to before?'

There was a smashing and a crashing noise, and the hi-fi store's roof fell in. We slung our rifles over our shoulder and made to leave – because those particular combatants were clearly dead, and there were other jobs that needed doing on that part of the battlefield. Three or four pings were asking for help. We didn't even need to discuss it amongst ourselves; the wiki showed a push of enemy combatants coming in behind three or four arm-cars, and we were off to join a concerted repulse. But Professor Such-and-such was eager we not go. 'Just a few more questions!' he cried, as we jogged off – folding his laptop and tucking it under his arm. He trotted after us head-high. How he didn't get a chunk of shrapnel or a bullet in his forehead I don't know. 'I won't take up too much of your valuable time!' Then, as we outpaced him, he called after us: 'research into naturally emergent functioning intelligences in high density computing networks could have material benefits—'

We went round a corner, and, looking back, I could see him trotting off in a different direction to find some more willing subjects to interview.

Did I say *bullet in his forehead*? I suppose I did.

9

But I've been over all that already. I have been scrupulous in giving you tips and hints, such that you can improve your battlefield success, and you have been consistently courteous and grateful. Or at least you have *performed* gratitude, you have *feigned* gratitude. Because you'll take none of this on board. You have your feudal ways, and you are attached to them even though they will get you killed.

You have no idea.

Let me tell you something. After Basingstoke and Reading, when we negotiated the first ceasefire, the British Army withdrew forces to an agreed number of barracks. Our force, on the other hand, dissipated into the country as a whole, as breath dissolves into the air. We all went to our various lives. Of course we were in contact with one another the whole time, though we were spread all about the country. And I'll tell you something more. We did not expect the enemy to honour the ceasefire – not because we considered them (you, I should say) to be any more dishonourable than any other army, but because you had been forced to accept a ceasefire after a run of lightning military defeats, the destruction of many millions of euros of your equipment and the death of many thousands of your troops. Which is to say, you had been compelled to accept ceasefire by force. And then, when you settled yourself in your barracks, and the Scottish Assembly declared Independence for Scotland, and crowds celebrated in the streets of Glasgow and Aberdeen, *you* would inevitably look around you and see no army in the field to pen you. In other words: we understood that the medium of the contract was force, and that when you assumed the force had disappeared you would break the contract. You thought, I daresay, that we had demobbed foolishly, prematurely, thinking our work done. But this is the core of your misunderstanding, and this is why all my tips and hints are of no use here. Because a member of a New Model Army is never demobbed, any more than the cells of your body decoalesce. The giant man you were fighting might flow and run about all over the place as perfect beads of silver, like the flowing robot from the *Terminator* films. But the beads are always quivering on the edge of reassembly.

The ceasefire had included a clause by which the British authorities agreed to treat NMA soldiers as legitimate combatants, and not harass them by law or otherwise during the cessation of hostilities. But although the authorities agreed to this clause they did not honour it in practice. Once they saw their foe dissipate they thought to disable it as it slept.

The first stage in this strategy was to use the civilian police forces to arrest as many members of the NMA as could be traced – which was many, since it is by our nature as a fighting force that we are promiscuously present online and in other modes of traceable interaction. Some of us were interviewed by the media. These, I believe, were taken to be 'ringleaders', or the equivalent to officers, by the police; themselves a feudal organization.

These soldiers were arrested. The police came for me too, when I was staying with friends, in a modest house on the outskirts of Woking. But I was not in the first wave of arrests, and so I was forewarned by the urgent exchange of messages with my comrades. So I arranged the pillows in a line under the duvet in the spare room and slept in the garden shed. When, at one o'clock one morning, the police turned on all the lights and staged their shouty-shouty, pistol-waving performance, I was able to take my pack and slip out the back of the garden. I was sorry for my friends, of course, for the inconvenience my presence caused them. I sent them money, months later, after we had comprehensively beaten the British, and it was safe to exist openly as a *homo NMAicus*. I was a cinder by that stage, but that didn't matter.

The majority of arrest warrants were for firearm possession, a technical illegality in the UK at that time. All eagerly, even hysterically reported in the British media. The illegality was a pretext, though, because we were still serving soldiers in a legally sanctioned army, and as such permitted to bear arms.

Seven hundred, give or take, of my comrades were arrested. The authorities intended, I suppose, to lock us *all* up pending a prolonged legal procedure – or if they did not aim so high as arresting all of us, then they sought to incarcerate enough to impair our ability to function as a military unit.

We were disinclined to play by these rules.

We reformed in al fresco units, and coalesced wherever our people were imprisoned. Mostly this meant towns where there were prisons. Sometimes it meant police stations or other facilities. Then we got such weaponry as we needed and we destroyed the capacity of these institutions to detain people. The British police, being unarmed, put up no fight. We got our people out, and released a good number of civilian criminals as well; although personally – I took part in the breaking open of Wandsworth prison – what surprised me was how many of these old lags sat in the corners of their cracked-open cells and said they preferred to sit out the rest of their sentences.

As we drove away from Wandsworth with a van full of newly liberated comrades, the conversation was taken up, for the first ten minutes or so, with a great deal of whooping and cheering and whistling. Fodior, our best driver, span the steering wheel to take and overtake and hurtle through lights, and we rattled westward and on to the M3. We got to talking. Several of our liberated comrades had fallen asleep. Those that remained awake were saying: 'The interrogations were constant. They kept hauling us off to ask us these questions.'

'Did they apply stress techniques?'

'Not so much. But they wouldn't *stop* with the questions. Back to the cells, and I'd lie me down to sleep, and just as my eyelids dropped – *bang*, and wide flew the door, and back once again to the interrogation room.'

'What were they after?' asked Raphael, wiping camouflage makeup from his cheeks with a wet-wipe.

'They tagged all our DNA, of course,' said Fodior.

'But what,' I chimed in, 'were the questions *about*?'

'Always the same questions! They wanted *ringleaders*! Give us the names of your ringleaders! Isn't that a crazy term, though, ringleaders?'

'Ringleaders,' agreed another freed comrade, waking from his sleep at this prompt. 'They kept banging on about ringleaders. Told them we didn't *have* any ringleaders.'

'Isn't that the point of a ring?' said somebody else, from the back. 'That it is a circle? That it's not led?'

'Arthur's *round* table,' said Fodior, in a loud and approving voice.

This seemed to me an ill-thought-through comparison – for didn't King Arthur's round table *have* a ringleader, after all? But I said. 'Did they ask anything else?'

'Told them we didn't have any ringleaders, they kept asking me about ringleaders. And they kept on asking us, over and over. They flat refused to believe that's not the way we're structured.'

'It's religious,' bellowed Fodior, over his shoulder. 'It's religious!'

'How do you reckon-o, my Fodio?' I called back.

'Folk see an army and they think it's been *intelligently designed*. They think: it must have been made by a single figure. Generals are Popes, you see, you see. But the world is full of complexity and functionality that has not been designed. People just don't like to see it in those terms.'

'The word makes me think, you know, Sauron's ring,' said somebody else.

The British authorities declared these actions to be in violation of the ceasefire; they occupied Edinburgh with military force and shut down the two-week-old Scottish Independent Parliament. They brought in a whole raft of new legislation, argued over and debated in their Parliament – supposedly a democracy, but in fact an archaic chamber of exclusion and privilege in which individuals are ranked according to an arcane logic from the bottom up: backbenchers, regular MPs, committee members, shadow ministers, Leader of the Opposition, junior ministers, senior ministers, Defence Secretary, Chancellor, Prime Minister. All these chickenlike pecking-orders carefully policed the debate and infractions of protocol were politely punished. That this place calls itself democratic is one of the pleasant ironies of which England has, historically, shown itself fond.

At any rate they passed their pronouncements into law. It became illegal for any shopkeeper to sell provisions to any illegal combatant. But, really: how were the shopkeepers to know? It is not as if we went into supermarkets in combat gear and shouted our affiliation to the tellers. It was made a requirement to display an ID card at all retail outlets; and at the larger stores they even checked these *cartes d'identités* against computerized databases. But there were plenty of smaller stores without the wherewithal to do this, and it was always possible to stock up from them; and besides ID cards were easy enough to get hold of. Easier than guns.

The Parliament also insisted on what they called a *border smackdown* – a wrestling term, I believe, and a peculiar one, in that context. *We need*, said the Prime Minister, *to stem the flow of illegal arms into our country*. Most unrealistic, really, especially given that much of the south-east of the country was in a state of war, a condition in which it is much harder than usual to caulk porous borders. We flew private planes down to the Med to collect some weapons; others we captured from the British – although it is fair to say that, after the first few weeks (when such seizures were easily effected) the enemy became more efficient at preventing these reappropriations. There was a certain difficulty associated with this for our enemy, in that ordnance, ammunition and supplies had to be constantly moved from place to place, which tied up a fair number of men, but it was better for the enemy than losing everything.

You want to know about Simic? They didn't arrest him. They didn't get old Simic. Perhaps they didn't know about him. He was being tended in a smart and expensive clinic, the best care money could buy. And then, when he was well enough, he came out and took his place again in the body militic.

We pooled a little under two thousand men in the country-side south of Reading. Back to our old stamping ground, the land still carrying the scars of our last visit. Another limb of our NMA hauled itself into being, gigantic muscles and sinews, outside Staines.

10

You want to know what was going on in my *personal* life? That's not the way it works.

I'll tell you about my father. He was not native, born in a town called Erm in Friesia. He had a little spiel about how the Friesians were the original English, and that this made him more authentically English than most of the resident UK population. But the truth is that Friesian, in modern usage, only makes people think of *cows* – which is spot-on, for my pater: he was a bovine, stubborn-skulled man. He came over to England to teach in a university, and he changed his name from Bloch to Block because, I believe, he thought it made him sound more English. In fact, of course, it made him sound less English (how uncommon is the surname *Block*!). But his subconscious prompted him to it anyway, because Block is what his head was. He was a broad-browed, wideset-eyed man with skin the colour of pink milkshake and he had white-blond hair and white-blond eyebrows and had he grown a moustache – which he would never do – it would come out milk-white too. He was not fat, although he did have a certain physical unavoidableness about him – because, I suppose, he *was* tall, and long limbed, and there was a lumbrous, awkward physicality to him. His neck was as wide as his head: as if someone had pushed a cannonball up through a pink membrane and drawn a face on the bulge. And he was rigid. When my mother moved to Turkey with a very nice man called Zafer his personality calcified even further. I was thirteen when Mum moved away, and Dad's first action was to send me to a boarding school – as if I were some infant from the nineteenth century. We argued over it. *Argue*, though, does not do the work needful, there, to convey what occurred between us. My position (a reasonable one I feel) was that I did not want to leave my current school; that all my friends were there; that I liked my school. My father's position was that he was a single parent now, and was too busy with his work to nursemaid a child. He said that boarding schools were one of the historical splendours of England, and that the experience would make me a man. It was not a reasonable position. I did not need nursemaiding: I was thirteen, and unusually independent for my age. I did not want to go away. He insisted. Understand: I do not offer you this as an exemplary example of his stubbornness, or of mine. His stubbornness was, rather, an absolutely consistent, continuous thing. He was like this *all the time*. I was my father's son. So we raged at one another: my rage taking the usual volatile adolescent forms, his rage manifesting its characteristic immovability, intense and placid-aggressive.

I suppose, now, after the passage of years, I could ask myself: why *was* he so angry? But I don't know the answer. I once had a boyfriend who, having met my father, diagnosed self-loathing. Maybe that's right. It's hard for me to imagine why he considered his self so loathsome. My mother was English and whilst my soul is like my father, I resemble her, physically, more than I do him; so perhaps there is a more straightforward psychological dynamic at work here – that he was angry at her for leaving him for another man, and he was punishing her vicariously by punishing me. At any rate I went to the boarding school. I had no choice. It was probably a perfectly fine establishment, but I was not in a state of mind receptive even to that possibility. I was hostile from the get-go to everybody:

teachers, fellow pupils, janitors, the school secretaries. There was some desultory attempt to bully me, ostensibly on the grounds that I was a poof, although actually because I put such effort into my fuck-you-ishness. But I was fairly strong, and physically brave, and I have the gift of vindictiveness. On one occasion I was ambushed by a dozen other kids, and debagged – which is to say, de-trousered – and dumped naked from the waist down in the middle of the school field. During this procedure I struggled like a person possessed by a legion of angry devils, but there were too many of them, and the trousers came away as a snake sloughs its skin, and I was left trembling violently with embarrassment and anger as they gambolled away over the turf waving my trousers and underpants in the air. I was forced, pulling my short shirttails down as inadequate loincloth, to creep to the school office. But here's the thing: I knew who had done it. Over the following fortnight I paid them back. I used a book on several. It was something I'd seen in a film. I would seek out one of my tormentors, when he was alone: leap upon him, push him against the wall, press the book against his face and then hammer the hardback as heavily as I could. I did it first to a boy called Tremain, and made a very satisfying amount of blood come out of his nose. Two days later I chanced upon a lad called Sinha who has also been part of that crowd, and punched him with my fists. Later that same day I gave another boy, whose name I can't remember now, the book treatment.

The following week I caught another of them, Dennis Corman, and actually broke his nose. He had to go to hospital, and I was disciplined by the school authorities. The Headmaster sat me in his office and gave me a talk about the Christian responsibility to turn the other cheek. I remember that conversation vividly, actually: because it was late afternoon and the sunset light coming through the windows made the

Head seem pinker than he usually was. That window was a tessellation of transparent panes except for two little inset stained-glass sections, Saint George, top left, and the Dragon, top right. George looked pretty cool, in his silvery armour and with a lance tipped by a blade shaped like a pack-of-cards spade and coloured like platinum. But the dragon looked much cooler, especially in the reddish light: its skin enamelled with ruby and purple, and gold coloured flames emerging from his open mouth. The Head was trying to explain a point of theological interpretation (a rather too subtle point, I'd say, for the context) about how turning the other cheek was the road to victory. If your opponent strikes you, he told me, you win by not striking back. To return the blow is to lower yourself to his level and so to lose. My thirteen-year-old brain refused to compute this. I asked, addressing the Head as 'sir' in that insolent way schoolboys have mastered, for clarification. Was he saying that defeat was victory? Wasn't that like Orwell's *Nineteen Eighty-four*, sir, where they say Ignorance is Strength and so on? Isn't that doubletalk, or ideology, or communism? Not at all, Block, said the Head. He sat behind his desk with both palms flat on the wooden surface before him. Christ is the Prince of Peace, not the Prince of War. But that's not to say he is the Prince of *Defeat* – on the contrary. He has shown us a better way to overcome our enemies. War is not the way to defeat our enemies: forgiveness is. By forgiving the boys who bullied you, the Bible says you will be heaping hot coals . . .

But *sir* doesn't it make more sense to say that Victory is Victory? But *sir*, doesn't God in the Bible say *I am that I am* – isn't that more God's logic? But *sir*, isn't God Truth, and isn't truth just another word for A = A?

He was patient with me, but eventually my stubbornness wore him down. 'Understand this, Block,' he said, eventually:

'what those boys did to you was wrong, and their parents have been informed. But you must let it go – do you understand? You broke young Corman's *nose*. I shall report it, officially, as horseplay; but it must stop with that. You are confined to house for a month as punishment, and after that we'll say no more about it. Do you understand?' I replied, in a surly voice, that I understood *sir* that I was to let it go because you say I must, *sir*. 'If that's how you choose to take it,' the Headmaster said, haughtily.

But of course I did not let it go. I beat a boy called Hilken whilst he slept, creeping like a Ninja into his dorm to do it: I stuffed a teatowel into his mouth and pummelled him, and ran away before the lights went on and all the hue-and-cry began. Then, the following morning, I tripped up Wray and kicked him pretty sharply in the ribs. I was confined to dorm, and told that my father had been informed. I was told that the governors were considering expulsion. But this was hardly a disincentive to me. I crept out of the dorm and followed Adrian Todd into the toilets. When he saw me he started weeping most piteously, telling me over and over that he was sorry, and begging me not to hurt him – offering me his trousers as a trophy if I liked and so on. But my father's stubbornness was in me, I suppose, and his show of weakness only infuriated me: so I bundled him into a cubicle and put his head down the toilet bowl, banging the seat down on the back of his neck as he writhed and shouting at him – I have no idea where this came from – *Todd means death! Todd means death!*

I was expelled. My father was very angry, in his implacably placid manner, at having to leave work and drive for an hour to collect me in the middle of a weekday. We drove back in silence, and as I sat in the passenger seat all I could think was that I had only paid back six of the twelve original malefactors.

I spent a month at home, sent to Coventry by my oxlike

83

pater. For a time he was involved in negotiations to get me returned to that school – negotiations with the Head over my contrition, undertakings not to reoffend, classes on anger management. In fact I was content to go back, not because I valued the school experience but because it would give me the opportunity to get to the remaining half dozen boys. But in the end it did not come about, and instead father found another boarding school, much further away, that was prepared to take me. I came there like Jane Eyre, with a reputation for violence, and was immediately subjected to a strict disciplinary regime. On the other hand, my reputation preserved me from bullying, although it also inoculated me against friendship. And I was miserable at this school. My only consolations were poetry and music – the music I liked tended to be old-fashioned, with an antique emphasis on elaborate lyrics poetically embroidering themes of alienation and unhappiness. I wrote a good deal in my Bible-coloured Moleskine. I did my lessons, and played sport with an aggression that intimidated the other boys.

I spent two weeks of the summer in Ankara with my mother and her boyfriend, and it was such a profound *release* – the sunlight, and the easy-going vibe of the house, and the sense of possibility – that coming back to the UK felt like dying. I decided that autumn to run away from the school. I knew enough to understand that I could not simply make my way to Turkey and present myself to Mum and Zafer with 'I've come to live with you!' They'd have to send me back, I knew. So I figured Spain, or the South of France, or Italy would be just as good. I was a tall fourteen-year-old by this stage, and was confident I could pass for adult. I ran away once in November, and hitch-hiked a ride from near the school gates, trying to get to London. Unfortunately for me the man who picked me up was married to one of the teachers, and had met me at some school event, so he simply took me back to the school. I tried again after Christmas and spent three days living rough before a police car happened upon me sleeping on a bench, and returned me once again to school. The next opportunity for escape did not present itself until much later in the year, and this time I managed to get to London, although then, maddeningly, I had an accident – I tripped on some wet red leaves on the pavement and broke my wrist. I carried this, in considerable pain, for another day and night, but I gave myself up at Casualty the following morning.

Thereafter they kept a close eye on me, and I did not run away again. Instead I joined the Officer Training Corps that the school ran, and dissipated some of my fury in drill and exercises. From there to a British Army sponsored university education at Cambridge, no less, since I am bright. And then into the British Army itself – and so here we are.

11

There's monotony in war, since fighting is always at root the same thing; but it is an ecstatic sort of monotony. We fought as individuals, and experienced the world as individuals do. But *as* individuals we were portions of a larger whole. We poured our misery in cups into that river and it washed it all away. We fought, day by day. Fighting was our whole being. That meant that we were constantly aware of death, and our resolve was tested every day with the danger and the loss of those comrades we loved. We recruited new men and women, and some of those grew in stature in the *demos*, and some died.

I kept seeing the boy with the key in his forehead. To think of all the dead people I had encountered – many of whom I had personally made into dead people – yet it was that little boy I kept seeing. Sometimes I would catch a glimpse of him out of the corner of my eye, and I'd turn my head and he wouldn't be there any more. But sometimes he would stand in front of me, in plain view, by moonlight or sunlight. A skinny lad, no more than ten, with those loose, ropy arms of youth, and those slouchy legs. But grinning at me, and looking straight at me. It is hard to concentrate on his eyes, because he has this weird little stumpy metal protrusion right in the middle of his forehead and it draws your attention. A short metal shaft, and the little piece of metal crenellation at its end, like a cyber-unicorn. The boy I saw, in Basingstoke, was white – death-pale, in fact. But when I see him about in the world he's as often black – not racially so, simply in terms of hue. Caucasian features inked dark grey everywhere, like one universal and unswollen bruise. He doesn't seem bothered to be dead. There's a question in his eyes. I stare at the key, embedded there in his forehead, and look at the end of it; as if the metal tines contain the answer to my question if only I could decipher it; as if they are not designed for a chublock but are rather letters in some other alphabet to be read: Љ or Ж or Щ.

You ask me questions. It isn't all about answers, though. Why do I keep seeing that boy, and no other corpse? I didn't kill him. It wasn't our bombardment that killed him, unless it was. I don't *think* we killed him.

Imagine a rocky coastline, trees growing close to the edge of the water. Imagine a sunny day, and the hours passing as the trees withdraw their shadow like sucking it up into their roots. And then noon passes, and the shadows start spilling out again. The pulse of balance, lightness and darkness. We breathe in light and it becomes darkness. We take the dry blue and cache it in the moist ruby of our lungs.

Simic recovered enough to come back to operations, and he and I hooked up with another man called Daltrey. He claimed to be part of the same family that gave the world the notable last-century rock singer, although a few quick web-checks proved he was fabricating this lineage. Not that we minded. We all have our little lies and performances, the little roles we play to unify the disparate portions of our consciousness, or to conquer our social anxieties, or to add flavour to grey lives. In the New Model Army we don't care about that; just as we don't care about your age, or your religious convictions, or your *lack* of religious convictions, or your ethnicity, or your sexual orientation, or sexual *re*orientation, or your gender, or those things the outside world considers handicaps. We only care about two things: that you fight, and that you be prepared to live democratically. These two things are hard requirements, of course; and some people come to us excited at the idea only to find them intolerable. Such people slip away, and that's all right. No harm is done. Our wiki firewalls get cleverer and more responsive every time the enemy tries to hack them. These ADAP patches and softwares integrate themselves into the fabric of the wiki communication itself. It's very clever; they're alive, thoughtful, canny. But in fact (listen now, this is important) I have come to understand that *fighting* and *democracy* are actually the same thing. Move the first term into the realm of the second we call it debate – democracy works best if debate is conducted briskly, candidly, sharply, with effective strategies such that the strongest case wins the day. If you reverse the semantic exercise and move the second term into the realm of the first, then what have you got, if not the NMAs?

You remember that old film in which there is a strange lumpy man, his body covered in a sheath of pink-yellow latex under which have been crammed various lumps and loads, bumps, cushions, silicon implants on his forehead, hot-water-bottles, all to give the impression of monstrous deformity. The film was called a number, in the hundreds, either three or seven – I can't remember, and because you've taken my webaccess away I can't check. Three, you say? Well surely it was always going to be one of those sacred integers. Nobody was going to make a film called *514* or *180*. But you know the story. Ancient Greece, and a Spartan story: a city-state sends a small army against a much larger decadent and corrupt feudal military force, to defend the gates at Thermopylae. According to the logic of that film the democratic force refused the service of the deformed fellow. That was where the narrative left reality behind. Any NMA worth its salt would say, You are strong enough to move about, canny enough to aim a weapon. Take this credit card and, with the help and advice of many people, accessed through this facelink wiki, buy some body armour and some weaponry. If you don't know from whom to buy such things then we will advise you; if you can't find the right stuff ask your comrades and they'll help. Then, when we go to war, contribute to the strategic debate, take on such tasks as are decided upon, fight as best you can. If you are too disabled to fight well then you will be killed – but if you (you know yourself best, of course) consider that a likely outcome, then it would make sense not to join us in the first place. That film with the numerous title got it wrong. We would *take* lumpy man, and he would fight with us, as he wished. If he tried, then, to betray us, then what could he do? If he tried to harm us from within, then we'd grok his wrongness pretty soon, and we would be able to act against him, because he would be inside the body. But why would he wish to do that? He would have gotten what he wished. He would be part of the whole, and no longer a remnant. No human being can live long outside the walls of the polis.

Betrayal, you see. Treachery, you see.

There are many different sorts of deformity, of course. The idea that deformity must always be visible, on the skin, or immediately underneath it (as in that film) is a foolish one. Look at *my* skin. Look – my hands! My hands!

We armed ourselves at Aldershot, and elsewhere, and converged in our swarming, coherent way upon Dorking. The enemy had by this time learned that they could not press us to a single decisive battle, after the historical model, and were trying to put in place plans to engage us with myriad smaller anti-guerrilla forces. So because they were not expecting it, we gave it to them – a large, pitched battle. Forces gathered at a large temporary camp south of Dorking, ready to go out – with police units as auxiliaries (in fact the authorities were spinning this as a police action with military support, rather than the other way around) – to scour the vale of the south in search of guerrilla bands. We moved in upon them at lunchtime, in force (and like a *thunderbolt* we fall) and caused a great deal of damage.

It was summertime now. A blue sky taut as a drumskin. Vivid quantities of birdsong.

There was a degree of panic amongst our enemy in the aftermath of this; them not being used (I suppose) to our mounting a single large-scale thrust-attack, after the manner of the old-style military tactic. They withdrew most of their forces rapidly into defensive positions inside the town of Dorking, leaving behind both large numbers of wounded and unarmed police. It is one curious feature of the police force of my native land that only a small portion of its officers is armed. They are supposed to enforce the law using, as I understand it, the moral force of their example and personality, as well as a piece of wooden broomhandle. Other countries are not so blithe on this important question, especially during wartime. But there you go.

We debated what to do with what amounted to a body of many hundred prisoners; and the debate took longer than these things usually do. Discussion was complicated by the fact that the national Chief Constable, the head of the civilian police authorities, immediately made multiple declarations on various media – in amongst a great deal of chatter about our lawlessness and our terrorism and our outrageous crimes and so on – that he would authorize *no* ransom payments for his men and women. He knew, he said, that the army had, previously, paid us ransom money, and he considered this a terrible tactical error, for it encouraged us in our kidnapping. The British Police Authority would pay *no* money to our illegal bandit mafia (and so on, and so forth), *no* funds from the British police would flow into the coffers of terrorists and wreckers and rebels (and so on, and so forth) and he *instructed* us to surrender our ringleaders to the processes of justice and law, to lay down our arms and to return to our homes.

It forced our hand, though. Some of us insisted he was bluffing, and that he would indeed pay us ransom, perhaps through private channels. Others advised taking him at his word, giving up the chance of ransom and ridding ourselves of the body of prisoners, either by simply turning them loose, or else by executing them. We could not simply sit on them. Events were moving rapidly.

What was happening, in fact, was that long-standing nests of disgruntlement, and principled objection, and local tribalism, were dissolving the bonds of the united kingdom. Some of this urge for independence was pseudo-national, or infra-national, as with Scottish, Irish, Welsh, Cornish, North Country, Asian-Muslim, Asian-Hindu, Polish and other knots and groupings. Some was simply oppositional, in that 'English' had for some decades been a signifier of generic oppression, and many sorts of people – religions, regions, subcultures – welcomed the chance to break that domination. Some of it was properly ideological, and some people welcomed the same technologies that had liberated the NMAs as a road to a wholly new social contract, in which all central authority would be rescinded and every woman and man would be their own country.

On the other side, of course, there was more than just the inertia of tradition. There were many people – the majority of the total population, probably – who did not want the united kingdom untied. They were brought together under the terminology of royalism, or successionists – those who wanted yesterday's UK to succeed into tomorrow – although I know many of them were not particularly wedded to the British royal family. But things like royalty stand in symbolic, not actual, relation to the world; and this was the banner that was raised. The British Army, for instance, had sworn an oath of allegiance to the King, and notionally fought for him. Those who supported the army included many Scots, Irish, Cornish, Northern, Asian, Polish and even Anarchist individuals; just as a good number of Southern English individuals supported the other side. But that is the nature of war. A country is never divided into two portions, a red and a blue. Try to pick up one or other half, and lift it from the map, and you will discover how many, how fine and how deep-reaching are the tendrils (red, or blue) that rip in scores and scars and channels in the other side.

We moved amongst the people, and to subsist we bought food and supplies, and sometimes shelter. Often these transactions went perfectly smoothly. Of course, because we were buying from shops in the same territory in which we were fighting we often encountered suspicion, and sometimes direct hostility, such that we were forced sometimes to buy at gunpoint, or sometimes leave empty-handed. But sometimes we would deal with people eager to be of help to us, and not always out of fear.

What I am saying is that the thing the media had been denying the very existence of for – literally – years, was now certainly in process: a war of succession. And whilst our contract was still officially with the Scottish Parliament, and they still paid us, it was clear enough that we were now fighting a bigger war.

Take that big battle at Exeter, for instance; the British did better against the NMA down there, which is what you might expect, since not every giant is as muscular as every other. Many New Model soldiers were killed. But the British were still beaten.

You want me to tell you about Dorking, and all those prisoners that had been thrust upon us. Understand that I didn't enjoy it at all. But sometimes things are needful. I don't say I was only obeying orders, because the shame of that defence – and it is a ridiculous, dishonourable defence – is not the orders, but the subordination of the actor to the authority of the person higher up the chain. To say that is to say 'I am not culpable because I'm a slave': who could bear to even try and avoid a guilty verdict on such terms? An NMA is not like that. I voted, and I shan't tell you whether I voted pro or contra, since that's not what matters. What matters was my fidelity to the will of the majority. That's what democracy means, after all.

The debate on what to do with the prisoners at Dorking resulted in a vote on a proposition from a trooper called Norris. The proposition was that we disable the prisoners and thereby free ourselves to move on. The vote was passed by a narrow majority, but a majority all the same. This, then, we did; and it was a squeamish and unpleasant process. We went among them shooting them in knees and shins, and the sounds in that field were very unpleasant: squealings like pigs in an abattoir, or deeper-throated howlings and bellowings. I wanted to say to these men: would you prefer we kill you outright? I wanted to explain to them that this was the consequence of their Chief Constable's public pronouncements, and that it had been properly and democratically debated amongst us. I wanted to explain that this was democracy and that this was mercy. But there wasn't any time for that; we had a lot of people to work through.

I discovered that putting on iPod headphones and listening to loud guitars helped me focus on the business; although I knew I was taking a risk doing this, since it made it easier for an assailant to come up upon me from behind. But it was better that than the alternative. I tried to aim for knees, since shooting them in the shins seemed to me worse. Either way, though, there was much blood, and little ricegrain flecks of bone, and they yelled. The bullets sometimes went straight through the kneecap leaving only a little hole and minimizing the bleeding. That, clearly, was preferable to a severed shinbone, or a carved-through thigh artery. But the problem was they *wouldn't* stand straight to be shot – they squirmed, or rushed, or tried to run away. They held up their plastic-cuffed wrists, both hands together like they were about to catch a cricket ball, and pleaded, and screamed, and begged. If they'd stayed still it would have been better for them. But they wouldn't stay still. Given these circumstances, and our own need for haste (let us say: for proceeding without delay) the amazing thing is not that a certain number bled to death in that field, but rather that this number was, relatively speaking, as low as it was.

I saw the boy with the key in his head with us, slinking in and out unnoticed between the people in the field, and hopping playfully over the prone.

When it was all done we informed the medical emergency services, and pulled out. We made our way eastward, towards London.

We talked a lot, in person and electronically, about what we had just done. I was even, I suppose I can say, a little surprised by how talkative we all were. We kept priority channels clear for tactical and emergency communication, but other channels blobbed into scores of little chatgroups, circles of justification and philosophy and anguish that swelled and burbled, connecting sometimes with other bubbles of talk. We didn't sit sourly on the thing. We talked it out.

The enemy was not ready to negotiate with us. That meant we were to keep fighting.

We fought the enemy at Chertsey, by the river, and then fought half a dozen skirmishes along the river, up to the bridge where the M3 motorway crosses the water. The banks were so crowded with boats and barges – pleasure craft, most of them – that it was as easy to fight on the decks as the grass. We commandeered some of these skinny boats and festooned them with explosives to blow the M3 bridge. Then we moved upstream to Staines where we snapped both the town's old stone bridge – a handsome two-span structure with a Victorian look about it – and also the bigger concrete edifice a mile or so upstream that carries the M25 over the river.

Once we had smashed these bridges we demobbed, dissolved into the country, eight thousand individuals loosed and disassembled for three days. We did this primarily to rest ourselves, and also to confuse the enemy – for they of course rampaged up and down to try and find us, and engage us. They assumed (which is to say, the media certainly did, and I believe army high command did as well) that the attack on Staines was a preliminary to a large-scale assault on Heathrow, the airport that stood not far away. Planes were all grounded, and a large concentration of troops dug into positions on the airport perimeter.

On the fourth day we reassembled ourselves. A pontoon bridge had been put together where the M25 bridge had been blown, and at Staines Town a wooden Bailey bridge was in process of being constructed. We targeted this latter and blew it up easily. Then, avoiding Heathrow (no planes were flying. It was heavily defended. Why should we bother with attacking the position?), we moved eastward into London. We spread ourselves widely, seeping through the outer postcodes, like mice through fields of wheat. As we moved we blew up bridges and mounted myriad small-squad attacks (six or twelve people) on police stations and official buildings.

A few hundred of us took to the underground railway network. This system had been subject to terrorist attacks in the past, but the authorities had done little to fortify it – to be fair to the authorities, and in point of fact, there was little that could be done. We took Putney and Queens Park tube stations without any opposition at all, moved the civvies out and blew up the rails. The authorities, naturally, closed the entire network; and the absence of trains actually made it easier for us to go into the tunnels at Hammersmith, move through them on foot, flashlight ovals wobbling on the walls, grey rats squeaking between the rails like they needed oiling. We laid down several dozen large-enough devices, all through the Circle and District lines, and then put some more in the central London stretches of the Northern, Victorian and Piccadilly lines. We cleared out and exploded them from above ground.

The underground railway was easier to disable than the above-ground network. It was an easy matter to snap the rails with explosives, of course; but the enemy repaired them with impressive rapidity. That hardly mattered. We blew a few more Thames bridges, and positioned other devices to break gas mains – making great bright feathers of flame that tickled the undersides of the clouds with light and heat. Then we broke open water mains and snapped the straws of the gas pipes. We brought down a few roadway overpasses. We did various other sorts of damage.

By the time we pulled back, south-west across Wimbledon Common we had done something better than seizing the city – we had seized it up. Modern cities are delicate corals. London depended upon a few, vulnerable systems for transport; and when they were interrupted the result was a disproportionate quantity of trouble for the British authorities. Military vehicles had to be used to ship in basic supplies; troops had to be stationed all about the city to keep order; there were demonstrations – as many were organized against us as against the government, but both sorts had to be policed – and riots. We were a little over nine thousand individuals, and we never committed more than a third of our number to the big city; but that was more than enough to bring the whole of London to a halt.

12

I was in a house in the outer suburbs of London – somewhere a long way west. The owners had, I suppose, vacated it, sensibly, and gone whither they could. East Anglia was a popular destination for refugees, apparently – the government established camps along the Norfolk coastline. Or maybe they'd fled south-west, joining the clogged M3 or following arcane satnav routes through country lanes to get to Southampton and Bournemouth. At any rate they had gone. So we knocked on the door with a grenade rather than our fists, and two dozen of us took up temporary billets. Two dozen is a good number. It means that two of you can take a guard detail every hour, and otherwise the rest of the day is free to sort yourself out; to rest or play; to browse online and improve your skillbase, or to catch up with friends. I explored the house. The top floor provided a good view of the grey length of the London orbital motorway – weirdly empty, despite being, on this stretch at any rate, undamaged. A few cars and vans were parked – discarded I mean – along the hard shoulder. Otherwise I saw only animals, going single or in packs, from abandoned vehicle to abandoned vehicle hoping for food. Once I saw three adults clamber over the low wall on to the motorway, hurry across it and hop over on the far side.

Behind and before the gorgonized river of grey was an olive-green and brick-orange landscape of trees and houses. The sun was going down behind the foliage line of the horizon, a mix of superb fruit colours in the sky: strawberry reds and peachy oranges and banana yellows. It was mine to look at, and the birds' to fly in (to rub against, it looked like) but otherwise nothing disturbed the evening quiet save the occasional, and distant, grind of a military jet flying somewhere away to the north.

All the street lamps were on, a tessellation of parallel landing lights lining empty suburban roads. Nor had the electricity supply been curtailed, so that we were able (we: a woman called Heron and a man called Hussein) to cook the supplies we had salvaged from a warehouse half a mile away, and enjoy a pretty decent meal.

We all watched the news on a television the size of the whole wall, a piece of kit that rendered the newscaster's face large as Goliath's. He had on that austere expression newsreaders wear when they deliver bad news. I suppose they practise it, in front of the mirror, before they go to work.

The news was all the war, of course. There was nothing else. All Premiership football had been suspended until the war situation ('war situation' was the preferred locution) was resolved. The Prime Minister had convened a cabinet of the talents, and addressed Parliament about the state of emergency. Aid had been offered by North America. In Croydon civilians had heroically, and spontaneously, resisted incursion by rebellists. There had been riots in Hackney. The rebellists had established a base at Kingston, hijacking boats, packing them with explosives, setting fire to them, and pushing them out to float downstream. The fire brigade, said the newscaster, had dealt with most of these suicide barges.

'Why do they call them suicide barges?' said a trooper called Porter, who was one of our number. She had her left arm in a cast, and wore an eyepatch, but had elected to carry on fighting, enabling herself to this end with a continuous supply of painkillers.

'Maybe they think we leave pilots on board,' I suggested.

'Which,' said Simic, clapping his arms around my shoulders from behind and embracing me, 'is tantamount to saying they think we're idiots.'

'Do you remember that boy, in Basingstoke?' I said, shortly.

'Boy?'

'We went into a house, you me and Tucker.'

'You'll need to be more specific than that.'

I looked at him. 'Think back to Basingstoke. We came in through the busted-up window, and checked the hallway. In the hallway there was a lad, ten years old maybe. He was on his back.'

Simic scowled at this. Talk of dead kids was, clearly, not congenial for him. It would hardly bring *good* luck upon us, would it now? And if not *good* then what kind? 'I remember him. He had a key in his eye.'

'In his forehead.'

'That's right. The key must have been in the lock – hey, Porter, listen to this. It's pretty weird actually.' Because what else do we do, faced with such a thing, than turn it into a believe-it-or-not, and stress its peculiar fascination? Weird shit happens all the time, but people's appetite for weird shit keeps growing. 'This kid, in Basingstoke, must have been in the hallway of his house when a detonation went off outside. The blast blew the key out of the lock and straight in his head.'

'Fuck!' said Porter, because it was the kind of response expected of him, but he spoke without heat. 'Was he, like, walking about, with this key stuck in there?'

'He was dead.'

'Oh.'

'Anything can be a weapon,' said Hussein. 'What you're saying is: the blast turned the keyhole into a gun, the key into a bullet.'

'Yeah. It's a shame, though. Him being a child. But it wasn't *our* blast.'

'You sure?' I said.

Simic turned his *you're harshing my buzz, man* expression on me. 'I remember they were trying to kill *us*. I remember running hither and yon trying to avoid getting blown up. Hey, I tell you what. Maybe he wasn't dead – you know? It's not as if we checked for a pulse in his jugular. Maybe he was just stunned. Maybe he got up afterwards, and he's now alive and happy and playing in the playground with the other little kiddikins.'

'You remember the way we had to dash out the back of that house?' I said. 'You remember that a plane came by and blew the whole thing up?'

'Oh, yeah.' Simic made the gollum-gollum noise he occasionally made, when he was trying to scratch an itch right in the middle of his head. 'Tony,' he said. 'I love you more than I can say, but why are you bringing up that kid, now? All the dead bodies we've seen, kids as well as grown-ups. Why that one? And, fuck, why now?'

'Because that kid – yeah?'

Simic nodded.

'He's standing behind you now.'

Of course this made Simic yelp and spin around, and then everybody decided that this was me making a big joke, and everybody laughed. At first Simic fumed and told me off, but then he slipped into the general vibe and laughed too. But here's the thing: the kid *was* standing right there, just behind Simic. He had the key poking out of his forehead. What is it with ghosts, anyway? The *inertia* of the spirit world – why don't they take the opportunity to pull together the gaping wound, to remove the dagger, to tug out the key that ended their lives? The boy stood there with a knowing expression on his face, his skin blue as woad.

Everybody ate, and key-boy stood and watched us; not hungrily, not resentfully, but patiently. As we ate we watched more news.

The bulletin was given over to a ten-minute segment interviewing survivors of Dorking Fields. A reporter walked around a hospital thrusting his chopstick microphone in the faces of various soldiers and policemen. Some of these latter were hobbling about on crutches or with calipers; some were supine in bed. One wept as he talked of having his left leg amputated below the knee. The interview was intercut with footage shot by embedded reporters travelling with the Medical corps, the first personnel (the voiceover said) to discover the atrocity. Wobbly images of people lying on the blood-messed turf, wailing and lifting their arms. A long pan of a disorienting sea of writhing humanity. The tape feed wriggled along the bottom of the screen at all times, like red tapeworm: AUTHORITY CONSTITUTES WAR CRIMES TRIBUNAL and those plus signs that separate items: ++ JENNY COBDEN IN SKIING ACCIDENT, FIGHTS FOR LIFE IN SWISS CLINIC ++ RENEWED FIGHTING IN CORNWALL ++ ULSTER ATROCITIES ++ COURT APPEAL PLANNED TO REINSTATE FOOTBALL. News pretends to be additive. It is not, though.

'It was a mistake,' said Simic, in a sober voice.

'It was hard *work*,' said Hussein.

'It was the yelling,' I put in. 'That's what I didn't like. I had to wear my iPod to block out the noise.'

'That's dangerous, listening to music when you're working,' said Todd – did I mention Todd to you before? I can't remember. 'It distracts you.'

'I know.'

'The enemy can creep up on you.'

'I agree. This was only because of all the shrieking. The shrieking was putting me off my game.'

The Secretary of Health was on screen, fixing us all with her beady eyes and promising the British People that the victims of Dorking Field would not be forgotten by the government. That they would receive the very best in medical care. That this atrocity showed the heartless savagery of the enemy we all faced. There followed thirty seconds of rhetorical boilerplate about how we were terrorists and rebellists and violent bandits and that the whole modern phenomenon of the New Model Army had to be rooted out and extirpated for the good of democratic society.

'Democratic,' said Heron, scornfully.

'That's rich,' I agreed.

'It was a tactical error, breaking all those kneebones and shinbones at Dorking,' said Simic. 'I voted against it.'

'The vote didn't go your *way* then,' said Macleod, crossly. 'That is how democracy operates.'

'Democracy is not infallible,' Simic pointed out, rather pompously. 'We can make mistakes, collectively, just as easily as we can come to the right decision. *That*,' and he pointed a thumb at the screen, 'was a mistake. It makes us seem like savages.'

'They'd be more furious if we'd executed them all,' said Heron. 'Or do you think we should just have brought them all with us, a long crocodile of prisoners trailing behind us wherever we go?'

'Killing them would have been better,' said Simic, firmly.

'Hark,' said Hussein, cupping his ear derisively. 'The *vrai* savage speaks.'

'I'm content to stand by the collective decision,' said Simic. 'Don't misunderstand me. I know what it means to be part of a democracy. But another part of democracy is the free and frank exchange of views.'

'Oh exchange away,' said Hussein, nodding, and biting another portion from his chicken wing. 'By all *means.*'

'If we'd killed them there would have been some pother, and they'd have called us barbarians, of course. But it would soon have died down, and the numbers would have been folded into the overall casualty figures. Plenty of people dying in this war, you know. *This* way, though, the media will keep parading the legless policemen and filming their tears, and it will keep hurting us.'

'I'm not hurt,' I said.

'You're saying,' said Heron, sucking on a chicken bone like a lollipop stick to get the last shreds of meat off, and pulling it with a smack from between her lips, 'that mercy backfires.'

Simic made a moue, as if to say: *well, yes.* Then he said: 'war,' as if that one word explained everything.

'You could be right,' I said. 'But it's the past. We need to look forward. Onward.'

The news had moved on, now, to an account of the fighting in the West Country, where a completely different NMA – the news stupidly conflated them and us, as if we were all part of one unified invading army – had engaged troops in twelve hours of intense fighting south of Barnstaple. We watched with interest, and broke out the chocolate digestives.

13

The following day we moved further away from London and hooked up with several dozen clumps of troops. And do you know what? Simic was right about Dorking Fields. The wounded prisoners generated more hostility than dead bodies would have done. Human beings aren't enormously logical about that sort of thing. We debated this, as we debated everything, and the wikis buzzed with chatter, and the software worms crawled in their semiconscious way checking the probity of the connection. Talk and talk and talk. But there wasn't much we could do, and so we went on with our campaign. We were warriors.

One night, a day or two later, I had to sleep in the open air, in the countryside south-west of London. It was on account of a skirmish that dragged itself on unconscionably. Sometimes fighting does just dribble on and on like that. We spent several hours in a field – hiding amongst cabbages, leathery great leaves like black-green batwings – and fought sniper-actions and contact fire until past midnight, anxious the whole time that the enemy might simply call for air support and flame the entire area. But they didn't; and we made sure our action was spread as widely as possible over the whole terrain, hoping thereby to inoculate ourselves against area denial from the skies. Either it worked, or else the enemy had other reasons for not blasting us.

Eventually the fighting eased off from the continual bang-bang-bang and turned into spittery gunfire following a random pattern. There were long stretches of nighttime silence only occasionally interrupted by jittery clusters of small arms fire, or else distantly coloured by the sounds of cars, yawning very far off; or of planes flying past, I suppose sweeping the ground with infrared. Simic and I cuddled together for the warmth of it, and dozed under the thickest vegetation we could find. I slept, off and on, for three hours or so; but holding him in my arms like that – the pressure of his body against my body – gave each of those hours a magical weight and intensity. That was the happiest I've been. That's quite a claim, actually, now that I look at it. That's a pretty big claim. But it's right, it's the truth, it's right. If he had not had his helmet on I would have stroked his hair. He wouldn't have minded, or been freaked out; he understood the nature of the connection between us, and understood that it was neither what he nor what I was used to in our relationships.

I had stood beside him at Basingstoke and seen him shot down, and I had known the terror he would die. To have him again, literally in my arms, was the purest intensity of resurrection and love.

As the dawn did its chilly widescreen slow-fade-in we poked our heads up to discover that the enemy had withdrawn all their forces – eastward, mostly, or that's what the wiki said. There were a couple of dozen bands in our area, each with a different localized task for the day. So we pinged one, pretty much at random, and went to join them.

I see how you're looking at me.

You think I delude myself. I know that Simic didn't love me the way I loved him. When you face death together, you bond closely; but I know better than anybody Simic was a thoroughly straight-o man. That didn't matter. My love was something more than that. This is my way of saying that it was more important than sex. And I'll tell you something else, too; something that only soldiers properly understand, because they face death all the time. What I mean to say is: because the *intimacy* of death is the very definition of what we do. Civvies tend to think that sex is itself a value (because it is genes, and because it is passing on our genes). But the truth is other. The truth is that the proximity of death is the core value. The continual proximity of death is the very ground of life. Genetics is just a wrinkle by nature to try and evade it. In the continual proximity of death a purer, taller, more sublime love is possible than can be achieved in the tangles of childmaking. In the service of life, love is always secondary; but in the company of death love shines as master.

You do need to understand how deeply I loved him. That's crucial. Excepting only that I am not the subject, here; and even Simic is not the subject. The subject here is giant.

14

We fought all round western London. Some of us came in at the north-west. Simic and I were part of several dozen warbands that picked a way up south-west. We fought through Esher, and up to Kingston. Mostly we avoided the open spaces – the heaths and parks – because built-up areas gave us better cover. Because we had no desire to hold the territory we did not leave troops behind to guard where we had been, and so we maintained our optimum fighting strength all the way up to the Thames. The postcodes we fought through were pretty empty anyway, and our actions emptied them further, so there wasn't much to hold.

We crossed the Thames on, and under, the bridge at Hampton; and as we passed along the northern bank the enemy detail guarding the Court opened up on us. That's never a pleasant experience – the sound of detonations all about, the bone-shocking surprise, swiftly followed by people falling over all around. There wasn't enough cover on the north bank. I sprinted with my head down through man-high snorts of concrete dust and hailstorms of dislodged tarmac pebbles. The next thing I remember is pressing myself in at the base of a long brick wall, along with a dozen or so colleagues, the barrage continuing, and people in every direction collapsing in mists and splashes and lava-lamp splurges of blood. We had stumbled blindly, and foolishly, upon a large concentration of the enemy at Hampton Court.

This was the severest massacre of my kind in which I have been involved.

The worst of it was that the wiki was overwhelmed, for five minutes or more, with a lot of senseless bellowing and screaming. It took us that long – five minutes, I need hardly tell you, is a very long stretch of time in the middle of a firefight – to lock out all those who were too injured, or too stunned, to be able to step back and let cooler heads discuss the situation. Once we got our communications back in proper order things eased a little. There were several knots of people in the vicinity, and they all pulled in to help. One of these had a nuclear bullet – about the size of a full gym-bag, this device, so calling it a 'bullet' is, I suppose, litotes. The group who possessed this weapon happened, by good chance, to be in Sunbury, which is upriver from Hampton; and they strapped the thing about with floats and a model boat motor and fitted a webcam on top. They pushed it into the river and told us to clear out.

The news talks about 'a nuclear bomb' being detonated at Hampton Court, but that's not an accurate way of talking about it. A nuclear bullet is not the same as a bomb. Its destructive capacity is considerably less. We did as much damage as we did only by virtue of the fact that, having steered the little craft down from Sunbury by watching its passage on a little screen, the remote-controller (a woman called Emma Clack) noticed an inlet off the river going in at the site of Hampton Court. Had we just exploded it on the river the banks would have dampened the horizontal spread, and most of the damage would have scorched east and west. But Clack was able to steer the little thing, put-put-put, in at this channel and right into Hampton Court itself. That meant that when the bullet blew it dismantled the house and sent a mass of incandescent masonry up into the air to hail down again. It was not a blast to watch with your naked eyes if you wanted to keep your eyesight. But by the same token, I was huddling against the wall of Hampton Court itself when the bullet was floated, and I had fifteen minutes to get away on foot; which I did, and I suffered no ill effects. I could not have managed that if it had been an actual atomic bomb. In fact not even all the troops stationed at Hampton Court were killed; although the fact that their superiors had positioned so many people in one place made them more of a target than they needed to be. We lost nearly three hundred of our people at Hampton, a figure of which the British can be proud. Then again, we killed many more of them with our bullet.

There was no time to lose. There never is, in war. I was filled with a kind of frustrated fury at the useless, avoidable loss of so many people. This fury was generalized throughout the body of the whole NMA. We went through Kingston in a rattle and a clatter, fighting through a blizzard of smashed and tumbling glass to take easy possession of the shopping centre, and therefore of the roofs, and so of excellent bazooka positions to bombard the four or five most obvious enemy emplacements in the town below. I was lacerated in a number of places, small cuts with some bleeding, and I had to keep wiping my goggles with a chenille shawl I'd grabbed from a department store on the way up. But we coordinated our shooting with a half a dozen other groups, and put an end to the key enemy emplacements. Then we vacated the roof, before the enemy could bring jets to bear upon it.

'[The bullet has startled them, some.]' This was McKibin. I had met her once upon a time – oddly, though, before joining the NMA, at a party; since being in the same corpus militis as her I hadn't seen her. ['They're sending along cars, but only from the east.]'

'[I can see them, half a dozen,]' said somebody else, name of Leggatt. I had never met this individual, although from his name, and doubtless irrationally, I believed him to be a tall and lanky fellow.

'[We're at Sunbury,]' came somebody else. '[There's a lot of noise up here.]'

'[It's set the cat down *amongst*,]' said Barnard. I knew Barnard well. '[They're all hurrying along. It's drawn them, like shit draws flies.]'

'[We're up on a hill,]' said somebody new: Myerson. '[Looking down on Twickenham, Teddington, google seems a bit uncertain as to where – so I guess the borderline between the two? I can see that crater you guys made, and no mistake.]'

I pitched in, here: '[Get off the ping, Myerson, if you're just rubbernecking. Some of us are *fighting* here.]'

'[I have priority news,]' Myerson insisted, in a hurt tone of voice. '[I can see a long way south-west, and there are a dozen helicopters. More than that.]'

'[Here come the *choppers*,]' tooted a man whose moniker, Snow, may have been either name or nickname. ['To chop off our heads.]'

'[At least a dozen, I'll confirm that.]'

'I can hear them,' said Simic.

'[Do they think this is, like, *half-time*?]' said Leggatt.

['Pinging that we're carrying a good set of chopper-choppers,]' said a man called Asherton.

'[Where are you?]'

The map was updated.

'[We're carrying too – this is Wilton, and we're a dozen ladies and germs, and we're setting up on the hill, north-west of the crater.]'

'[Take them down – sorry, this is a formal prop.]' The lights lit up on my arm. '[This is a strategic needful. Take them down and pull north up towards Hammersmith. It's built up, heavily housed up there.]'

'[Counter proposal,]' said somebody, also lighting up the priority. I couldn't, for a moment, see what a counter proposal could even be: going north was the only sensible tactical call. I checked the tag: a woman called Lee (again: surname, first-name, nickname, I don't know). What was she going to suggest? Pulling east? Going west past the crater?

'[I counterprop we let the choppers alone, pull south out of the fighting and let the world know we're a fucking *merciful* warrior-giant.]'

I swallowed air in astonishment. Simic, Ridgway, Levy and I were jinking our way quickly but cautiously through Kingston in the general direction of the river, so as to be ready when the prop was passed and we had to pull north.

Straight away a dozen debating pings queued. '[Mercy?]'

'[I call it weakness.]'

'[If this is a serious prop, then it's tantamount to ceasefire.]'

'[I say no.]'

And one: '[Smart – they know their choppers are vulnerable, the fact that they're sending them at all suggests they're undertaking this manoeuvre more as a humanitarian gesture, perhaps to evacuate the—]' He ran out of time to make his point.

This led to another dozen. '[*Too* soon to ease back on the fighting.]'

'[Agree. *Way* agree.]'

'[One week minimum, two weeks likely, then negotiations.]'

'[We've shot a nuclear bullet. Showing mercy to helicopters isn't going to be noticed as mercy after that.]'

'[The nuclear bullet was our Paul Atreides play. Our genius play!]' said somebody, very eagerly. He was yelled at: '[What does that even mean?]' '[I move we lock this idiot out of debate]' and so on.

And in fact a surprising number of people were behind the

counterprop. '[Atomic bullets are serious. They have serious consequences. We need to rein it in.]'

'[One atomic explosion is enough shock and awe for one day.]'

I flicked through, but my mind was already made up. Time to vote. The sound of the approaching choppers was swelling in the afternoon air: 'Move,' I pinged.

I was one of thirty or forty who were pressing the vote in this manner.

'[Move!]' '[Move!]' '[Move *now*!]'

We voted. The four of us slunk through an underpass, came out round a corner and saw Kingston Bridge spanning the river in front of us. The vote was closer than I might have thought, although the majority was clear: we would waste all the helicopters, and pull north. '[OK,]' said Lee. This was sort of traditional: that the defeated proposer be the first to press the majority decision: '[Let's take them down and go north.]'

'The bridge looks clear,' I said; and a fraction later somebody confirmed. '[Also at Kingston Bridge, and it's clear.]'

The choppers were twanging the sky noisily now with their trippy, dance-club reverb; that How Soon Is Now shudder, multitracked a dozen times. Something else was folded into the noise. Words. We rushed the bridge, keeping close to the stone balustrade, peeking over the side to check the river below, flowing strenuously, silently, dark and thick as stout. I was nearly across when they were close enough for me to be able to make it out: loudspeakers on the choppers broadcasting an urgent, booming voice: RADIATION HAZARD, RADIATION HAZARD.

We four jogged over the bridge and on to a roundabout on the far side, completely traffic free. Beyond it was a fuel station; and there, behind the twin banks of recharge plugs, was a row of petrol dispensers; and behind *those* – amazingly enough – was a delivery tanker, parked up. 'Sometimes,' said Levy, 'they make it *too* easy for us.'

I pinged through to the rest of them that we wanted to explode a petrol tanker, fortuitously abandoned in the midst of the fighting, on the northern side of the bridge. It was a nobrainer, really; but given how sizeable the minority had been of people who wanted to spare the choppers I thought perhaps we should run it past a vote. It came straight back, unopposed, maybe a third of people even bothering to click their voting buttons.

The choppers chuntered closer. Levy broke open the cab and used his clever phone to jump-start the truck. Simic got up there too, and propped his rifle on the hinge of the open door to give him cover. I took up a position on the roundabout, watching our people come driving or running over the bridge, checking their pings and counting them off. Away to the west was a stretch of parkland; and smoke was sifting upwards from this like chaff in the wind – myriad flakes of soot, like Goth snowflakes, dropping and blowing all about me. The weather was damp. We had set fire to a lot of vegetation.

Then, several groups, working in unison, pulled the enemy choppers out of the sky. Light, abruptly, flared; the sky roared as if in pain. Missiles seared out from four separate positions, and four enemy helicopters became four fantastically expensive firework displays. The two remaining choppers started to bank, turn, the chuggety of their rotors increasing in pitch as their engines strained.

Levy was backing the petrol tanker out of the fuel-station, and it was making that sleekit cowering 'eek! eek!' noise huge trucks make when they back up.

'[General ping, Kingston area,]' I said. '[We're going to snap the Kingston Bridge in two minutes; so if you're south of the river you'll need to go round.]' I was coughing with all the smoke.

'[I'm right here,]' came a ping back: man called Coates. I could see him waving, on the other side of the bridge.

'[Coates, hurry. Everybody else, find another route.]'

The remaining helicopters had turned, and were on their way back south. A squad in Esher put out a general ping that they had them. Away to the west the sounds of more than one localized firefight were sporadically audible. Behind me the tanker's engine made its hungry-belly growl, and Levy drove it out of the fuel-station and on to the bridge. Sheets of smoke folded like theatre drapery through the sky. The moon, visible westward through the gaps in the smoke cover, was almost full. I was struck by it. There wasn't anything in the least cratered about it. It looked, indeed, like a smooth silver shield, that a giant might carry, if only he could find a sword massive enough to match it.

Levy dashed back to the roundabout with Coates and his half-dozen others. Just at that moment we came under small-arms fire: snap, snap, snap, like sticks in the fire. At first it wasn't clear from where. I pulled my head down, put out a help!-ping and checked the wiki for updates.

Then one of the people with Coates, a chap called Durcan, did the most extraordinary thing: he suddenly performed a perfect backwards somersault, like an inadvertent circus acrobat. What happened is that he took two rounds, simultaneously, in the armour of his chest; and the double impact absolutely flung him backwards with such vehemence that he went down and his legs came up. He stood on his head, for an instant, his boots waggling. Then he went down right over, and lay on the ground on his front. Coates and somebody else had him, hauling him by his armpits and he was coughing and coughing like an eighty-a-day man. He was fine – alive, although more than one rib was broken and his phlegm was coming up bloody. But the bullets had not got underneath his skin.

We had moved the tanker to the middle of the bridge. Levy dropped two lob-rounds. One, deliberately, missed the tanker and cracked the stone of the carriageway so that the big truck sagged into a new declivity. The second hit the tanker squarely and the whole thing went up exactly like a Hollywood explosion – a rare sight, rarer than civilians might think. But we were already hauling ourselves north, taking turns to drag Durcan with us.

15

You asked me, Colonel, what I'm reading, in between our conversational sessions together. I'm reading a book called *Seeding Neural Networks*. Popular science, pretty interesting. I am reading it because I want to come to terms with the logic behind this new awareness. It is not very forthcoming on that subject.

By dusk Kingston was far behind us, and we had made our way more-or-less unopposed northward into the dingier streets of Hammersmith.

A couple of dozen of us found a good-looking building to hunker down in for the night, and scattered ourselves about the place in threes and fours: settled ourselves in with good lines-of-sight and supplies to wait the night out. We did debate pushing on, through the dark; but the heart of the group wasn't in it. I think the bullet had thrown a fair few people, on both sides of the fight. It was, I concede, a lot to take in. We were tired. So we bedded down.

There were sporadic sounds of gunfire, and the occasional more distant detonation – for there was some nightfighting on the other side of the river at Barnes. We ate and chatted and dozed.

At midnight, or thereabouts, it started raining. Simic was of the opinion that this would wash radioactivity down upon us, and became indeed fairly peevish about it. I thought it an ill-informed opinion and told him so. But, you see, people are irrational when it comes to radioactivity. It is all around us all the time. Sometimes (as when the dentist scans our jaw, or when we make camp a couple of miles away from a recent nuclear bullet detonation) it's more intense. Other times less. It balances out, overall. A bullet is not a bomb.

Simic and I bickered over this subject, but pleasantly, and with laughter, as friends do. He was straight. I couldn't help that. Better, I suppose, that he was the way he was and I got to spend time with him, than that he was queer too and with somebody other than me. Best of all that he could be both queer and near, but life doesn't shake itself down like that.

So, on the subject of love. I will say this, honestly not intending to evade the responsibilities of truth: love is a difficult thing to write about. This is not because it manifests itself in the world in impossible ways (I mean, impossible to apprehend, impossible to talk about) but rather because love by its nature inflects so large a quantity of desire that its representation gets pulled out of shape. The desire in question is complex, not simple; it is laminated on several layers. Love in fiction, for instance, becomes the written form of how we desire love to be. As a result we are of course continually getting it wrong. Love is not a representation of love, you see. I'm talking about more than the simple form, the familiar erotic-romantic fantasies where you get the guy, and he's a splendid fellow; or you get the girl and she's a doll (though that's clearly one way of getting it wrong). I'm talking about more complex forms too. More nuanced understandings of love still don't escape the black-hole-tugging ellipses of desire, the way those forces distort the otherwise flat map of lived-experience. All those films and books about the woe that is in marriage, about desperate affairs or exploitative relations: they tend to represent sex as mind-blowing, love as life consuming. But this is only the shape of our desire for desire. It's not the thing itself.

My desire for Simic was unsimple, but I want to try and put down here what was important about it. It's not that I didn't want to have sex with him. Of course I did. And it's not as if I was the first gay man in history to fall in love with a straight man. Let's not get into the business of embroidering that cliché. Love is something else, you see. Love is like a car on ice: it needs a little grit to get purchase.

We've had this conversation more than once, Colonel. It was one of the first things you said to me, in fact. The two of us, grizzled old soldiers, bent and dinged and broken by war, and the first thing we talk about is *the question of love*. No, not as strange as you might think, I suppose. It all came about because you were so unreticent about your religious beliefs. I suspect you were trying to save me for Jesus. Sweet of you, though not needful. And your beliefs were exactly what we might expect a person such as yourself to hold. It *fits* your consciousness to think (naturally you didn't put it in these terms) of God as hierarchical order, a supreme leader whose orders are passed down through the chain of command (archangels, angels, popes, bishops and priests, the godly and the ungodly) – so, so, then, if that is the way the cosmos is, then the cosmos *is* undemocratic, and democracy itself is a sort of violation of divine order. I believe you're sincere in your inability to conceptualize a model of the divine that wasn't like the feudal army to which you have dedicated your earthly life. I'm not trying to be offensive. But there are other ways of imagining the divine. It's just that you can't see them. I remember saying something like: 'hard to believe that a religious system that is so hierarchical and autocratic could have done so well in a democracy like the United States.' You didn't bridle at this, because for you *autocrat* is not the term of abuse it is for me. It was when I started discussing the mendacity of calling fundamentally feudal and anti-democratic political systems things like Republic and Democracy that you bridled and became annoyed. Anyway, I remember you saying: 'what you don't understand,' in that slightly pursed lip, vowel-flattened way you have, 'what you don't understand is that God is Love. A *human* supreme ruler would be a Hitler, a Stalin, yeah. I concede that. But a supreme ruler guided by love – a being that is pure Love – see, that purges authority of all negative possibility.' I quote from memory and may not have got this quite right. But you'll concede that's, pretty much, how you speak.

What can a rational human being say to that? I probably mumbled, and looked away, and adjusted my face-plate in that fidgety way I've gotten into the habit of doing. Yes, I've noticed myself doing that, as I know you have.

What I probably didn't say, or at least didn't say with needful eloquence, is: love is obviously a wonderful thing for a human to experience; a self- and other-validating thing; an exciting and pleasurable thing. And actually we can say more, because in terms of, to use the Attenborovian phrase, Life on Earth – the successful transmission of genes – love is clearly an immensely *useful* thing. But that's not what I'm trying to get at. Maybe I can put it this way: what might an alien civilization that had no concept of love think, observing the way we elevate Love to transcendental, cosmic and godly proportions? Might they not think it a little *self-regarding*? A little *peculiar*? As if because I enjoy eating beefsteaks, and because beefsteaks serve the useful purpose of keeping me alive, I therefore declared the universe to be beefsteak, God a beefsteak and beefsteak the universal core value of everything?

There are plenty of religious people in our NMA, and I would not want to generalize about their beliefs. But I'd hazard this: they don't worship a Fuehrer God. Who but a slave could love such a concept?

Did I say so? Were you offended? I can't remember. I may have been, I suppose, a little belligerent. It was early in our relationship.

There was another conversation of ours that I *do* remember. You told me that your troops fight with discipline, and that our people didn't know what discipline was. I said that free men fought better than did automata. And you *did* get a little riled at that, and said that being dedicated to *service* didn't mean that your men lacked *passion*. Do you remember that? Maybe that was even part of that same conversation as before. Perhaps I'd said that your army is an army of slaves, because everybody is bound by the hierarchy in which they live. And you of course wouldn't have conceded the point about slavery. But you would counter it by saying that provided they fight with *passion* it doesn't matter if troops are following orders from above, or debating their own strategies with their fellows. This is what I said: I said the word passion is linked etymologically to concepts of passivity. We don't think of it this way any more of course: we think of passion as a positive force (a positive good, often). That's a wish fulfilment thing. 'I feel passionately about this . . .' 'I feel passionately about you . . .' These expressions actually mean 'I have surrendered the agency and activity of my feelings; I am in a merely reactive and passive state.' Dominoes fall with exactly this passion.

But – and this is *my whole point* – it does not follow from this that we should cultivate a stoic imperative to escape our passions. To attempt to be free of passions is to be seduced by a dream of perfect independence: power, active control, the ideally circulating Unaccommodated Man. But that's a false flicker. Passion is a relational term, and it is our relations to others that define us as fully human. That's the great truth at the heart of democracy. Nobody can be passionate about themselves (I mean passionate in the conventional sense) –

you can be enthusiastic, excited maybe, but not *passionate*, any more than the universe could ever passively react to the universe, or the Singularity be passionate about the Singularity. It's a misunderstanding of the term.

The original meaning of the word is now only recalled in archaic linguistic fossils. That Mel Gibson film you think so highly of, *The Passion of the Christ*. People don't understand what the title means. It's not about the furious or intense desire of Christ. It is about the period of agonizingly *passive suffering* of the Christ. But even here the modern and original senses blur, semantically: for in Gibson's film the quasi-erotic objectification of Christ's naked body in pain parlays passivity into the passionate lust-for-pain which is so much the currency of contemporary cinema.

This is a roundabout way of saying I prefer that the individual organs of our NMAs not be seduced by rhetoric of passion. Our giant, I know, is not a passionate giant. Our giant has his seven views of Jerusalem.

So, yes, there I was, in Hammersmith, with the man I loved most in all the world; and with other friends, too, present physically or present virtually. And I was part of a single organism, a Pantegral being, and was gifted with purpose and meaning and strength and agency in my life. It is true that Pantegral had reached his arm over the bridge at Hampton Court and received, unexpected, a savage slice from a sabre. This had opened the skin and severed some of the fibres of the meat. But he had struck back at once. And now this Pantegral creature was lying and gathering his strength. And in the morning we would rise up, mightily. For the heart of our creed is: rejoice not against me, o my enemy.

16

The rain fell hard all night, and I lay in the darkness in the chaste embrace of my Simic, sometimes dozing and sometimes waking with the sheer pressure of happiness.

By morning the shower had reduced in intensity, although rain was still falling, and it washed dawn in greys and silvers. We roused ourselves and ate some food. We opened the window to clear the fug accumulated from half a dozen bodies in a small room. From the window, the sound of water pouring ceaselessly from a drainpipe on to the flags of the pavement: an endless sheet of silk being continuously ripped in two.

'This place is pretty much empty,' said Simic, coming to stand alongside me. He meant: the civilians had pretty much vacated Hammersmith.

It stopped raining. The sun came out.

We moved out and made our way through streets that were all oil-glisteny in the aftermath of the rainfall. Versions of ourselves, painted in fat sines and cosines, walked upsidedown through the ground beneath us. We made our way house to house, and updated the wiki, and tooted other squads in the ground. '[We need to clear out,]' said a trooper called Armistead. '[There are no civilians in a mile in any direction.]'

I saw one civilian, lurking in a doorway, and I almost contradicted him, 'Not all the civvies have vacated the theatre of operations, I just saw—'. But I looked again, and it was the boy with the key.

We came to the elevated section of the motorway, and

trotted up a sliproad to check the lay of the city from up there, looking east. East, in the heart of the town, was where the wiki said most of the enemy troops were concentrated. Without civvies to shield us we all felt exposed and vulnerable to air attack. Traffic was not moving, of course. Cars were abandoned irregularly along its length; not parked neatly at the side as I had seen on the M25. There was a line of street lamps down the middle and each pole crossed with two metre-length light-casings. Upon every one of these casings sat perched a dozen birds, silhouetted against the dawn and looking exactly like eyelashes against the apricot sky. 'Quiet, ain't it,' said Simic.

We kept checking the sky for airborne ordnance. Personally I figured that the British would prefer not to destroy acres of prime London real estate just to liquidate a couple of hundred NMA soldiers; but – Coates made this point – the British didn't necessarily *know* that our numbers were so few. Also we had fired an atomic bullet, and that might well have changed the game. Might have moved it out of the realm of rationality.

There was a great amount of e-chatter, but nobody had enough of a sense of things to put a formal proposal to the whole corpus. Only a few groups were engaging the enemy; most of us were moving through a deserted cityscape. This gave the debates a longer, more prolix quality – there's nothing like being in the middle of a combat situation to *focus* democratic debate. By mid morning a consensus was emerging: majority view – the enemy were gathering themselves for a counterattack from the east. Minority view, they were stunned that a nuclear cap had snapped in their own back garden, and just sitting there in shock. The point of the minority view was that this was the chance to press a negotiation angle. But I cleaved to the majority view – correctly, as I can now say, with hindsight. My reasoning was thus: the British knew that they would have to negotiate, but they couldn't *not* react to the bullet, and the only reaction that counted in such circumstances was a great deal of boom-boom and bang-bang. Give them a week of smashing about and things would calm a little. Meanwhile we could vanish, dissolve before their advance and give them nothing to fight. There were three thousand of us, give or take, in the northern portion of the city. Three thousand people can vanish like breath into the wind in a city that size.

Then, a little before lunchtime, the British forced the issue. A bombardment opened from the east, and a massive advance – tanks, many thousands of troops, with air support – began moving west through the central city. A quick proposal didn't meet with any counter-prop: we would fall back and give way. This meant (it was hardly the first time we had done this) putting up enough resistance for the enemy to think they had a proper fight on their hands in order to give people time to slip away. Then we would let things settle down, a little while, before recoalescing and striking back. But we had to handle this carefully, or Houdini disappearance would become a rout.

A couple of hundred of us picked out likely looking spots, and checked the wiki, and noted the advance. The British were moving cautiously, but in massive numbers; and they were taking particular pains to knock down our toy planes and limit our surveillance. This wasn't too much of a problem. You can't keep the advance of many many thousand men a secret, after all.

Simic and I went into a multi-storey car park to set up an automatic cannon. This was a small part of the general strategy of covering our disappearance.

'Where will you go?' Simic asked me, as we climbed the car park's urinous, grey stairwell. It was the two of us, none else.

We could have done with a few extra hands, actually, to help lug up the canvas bags of ordnance.

'Cambridge,' I said. 'I'll put up with a friend there. He'll tolerate me for a few days, at any rate. A couple of days. You want to come?'

'I'll go south and round I think. My girlfriend has a place in Canterbury.'

'Girlfriend,' I grunted.

'I told you about her.'

'Oh,' I said, in my Omar voice, 'in*deed.*'

We came out into the penultimate level, and dragged our bags across the concrete floor, over the oil stains and the enormous white-painted arrows, to the edge. The boy with the key was sitting on the bonnet of one of the parked cars – there weren't many cars inside, actually, and he had picked one of the cleanest. A Range Rover. I tried not to catch his eye. I had work to do, after all. I wanted to concentrate upon that. Actually there was something strangely insistent in his presence. I say *strangely* because it's hard to pin down precisely by what means he communicated insistence. He did not speak, of course; and he did not seem any more agitated than usual. But somehow I sensed something amiss.

Still, as I said, we had a job to do. The concrete balustrade was rough-textured, and the stone ceiling loomed overhead. We had a good view down towards Westminster. Some token fighting was happening in that direction. The sounds of detonations carried easily; I could even see little cigar-puffs of grey and brown in amongst the clutter of roofs and office blocks.

I set up one of the automatic cannon, fiddling with its tripod legs. Simic did the other one. Stupid thoughts kept crowding into my head. I remember this with peculiar vividness – the daftness of the thoughts, I mean. I ignored key-boy. I looked back across the mostly deserted parking tier, and thought: *it's a pity those white painted arrows are bent* – they were curved, you see, to direct traffic round and up the ramp, or else round and down – *or they'd go nicely in the quiver of the same giant who wields the moon for shield.* But there's no point in broken arrows. No military point, I mean.

'So,' I said. 'Is your girlfriend going to be OK about stowing your kit at her place?'

This was on my mind. I was wondering if it was going to be a problem for me in Cambridge. Not that I expected Harry to be a problem. I was confident he wouldn't try and turn me in, given our history. But Harry had a new partner now, and *he* – on the few occasions we had met – had manifested a focused and intense hostility towards me, a hatred that was prompted by more than the fact that Harry and I had once been a couple. I don't know where the loathing came from: not the severity of it, I mean. I can't say I cared. The point was: Harry would accept me for a few days; but Joram might well call the police as soon as I turned up.

'She'll be OK with that,' Simic said. 'She's pretty boho.'

'What does she do?'

'She's in a band.'

'I don't mean,' I said, sighting the cannon and twisting the dial to angle the barrel further downwards, 'what she does *in her spare time.*'

'Seriously,' he said. He was checking the wiki, noting the advancing line of enemy. 'That's her job.'

'Your girlfriend is a rock star?'

'Yes.'

'She has no day job?'

'No.'

'Fuck off. She knows you're NMA?'

He didn't answer that. So I tried: 'What's her band called?'

'They're called *Monkey Fetus.*'

'And I have never heard of them.'

'Unsurprisingly, since you refuse to listen to any music released after 1979.'

'Not true!' The webcam refused to settle into its bracket, and I fiddled with it, and swore, and fiddled with it. 'I own, uh, *dozens* of post 79 albums.' The webcam went into its slot.

'Dozens?'

'Well. Some.'

'We're set here,' said Simic.

We jogged back to the stairwell. The aerial growling noise of jets had swelled a little. Distant silhouettes dashing about the sky like blown leaves: it was the royal air force bashing their snouts on the firmament. I was singing as we went:

> *And what can a poor boy do?*
> *'Cept to sing for a rock and roll band?*
> *'Cos in sleepy London—*

At that moment the world exploded around me.

It must have been like this inside the Twin Towers, when the world changed. One minute you are moving through an interior space, designed as such things are to fit neatly about a human being, enveloping without being claustrophobic. The next, with a roar and a hugely forceful compression, a snapping-over of the air upon itself, everything disintegrates. It's all dark, suddenly and you feel (your heart like an epileptic doing its fish-flop on the hard ground) that it will be dark for ever now. The walls have turned into a sandstorm, and the ceiling comes down, and the floor turns to fire, and everything clatters and shears and burns.

Darkness.

A cosmic finger had flicked the Great Mute Switch and all the sounds of existence had been instantly eliminated – all sound with once exception: for there was one lone football referee, standing on some impossible drizzly school football pitch somewhere, and blowing on his whistle with impressive force and consistency.

It was black as midnight. My head hurt.

I was lying on my front. It was dusty and dark and I couldn't see anything. The whistle continued blowing its unyielding monotone.

I knew at once what had happened. A jet had spotted the muzzles of our cannon, poking over the lip of the car park and had decided to take them out. I say decided: I daresay what happened was that the pilot reported it, and his superiors considered the report and ordered him to fire a missile and destroy those cannons. We had been, of course, foolish – stupid – careless. We shouldn't have set the guns up so close to the edge. We should have positioned them deeper inside the car park; perhaps on the bonnet of a car, angled out in decent obscurity.

I dragged myself round. The whistle was still blowing. Penalty. Foul. Stop the game.

I was dazed. I had a sticky gel all over me. I had blood all over me. I blinked and blinked, and saw what had saved my life. When the missile struck I had been between a stocky concrete pillar and the inner concrete wall of the car park. The blast had caught a 4by4, shove-ha'pennied it, thrown it directly at me. The front of the chassis had slammed against wall and the rear against the pillar and the thing had stuck there, such that, although I was knocked down, the body of the vehicle had kept the worst of the blast off me.

My left hand wasn't there. The whistle was blowing. I searched frantically with my right arm, and pulled at the sleeve, and found the hand – it was still there, after all, still attached to my arm, though the hand itself was numb and I couldn't feel it.

My *arm* ached, though. The wrist had been bent back, or broken, or something. And, yes, now that I looked at it, I noticed that there was a considerable amount of pain in that wrist. Now that I noticed it, my wrist hurt like *fuck*.

All dark and dusty, nothing to see.

With an inward pop the whistle stopped blowing. Sound came back into my ears, though muffled: a distant roaring; the sounds of sifting and things falling; the scrunching-tinfoil noise of flames.

That was when I finally thought of Simic.

I got on all fours, or tried to, but I couldn't put weight on my right hand; so actually I got on all threes, coughing and trying to spit dust out of my mouth, and I did a sort of lame dog crawl, two knees and one hand, through the smoke. I tasted tar, and charred tyres, and death.

And as I looked about me I could see that the scene was not altogether dark, after all. There was an orange-yellow smear of light and heat away to my left. A burning car, I supposed.

Where had Simic been? Until a moment before he had been standing four yards to my right.

I found him. My left hand touched him as I crawled. He was lying on his side. I couldn't see in the bleary orange-dark. So I sat back, and scrabbled through my pockets with my good hand to find a torch. Fumble fingers. It took me a shaky while to locate the torch and turn it on, but finally I directed a beam of light at his body. I wished I hadn't immediately. Something more rigid than flesh had passed through Simic's back, on the dexter side, and had torn off his right arm and right shoulder-blade and a sizeable piece of his flank. A rope of raw meat, slathered with eggwhite and oil and cream-of-tomato soup, had spilled out of the hole in his torso. Everything else was scorched black. The hair on his head was smoking with an odour I could smell even over all the other baked and scorched and dusty smells of that place. The uniquely astringent stench of burning hair.

I fumbled the torch away. I was shaking pretty seriously. It was a proper late-stage Parkinsonian tremor, all over my body. But I couldn't stay in that place, shakes or no shakes, Simic-corpse or none. I crawled over to the crushed-up 4by4 because that's where my weapon was. I reached out to pick it up, but instead of managing to grasp it I acted as if I was trying to fan it cool. Like I was waving bye-bye at it. I couldn't stop my hand shaking. I sat back, and suddenly vomited, turning my head to avoid getting it on my clothes. Pull yourself together, I told myself. I said those actual words to myself: *pull yourself together*. I wiped my mouth on the back of my coatsleeve and tasted ashes and blackness.

I couldn't stay where I was.

So I pulled myself together, and hooked my shuddery arm through the strap, and dragged the weapon over the stone to the exit, and through the place where the door had been, and out into the stairway. I came down shuffling on my arse, step by step, and my gun came clattering down with me.

That was the last I saw of Simic.

17

I want to say one more thing, here, about Simic. This may not be interesting to you, or relevant to your purposes, but it matters to me. I said earlier that I'm not the first queer to fall hopelessly in love with a straight man. People have always fallen in love with all sorts of unsuitable and unavailable other people, for as long as we have been. But, you see, it *felt* like I was the first. You see, however much a man-of-the-world you may be, however varied your experience, there's an element of love that necessarily makes you the first person to experience it.

Sometimes I would look at his face and be struck by how beautiful he was. I'm not talking in terms of conventional beauty. His features were regular, and his complexion wasn't bad; but his hairline was being swept back by the tide of age – he was nearly forty, which in gay-years is something over a hundred – and there were all these little pleats and wrinkles in at the corner of his eyes. One thing that I always look for in a man is good breath; evidence of a good dental hygiene regimen. I can't be bothered with sour breath, or coffee-breath, or the hint of decay. Who wants to kiss that? Simic was never too careful with his teeth. I never kissed him, but I sometimes caught a whiff and it wasn't pleasant. When all is said and done he wasn't really my type – and all this is quite apart from the fact that he was straight.

Nevertheless, he had the bluest of blue eyes. I might be talking to him, chatting about nothing at all, and suddenly I would stop, my heart chirruping, because I had just that moment caught a glimpse of the sky inside his skull.

I didn't fall in love with him because he was unavailable to me. That may be what you're thinking, but it's not true. Quite apart from anything else he *was* available to me: he and I were closer than most human beings ever are. Comrades in war – you know how it goes. We shared everything. I know he loved me, and he knew I loved him. What we didn't have was *sex*. But what does that mean? Look. The key thing here is intimacy. Sex and intimacy are not the same thing. In lots of cases sex and intimacy are mutually incompatible. But love and intimacy are connected things, of course that's true. You'll surely agree that intimacy is the currency of love. No? Imagine true love without intimacy – or imagine it, if you like, with only glancing, occasional intimacy: a slap on the back, an arm round the shoulder (but the face looking in a different direction), a shared cup of coffee.

You see there's a grim secret hidden in intimacy, and this has to do with the awkward fact that pain is more intimate than pleasure; and death is the most intimate thing of all. I tell you this expecting you to understand, because you are also a soldier. A human head deformed by some killing impact into a bell-shape, the features stretched and grotesqued upon it like wax. That leer. A body lying on its back on the pavement, its juices oozing and running from all its loose joins and threads. Blood and engine oil mixed copiously together. The day-glo orange and red and streaky yellow of intestines in bright sunlight. That old song:

> *I want the doctor*
> *To take your picture*
> *So I can look at you from inside as well.*

Of course you might repress it, might *need* to do so, but it's the truth of love regardless of that. You want to dismantle the loved one. If you properly love somebody it's not enough to love their exterior surfaces only. This reason, or one very like it, is why love and war have always been so completely intertwined, from Homer's day to our own. I'll eat you up, I love you so.

Simic's death was a terrible and a pitiable thing for me to endure. The phrase is *a blow*, and once you've experienced it you understand the force of that metaphor. Death had swung his meaty fist and connected hard with my chest – slammed me in the middle of the ribs, sat me back on my arse and heaved all my breath away. I was drowning in grief, like a man in water. Like a fish in air. That is how I was. But how I was and what I did were different things.

That car park in Hammersmith. I got to the bottom of the stairwell, scraping my arse from step to step. My pack was at the bottom – I'd had enough to do with lugging the automatic cannon up the stairway without trying to bring my pack too – so I tugged that outside on to the street. The concrete structure was groaning above me. I got it into my rabbit-panicky head that the whole car park was about to topple in upon me, so although I was sobbing and shuddering hard I forced myself to scurry through the ground-floor level and out the main car entrance. I wasn't thinking. I should at least have checked the wiki – there might have been squad upon squad of enemy troops right there. I might have been gunned down like a fairground target, dusty and blinking in the light. That might have been where my narrative ended, when the freeze-frame goes from colour to sepia, though the soundtrack carries on to broadcast volley upon volley of gunfire. And maybe there's an inadvertent truth in that. Perhaps hearing continues even after sight has gone; blackness and the body's pulse frozen, and the lung's cul-de-sac no longer throbbing. Only the sound of the voices in the darkness *He's gone, yeah, he's done – he's done. Cooked like bacon.*

There was nobody in the street.

I staggered left and lollopped away. Ten minutes passed before I thought to check my wiki, and since I couldn't get my right hand to work I had to stop and put down my kit to do this. I pinged the destruction of the car park, and Simic's death, but the former piece of news – which, tactically, was the more significant – had been noticed by others and added already. I discovered that I was going the wrong way, and liable to stumble into an enemy patrol, so I turned about and ducked left up a long, empty street. The sporadic sounds of battle seemed enormously distant to my damaged ears. Pings were coming in constantly. Mumblings in my ears. Dust in my eyes. Checking the wiki was a tiresome process; the readout kept blurring.

Was I crying? Of course not – a warrior, like me? The idea.

I passed a Boots Metro, and blew a hole in its shopfront grille with a grenade shell. Inside I grabbed a bagful of first-aid: splinted up my right wrist there and then, and took the rest with me, stumbling away. Then I followed the wiki as best I could. It was a good guide; my comrades were still updating it, and enemy positions were charted pretty accurately. I'm afraid I added little to it. Prolonged jogging was awakening a series of specific pains inside my body. My wrist seared with every jolt. My hip seemed not quite right in its socket, and flared pain with each step. I ran into the enemy only once: turning a corner and seeing a tank and several dozen combatants, several hundred metres away. I don't know if they saw me; but I pulled back sharpish. I tried to update the wiki – which is to say, I tried to focus my jammering heart and trembly fingers, to steady myself sufficiently to note this advance. But by the time I had got myself sufficiently under control to input data somebody else had noticed it.

I jinked round again, and ran through a shopping mall, keeping tight against the shopfronts. A simulacrum of me ran through the glass frontage, leaping towards me or jolting further away as I passed shop window, or inset glass shop-door. A surveillance camera began shaking its head, glacially, in disapproval.

I came out at the back into the delivery area, a petrified lagoon, where the sunlight cast parsimonious shadows from nearly straight overhead. Two trucks, both electric, were parked on the yellow crosshatching; and I took the nearest, cracking the doorlock with my rifle butt and starting the engine with my smartphone.

There was a spycam tucked into the corner of the ceiling like a tiny black limpet. Some people like to stick the lens over with chewing gum; but I hardly cared. What did it matter? I backed up, the truck peeping like a sparrow, and then I pulled round in an arc. I set off. As I went over speedbumps, pallets in the half-emptied back clashed and chimed.

A vote was called. I almost didn't participate because I felt so discombobulated. But I make it a point of principle always to vote. The vote is the lifeblood of democracy, after all. The prop was that we not scatter but rather pull back and counterattack to the south. Some NMAs must have spotted a tactical possibility down there; but I couldn't really follow all the debating, not whilst I was trying to drive and to contain my sobbing and shaking, and to swallow down my pain. And I preferred the earlier plan. So I voted no; and no was the overall vote. Accordingly we reverted to the earlier model, and disappeared; and the enemy's knife met water, or mist.

This van took me all the way out of London. I followed the wiki, and it did me proud: no roadblocks, almost no enemy activity. What I mean is: there *were* roadblocks, and there *was* enemy activity; but we had people all over the area and it was an easy enough matter to slip through the cracks. I passed underneath the M25 near Waltham, and made it up past Harlow before the van ran out of juice. I parked it by the side of the road.

By this point I had calmed down a little. I took a good look at myself in the rear-view mirror. My face was speckled with cuts, the scabs already turned ruby, by the body's own alchemic processes of metamorphosis. I was so grubby it looked like I was wearing nightassault facepaint. Wet wipes from the bag of Boots stuff I had grabbed made some inroads in this dirt, and opening up several of the lacerations. Then I took off my body armour, and scrubbed at the clothing underneath – jeans and top – as best I could, to take off some of the worst dirt. I still looked like a tramp, of course.

It was mid afternoon. I was suddenly ravenous. In the back of the van I found crates of easymeals – microwaveable curries, ready-to-cook pizzas. I unsheathed one of these latter from its cardboard, cheese and tomato, pulled off its condom of cellophane. I ate it raw, in big bites. I drank a can of milk. Then, still shivering slightly, I discovered to my surprise that I was absolutely, deadbeat, couldn't-keep-those-eyelids-open exhausted. I lay on the floor of the van and fell asleep.

When I woke it was gone midnight. I experienced for the first time (the first of many times) that horrible visceral wrongfooting, like the sensation just before you reach the top of the hump of the rollercoaster, when the thrill of anticipation turns over into the low-in-the-gut terror and nausea and horror. I might wake, and for the briefest moment the grief has gone, and the day is all possibility. Then the car goes over the lip and the reality slams into my stomach: that he is dead and will never come back again, and I feel sick and full of fear and crushed. The key had been propelled forcefully into my cranium, and there it stuck, like a poisoned thorn, a torment to my flesh.

Through the windshield everything was black. The sky in mourning for the death of Simic.

I gathered myself; packed up my kit and clambered painfully down from the van. Then, without looking back, I limped away into the dark, my useless right hand tucked in at my jacket pocket. It was a clear, huge night. Tyre-black sky. Bullet-sharp stars. The moon, very low in the west, made larger by its proximity to the horizon as if gorged on its own delicious, fluid light. Night is a more intimate thing than day; but the last thing bereavement wants is intimacy. Nothing to be done. I pushed on.

Twenty minutes of helping along and I came into a village: all asleep under the English sky. I advanced cautiously, but unnoticed, beneath tangerine street lamps, past short-back-and-side hedgerows. Most of the houses stood a long way back from the road, dark and quiet. My mind was fizzing. It circled round and round. A tisket, a tasket. On and on and on. I dream I'm an eagle. Here's a mock-Tudor house with a Ford Tiger in the driveway. I stepped up to the front grille of this vehicle, half-thinking of taking it and driving away. But these new cars are slathered in theftproof devices. So I stood there trying to think it through: I couldn't smash my way into the vehicle, and even if I somehow got inside it would take more than a smartphone to start the engine.

I lay my hand on the bonnet, unthinking. Straightaway the alarm started: a colossally loud, strangulated high-pitched yelping. All the car's lights winked together. It made my heart jump, I don't mind telling you, and my right hand flopped out of its pocket to dangle uselessly. I didn't so much step away as lurch backwards up against the hedgerow and into shadows.

Then, getting a grip, I took my right wrist in my left hand and tucked it back in its pocket.

I stared, to be honest. There was something hypnotic in the son et lumière. I'll tell you what it was: the car in front of me was giving voice to my grief, although it was a nerveless and bloodless device. It was a mourner. The machine mourned as man could not, with a force and a relentlessness: and as it did so it occurred to me, thinking of all the tasks mankind had delegated to machines, that it was strange we had not devised some machine for grieving. Of all human activities grieving is surely the one that calls for the greatest perseverance, the greatest regularity and stamina, the greatest inexhaustible perfection.

The keening of that car. There was something terrible and beautiful about it.

The cuts on my face had opened up again – I could feel the slick and ooze on my cheeks, and running into the corner of my mouth. But it wasn't blood, and the cuts had not opened up. The lacerations, there, were still sealed just fine by their ruby plugs. I was weeping to keep the car company. Ach, ach, ach.

Isn't crying a shocking thing?

A rectangle of light came on in the mock-Tudor house's flank: bright yellow against the darkness, with an attendant trapezoid of rather dimmer yellow upon the grass beneath it. Then, a few moments later, the front door – two inset stippled glass panels – lit up. I reached into my pack with my good hand as the door swung open.

A man came out, still fitting his right arm into the sleeve of his dressing gown. His was a large bald head, and it was briefly silhouetted against the light in the hallway behind him like the dome of a Van de Graaff generator – a few wild hairs standing straight up off it under electrical prompting. He padded over the drive, and aimed his key at his car to switch off the wailing. I recognized my cue.

I stepped forward. 'Give me the key,' I said. I may not have articulated the sentence very well. My mouth was gummy, and tears were still leaking out of me.

'What?' he cried, turning to face me. 'What?'

I came further forward. The car was still shrieking, and shrieking, and shrieking.

'What?' he said again. 'You what?'

Aiming the pistol with my left hand was a tricky business. I didn't want to shoot him by accident.

'That,' he demanded, crossly, 'what have you *got there?*'

'Give me the key,' I repeated. I felt a huge pressure of will inside me. He was *fucking going* to give me the *fucking key*. 'Hand it *well* over. Do it now, or I'll rip open your body with this, this, this.'

But he ignored me, from dazed incomprehension rather than bravado, stepping over to his car and pressing the key against the roof. The lights stopped flashing. The song of sharp grief was ended. I felt a flare of rage at this, bright as a welder's torch. What right did he have to stop the shrieking? He was supposed to give me the key. He hadn't given me the key. I resented the curtailment of the car's song. Simic deserved much more than this.

I aimed the pistol at the ground, not far from his feet, and fired. It felt awkward, firing left-handedly. But the round passed from the weapon and into the ground, and it shook my ears as it went, and it woke *him* up. He did a short-lived impression of his car alarm; and then he dropped the key on the gravel and threw his arms upwards. I made him pick the key up, place it on the roof of the car, and back off into the garden. 'Lie down,' I shouted, weeping like a child, barely comprehensible, bitterly conscious of how stupid I must look.

139

But raging, too. 'Lie on your front.' It would have been the easiest thing in the world to shoot him through his ridiculous bald head.

He kept saying Christ's first name, over and over.

I had never before seen a skull so idiotic, so puffed-up and shell-like. His head ached to receive my bullet.

I tucked the gun into my trousers, picked up the keys, opened the car, put the keys in my pocket, threw my kit inside, got in myself, and freed the keys to start the engine. And then I drove away. The street lights were smeary blurs that leapt and danced when I blinked. I could hardly see.

I kept to tiny roads, synchronizing my NMA wiki with the machine's satnav and making my way past a succession of signs all offering WELCOME to CAREFUL DRIVERS and, by implication, with no hospitality for me: Much Hadham; Patmore Heath; Brent Pelham; Nuthampstead; Great Chishill; Fowlmere; Haslingfield, and finally along the road into Trumpington.

It was still dark, a little before dawn, and the broad road from Trumpington to Cambridge was deserted. In no time at all I was in Cambridge proper, patrolling along the narrow streets, with the stone trench on each side, sliding between the tall, silent and unlit edifices of Gothic and Classical colleges. My tears had dried. The skin of my face felt caked and stiff.

I parked outside an all-night coffee bar and bought a cardboard cup of black, tasteless to my gummed mouth but palpably hot. A few panda-eyed students were clustered at the back of the place, giving all their attention to their screenbooks and paying me no heed. The server was a dark-skinned woman, and she looked at me, but not in recognition or suspicion, and not with any interest: in fact with a settled form of indifference. I don't know if she considered me a suspicious character but didn't care, or if all her customers looked like me.

I paid one euro for a screen and spent an hour browsing newssites, my mind numb. I was exhausted but wide awake: a strange combination. The thing was, I was curious how subscriber newsgroups were reacting to the ongoing – but it was the same sort of stuff I could get through my own link.

A great mass of outrage and hostility focused on my NMA, expressed in a great variety of forums; and a lesser quantity of Scottish nationalist or other support for what we were doing. *England brought war to half the globe for two centuries; now war has been brought to England* was one commentator's opinion (or words to that effect), and her feed carried two thousand reader comments. *In the twentieth century the enemy was dictators; now the enemy is terrorists* wrote another, with eight hundred comments. *Any means necessary*, was a common tag, and the means included all-out nuclear assault, gas, white phosphorus, targeted gene-weapons or 'sonic lasers', which (the commentator insisted) were in development in a secret lab. But the thing deemed 'necessary' varied from annihilating NMAs to humbling the UK Government. Above all the web hummed with the palpable excitement of it. Nothing more exciting than war, after all. The best kind of war is one close enough to you to raise the thrill, but not so close that it actually incommodes your day-to-day. *Homeric*, was one very popular tag, which didn't seem to me very accurate. *Heinlein*, another. *Churchill*, another.

I couldn't get used to tapping the mouse with my left hand. It didn't feel natural, or right.

When I went outside again the sky was mother-of-pearl overhead and rosy nearer the rooftops. I drove out to the north-east of the city, where Harry lived.

This was Harry's road: two lines of fancy terraced housing. Both sides of the street were crammed with parked cars, but I wasn't in the mood to drive about looking for a free space, so I stopped, fished a tyre-lever from the boot to use as a makeshift towline, and dragged a car by main-motor-force from the side of the road. There was a satisfying sound of metal complaining, and of course the parked vehicle's alarm started whooping. I towed it round the corner; and because I had a little difficulty unsnicking the tyre-iron (for it had bitten hungrily into the metal), I left it there with the wailing machine. Then I drove back round and parked up.

I tickled the belly of my smart phone until Harry's number came up.

It rang eleven times before Harry's breathy voice mumbled, 'You'd better have a fucking good reason for ringing me at this hour, Caller Unknown.'

'It's me.'

But his mind was obviously blurry. 'It's me?'

'It's Antony'

'Tony Block Jesus. Tony Jesus Block.' The o vowel was inflected with a groan. I heard him coughing. Then: 'Jesus you know it's not even six o'clock.'

'Did I wake you?'

'You remember the times we spent together? You remember how I wasn't a vampire, and needed to *sleep* in the nighttime, like every other fucking human being? That's still the way it is with me.'

'Can I come over?'

He coughed again. I could hear a voice, indistinct, in the background. 'I'm not sure that's,' he said. 'Look, that may not be.'

'I'd really like to come over.'

'Where are you, Tony?' Harry asked. The voice in the background became more distinct: *you are speaking to* Tony? *you are kidding me along?*

'Cambridgeshire,' I said. 'I am in the English county of Cambridgeshire.'

'Are you outside my house, Tony?'

'I am outside your house, Harry.'

I could hear Joram, in the background, harrumphing. Harry asked: 'Have you come from London?'

'Brew me some proper coffee, Harry, and I'll tell you about it.'

'Jesus Tonio, couldn't you give me a little more notice?' Everything he said, from this point on, was accompanied in the background by Joram's squeaky little voice saying *no! no! no!*, like that Simpsons' episode in the radio station where Bart shouts *I want my elephant!* in the background of all the songs.

'I'm a little hurt,' I said.

'Hurt? Like, hospitalizable hurt? Hurt hurt? Or just hurt?' *No! no! no!*

'I need to come in, really.'

'Come in for, what, hospital care? We're not a hospital.'

'It's a sprained wrist,' I said. 'A broken heart, maybe. I'm not sure about that.'

'How long, Tonio?' He meant *how long will you be staying?* In the background: *No! no! no!*

'Couple of days.'

'Do you know how outrageous this is, turning up like this?' *No! no! no!* 'Do you follow the news? It's illegal now to have military kit in your house. The police could arrest us.' *No! no! no!*

'Please, Harry.' That was a word I almost never used. Harry knew that.

So I was in their kitchen, drinking coffee and eating a freshly toasted crumpet, the butter oozing from its giant pores like – but I didn't want to think what that oozing resembled. The news was on in the corner, and Harry was fussing at my face with a blob of disinfectant-soaked cotton wool and some tweezers. Joram was sitting on a stool glowering at me with his arms crossed.

'Bits of – is this blackened glass? Is that what this is? Did you go through a window?'

'I presume it's stone.'

'Don't move your mouth for a moment. There's a piece the size of my little fingernail in your chin.'

'Concrete. Or metal – or maybe it's glass, yeah. Could be lots of things.'

'Don't *move* your mouth.' He fussed for a minute. 'Oh but you look a mess, Tonio.'

'Why don't you go to the hospital?' said Joram, with a hint of Hispanic *ch* to the *h* of the last word. 'They can look after you better at the hospital.'

'Don't mind Jory,' said Harry plucking something that wasn't a hair out of my eyebrow. 'He doesn't mean to be unwelcoming.'

'You're a fucking cold-eyed killer,' said Joram. 'Is my opinion, Tony.'

'And lovely to see *you* again Joram,' I said. 'Do you know what? You're the only person I know who pronounces a "u" in the middle of my name.'

'I ought to call the police,' he snarled.

'You ought not,' said Harry, severely. 'Don't you worry about Joram. He's not going to call anyone.'

This, of course, was a worry. Perhaps I should have checked into a hotel, after all. But my sense was that the bullet at Hampton Court had changed things – we were probably in for an intense week, or fortnight, before the government finally accepted the inevitable and agreed to ceasefire and negotiations. During that time a lower profile would be best; and having my face snapped by the lobby camera of some hotel and stored on some police-accessible database might not be the cleverest thing. This, though, would depend upon Joram. And here's the thing: if it had just been myself and Harry in that house, I would probably have started crying, and I would have wept and wept. Joram's hostility at least gave me a notch against which to brace my grief. He gave me something to do that wasn't crying.

'Are you going to call anybody, Joram?' I asked, concentrating my words and aiming them directly at his head.

His fuzz-bearded face gave me a Paddington Bear Hard Stare. 'There's a terrorist hotline,' he said. The *ch* as in lo*ch*: *ch*otline.

Of course, him saying so meant that he wasn't going to call. At least not right away. If he'd been planning to do so he would not have mentioned it to me.

I got to my feet and picked up my kitbag with my good hand. 'Spare room in the same place? Or have you converted it into a home gym?'

Joram hissed.

I got upstairs and into the spare room – it was exactly as I remembered it. The curtains were drawn. The lampshade, when I flicked the switch, illuminated shapes from the Elgin Marbles and projected them dimly along the top of the walls. There was a smell of furniture polish, or of new carpet weave, or at any rate of a long stretch of prior non-occupation.

There was a mirror on the inside of the wardrobe door. I peered at my scratched and patched face for a while, hearing but not listening to the bicker of voices downstairs: Harry's deeper, Joram's higher-pitched. I put my head round the curtains to check the view from the window – a line of houses directly opposite, parked cars hemming both sides of the road. I calculated the exit line: a jump down on to the roof of the dark blue 4by4; good cover all the way along in either direction.

And when I had done all this I lay on the bed and looked up at the ceiling. The skin of my face throbbed a little from where Harry had gone over it. There was a square of wood inset into the ceiling. I got up again, and standing on the bed, was able to push this up and into the attic space. Even with my bad hand it wasn't too hard to haul myself up; to switch on the light and look around. Nothing but boxes, and the Λ beams of the roof. I took my rifle out, put it on one of the beams, and closed the hatch. Then I got my pistol, checked it, readied it, and put it into my waistband. Then I opened the spare room door, and went across the landing into the bathroom. I pissed, washed my hands, and took a good look out of the window there at the property's rear aspect – the ground floor roof stretched a good distance into the garden, which would be easy to go along. From there twenty yards to some bushes, and the backing garden a fence away. This was a better exit. Getting across the landing wouldn't be hard.

I went back into the spare room, put the pistol under the pillow and lay on the bed. Then I got up again, retrieved my pistol and tucked it into my pants. I checked under the bed and behind the wardrobe. Nothing there. I lay down again. There was a picture on the wall – a horse, done in blocky torn splotches of red and yellow and green. I didn't like the look of it, so I got up, took it down and leant it, face to the plaster, against the wall.

I lay on the bed again. I was crying, I remember that. I don't remember what I was crying about, or indeed if I was crying in response to any particular mental prompt – whether, in other words, I wasn't crying in the same way that I was breathing, or whether it was a more proximate reaction to the beating of my grief inside me. The localized rhythm of being-in-the-world.

The handle of my pistol was digging into my stomach a little. I shifted it round a little.

I dozed, I think. I couldn't say for certain that I slept, nor could I say for sure that I was awake. I had a half-dream, which is to say I experienced dreaming stripped of narrative or personage. There was a great plain, wide and green, and over it moved mighty parades of clouds, billowing structures of bright and bone-coloured splendour, darkening to blueberry in the middle of their undersides. The clouds were constantly decanting their contents on to the dark-green grasslands below, and the grasses were constantly soaking it up. There was not one sign of human habitation anywhere, and the air was neither warm nor cold, and the clean smell of rain and pasture possessed the whole of the landscape. The rain came down with an almost spiritual tenderness and completeness. And my point of view soared, and swept over the grasses: it was not just pasture – here were forests and copses, and here were ripe orchards, branches doing their actorly-melodramatic reaching-for-the-sky thing. Nettles like ruffs about the base of the trunks. A cidery scent or tang on the wet moss, and the grass between the trees. Crimson Queen, Early Bower, Green Longstem Pippin. Cobwebs strung with all the rain's clear globes, like miniature glass fruit. A boy in amongst the trees. I thought for a moment it was myself, as a youngster, but it wasn't. I knew who it was.

The key, the key.

A rat-tat knock at the door.

I was upright and the pistol was out and aimed at the door before I knew anything consciously – my finger light on the trigger. I had instinctively quietened my breath.

From the other side of the wood: 'Tony?'

The aim would have taken the bullet through the wood and into Harry's chest. I would then have dropped my aim a little, to take into account the fact that his body was falling, and fired again.

Croaky: 'What is it?'

'I'm going to work, Tony.'

I checked all around the room. Sucked in a silent breath, blew it silently out. I thought of putting my gun away, but felt more comfortable holding it out.

'OK.'

'I've got a spare key – shall I leave it *on the side* downstairs?'

I became aware that my face was sticky: the phlegm and salt aftermath of tears, glue on my cheeks. 'Key?'

'A doorkey, yes? Front door key?'

'OK.'

'I'll put it on the side downstairs.' A pause. Then: 'Joram's working from home, yeah? Is that OK?'

'Fine.'

'Tony – are you . . . ?' I was watching the twin lines of shadow in at the slit of light underneath the door. From those I could be sure my aim was at Harry's heart. He shifted his weight a little to the left and I moved my gun fractionally. 'Are you all right?'

'Fine.'

'Try to go easy on Joram, yes?'

'Sure.'

I lay down again and stared at the square in the ceiling. I heard him go downstairs. Then I heard the front door, and, through the window of my room, I heard the diminuendo of Harry's coughing as he walked away up the street.

I went to the bathroom, put my pistol into the soap dish and undressed. For the first time since Simic died I examined my body minutely, going inch-by-inch over it; bruised in a dozen places, new bruises layered upon old bruises. I found a thumbnail of something hard (metal, glass, stone) half-embedded in my thigh, and connected it – belatedly, stupidly – with the consciousness that I had had the sensation of discomfort in that leg. It came out and a slurp of blood came after it. I put a waterproof plaster over the cut.

I showered.

Then, wearing only a towel and carrying my pistol in my good hand, I went through to the master bedroom. The neatly made double bed: window opened a crack to air the place.

Harry, I knew, was the same build as me, give-or-take; and without compunction I went through his wardrobe and his chest of drawers and clad myself in his gear. It took longer than it might have done, on account of the awkwardness of dressing oneself one-handedly. The gun lay on top of the duvet whilst I did this, like a pet, watching me with its one eye.

I took some trainers, too. Then I strapped my wiki screen to my no-good arm, and made a sling from one of Harry's handkerchiefs. My right hand was tingling, which was either a sign that life was returning to it, or else that it was getting worse.

There was an enormous high-res photograph of the two of them hanging on the wall opposite the bed: shoulder to shoulder each with his arm about the other, beaming at the camera. It was pretty much life-sized; that's how big it was. Examining it I could not see any of the usual photographic grain or roughness in the image, so I daresay it had cost a fair bit. They were both dressed up, standing in front of some nondescript doorway. In the corner of the image, at a jaunty skew, had been written in silver ink: *Harry & Joram*, with a little flourish on the downstroke of the &.

There was a muffled clatter downstairs.

I took the gun and slunk into the hall, coming down the stairs stealthily. It had been the postman. The post lay on the mat beside the cat-flap. I tucked the gun away and stooped to pick it up. HARRY VAVASOUR, HARRY VAVASOUR, HARRY VAVASOUR, all official looking, and here was one: JORAM VAVASOUR. For some reason I found the juxtaposition of that forename and that surname comical. Some things just don't go very well together. Perhaps I was thinking, subconsciously, something along the lines of – you know: TONY VAVASOUR, or maybe HARRY BLOCK. Or something along those sorts of lines. But I can't honestly say that I *was* thinking that. I'm pretty sure that I wasn't feeling anything, on any level, at that particular moment. That might be an index of repression, or just of exhaustion.

Joram was in the doorway at the far end of the hall. 'I don't suppose any of that post is for you, Tony,' he said. The way he turned my name into three syllables. The way he *bent* it around its vowel.

I held the mail out to him. 'You took Harry's surname?'

'We're married,' he said coming towards me and taking hold of the envelopes, 'and I come from a traditional country.' I thought about arguing for the incoherence of this statement; but of course it would only have antagonized him.

'I'm going into town for a bit,' I said.

'He left you a key on the side. In the kitchen.'

'He said.'

As I went through, Joram called after me: 'How long will you stay?'

'Tomorrow. Or the day after, maybe. Not long.'

'Good.'

'Or maybe *months*,' I added, with a little dazzle of spite in my smile.

I put some milk and muesli in a bowl and sat in the kitchen. Joram stood in the doorway looking at me, but I didn't let myself be rattled by that. I checked my wiki as I ate. My people had scattered, and the British Army was stomping all over London with their heavy feet and rage in their hearts. But their knife had met only water. There were several discussions going on simultaneously about the timing of our reassemblage; which in turn was tied to the larger question of how long before the English government accepted the inevitable, ceased fire and entered into proper negotiations. One week, said some. A month said others.

'When *I* die,' said Joram, out of the blue, 'I'll go to my grave happy I got through my whole life without killing nobody. Without,' he added, flushing, 'killing anybody.'

I looked at him. I could see how thin his bravado was from the way he twitched and fidgeted under my gaze. From the way his own eyes looked left or right rather than directly into mine.

'Anything you need from town?' I asked.

As I was going out he hovered behind me in the hall, and said, again apropos of nothing: 'I make him *happy*, you know? Did you ever really make him *happy*?'

There really wasn't any point in getting into that.

I had left my helmet in the car. I didn't want to lose it if the car were seized (it was stolen, after all) so I transferred it to my room. Then, with a little black tape I'd found in Harry's toolbox, and some nail scissors, I turned the 3 of the number-plate into an 8, front and back; and for good measure I changed the P into an R too.

It was half ten before I walked into town. The day was bright, though cloudy; a few twisty ribbons of blue visible between tremendous swagbellied clouds, all fat white and cream brushstrokes and swirls. The closer to the centre of Cambridge I walked the more thronged the streets became. There were innumerable roadside stalls selling coffee, or bagels, or second-hand stuff, all operated by students presumably supplementing their income – or reducing, howsoever slightly, their debt. In the central market square there was a not unpleasant cacophony of musics: dance beats and brass, plainsong and acoustic guitars. I watched break dancers throw choreographed conniption fits around a hat – an actual homburg hat – that was almost half full of coins. Then I watched a lone trombonist, standing behind an almost empty plastic tub, angling himself down and up as he parped and blew: going as if to punch the ground, pulling back. Heiling at the sky.

Somebody jostled me from behind and I had them over, my trainer on the back of their neck, before I started thinking about what I was doing. He was whimpering. I've no idea why he bumped into me, accident or design. People were looking. My right hand was throbbing, its fingers twitching, as if straining to get back into the action and clasp his throat.

I took my foot from him and moved as quickly away as was compatible with inconspicuousness.

After that I tried to avoid the crowds. I wandered down to the river and sat on a pub terrace with a pint of beer, quite alone, and pleased to be alone. There were few other patrons, but they left me to myself. I had no thoughts. There were no thoughts in my head.

I browsed the wiki and added my contribution to a few of the debates. Being in this city felt wrong: the shops and the colleges; the crowds, all busy with their day-to-day stuff. There was a degree of war austerity, it is true: police patrolling, the occasional military Land Rover thundering along the road. But the city was mostly just carrying on its usual thing. The mundaneness of that seemed to me an affront. Or if not an affront, precisely, then certainly a kind of weird irrelevance. I found myself wondering whether I ought not to go to Kent – whether I did not have a kind of duty to go down to Kent, and find Simic's girlfriend, and tell her the bad news in person. Should I do that?

Apple orchards. Rain, being neither of the sky nor of the sea, is its own thing. The enormity of clouds; those giant objects.

Early evening news, and the three of us sitting in the TV room; and the newsreader folded his hands together on the desk in front of him and peered out from beneath a crinkly brow. To his left a slideshow of images from London; below him the red tape wormed its way right-left, detailing casualties; damages in euros; Newcastle peace talks; dangerous malfunctions on the EU Aeroscaphe, up in Earth orbit. The lead story was that the peace talks had broken down. Images of men in suits and women in smart dresses stomping out of a large grey building as reporters darted amongst them, prodding chopstick-mics in their faces. Then there were images of scientists suited up in tentlike protective suits, strolling languorously about Hampton Court, or what was left of it. 'Peace talks at Newcastle have broken down for the second time,' the newscaster said, drawing his face into ever tighter modes of seriousness.

'How they *love* this!' said Joram; a little toot round the edges of the tight lid crammed over his superheated fury. 'The news – oh it loves war, it loves all this *misery*.'

'You can hardly expect them not to report the war,' Harry noted.

'It's *our* misery,' he said. I thought: you don't know the first thing about misery, but I buttoned my lip; I zipped it. My lips were Velcro. Joram was on a roll: 'News and entertainment, now it's all the same newsertainment. They are *revelling* in it. To them its just ratings.' Rrrratings. I looked about the lounge as the telly burbled on ('. . . representatives of the so-called

Independent Government of Scotland deplored what they described as "bully tactics" on behalf of the British negotiators . . .'). Wealth was everywhere in this room: two original canvases by Konstantinou, a signed Turner print; Ultra High Def screen half the size of the wall; vat-grown beeskin sofas. I saw no evidence of misery here.

'I bumped into Meirion. Somebody vandalized his car,' said Harry. 'He said he parked it outside ours, but I don't remember that. Somebody tried to break into the back with a tyre iron, he said.'

'Hmm,' I said. I was thinking of a piece of paper cut into the shape of a human being – this piece of paper, you see, was Simic – and then I thought of this paper man taken between two impersonal hands, and ripped in one sharp gesture into two unequal pieces. But this being magic paper, imbued with the consciousness of Simic, and all his sly wit, and his blue eyes, and the beauty of his observations, and his capacity for feeling pain and his human terror of dying – this was a hideous wrench, and agony and death.

'Look,' Joram was saying, and he was looking at me and pointing at the screen. 'Senior sources in the military,' the newsreader was saying, 'have confirmed that the recent military surge has flushed almost all illegal combatants out of London.' And there was a headshot of a senior feudal officer, face as shiny under the camera light as a newly scrubbed child's: 'Hampton Court was a last, desperate throw of the dice for these bandits,' he said. 'We have beaten them in open battle. What remains is a mopping-up operation.'

'*That*'s why you're here,' said Joram. 'With your tail between your legs.' He had the linguistic ingenuity to turn even *legs* into a disyllable. It was rather winning.

'Cluck cluck,' I said.

'You could at least have the decency to admit—'

'One week,' I said, the torn paper figure of Simic scattered on the floor. Blood was coming out from the broken weave of the paper – each fibre tucked-in with blood. 'Two at most.'

'You said a couple of days,' said Joram. It was a shriek.

'Not how long I am staying,' I said, raising my own voice. 'How long until we have properly *broken the British military.*'

At this Joram opened his mouth so wide I could have put my elbow in there. His eyes were perfectly round. It was the most Mediterranean of dumb-shows; pure theatrical astonishment – for my benefit, of course. I sat forward and reached around to where the pistol was tucked, into the back of my trousers; but I contented myself with resting the hand there.

'Hungry?' said Harry in a loud voice. 'Don't fight, boys! I'll start the food.'

Harry cooked a fancy meal. The three of us sat around candles with Radio 3 on the speakers and ate in a weird pastiche of an actual civilized dinner party. Harry joked and talked small, but there was a high-pressure quality to his good humour. Joram made no attempt to disguise his hostility. He drank most of the first bottle, and as Harry opened a second he said: 'You don't even have uniforms.'

'Who,' I said. 'Me?'

'Who else?' The *Who* was kicked off with that lo*ch* throat-scrape sound.

'We do indeed have uniform. Oh, unless you mean clothes? We don't wear uniform *clothing*, no.'

Perhaps Joram thought this an obscure dig at his command of English, because he said: 'What other sense of uniform is there?'

'We have a uniform wifi, a uniform wiki. Clothes hardly matter. Who cares how you dress online? Even the British Army have given up wearing red coats.'

'The news call you a rabble. Yesterday it was terrorist militia, now its rabble – because you all turned your backs and ran away when the real army took back London.' He made one polysyllabic tumble out of *took back*.

'Jor!' cried Harry. 'Tonio, ignore him.'

'No *Tonio*,' said Joram. 'Don't ignore me.'

'It's the wine speaking, Tonio.'

'It's not the wine speaking, it is I.'

'Joram wouldn't hurt a fly,' said Harry, rather louder than he needed to.

Joram's face bulged at this comment, but he didn't say anything. He poked a fork through his pasta, trailed a strand though the bloodred sauce, then put the fork down and took another glug of wine. 'Let us talk man to man, Tony.' Trisyllabic Tony. It rankled, that mangling of my name. It's not a complicated or unusual name, after all.

I looked at Joram. 'Man to,' I replied, and deliberately stopped there.

'I can understand you wanting to be a soldier, but if you want to be a soldier why not be a real soldier? Why not join the real army?'

'He was in the real army,' said Harry; and with a wholly unconvincing laugh he added; 'You left me for the army. I used to say, *most* people, their boyfriends leave them for another guy; but *you* left me for ten thousand other guys.'

'You were in the real army?' Joram pushed.

'I *am* in a real army, you pair of fuckers,' I said, in a pleasant, well-modulated voice.

'You don't think there is a difference between a public army and a militia?' Joram insisted. 'You don't recognize the difference? So, by your book any group of terrorists or mare, or mare—'

'Jor,' said Harry, his voice loud and brittle. 'Put a *cork* in it? Maybe?'

'—terrorists or mare-*marederers* can call themselves an army? You don't think anything else is necessary?' He had a bit of trouble with the sibilants in that last word, but he got it out.

'Like what?'

'Like a government, like a properly constituted *authority*. And not just some gun-happy shooters all running about.'

'My army,' I said, 'is presently in the service of a properly constituted ow-thority. The Scottish government.'

'Afee-glif!' Joram hooted. 'Afee-glif!' It took me a moment to realize he meant *fig-leaf*. 'It's any excuse, you take any chance to play at soldiers. A trillion euros damage, the news said. A trillion! Not counting the dead, of course, or—'

My pistol, which I had tucked into my waistband, was digging in to the top of my right thigh. I put my fork down, pulled the weapon out and placed it on the dining table, next to my plate, where my left hand could get to it if I needed it. This shut them both up.

I suppose Joram raising his voice jangled my nerves a little. My nerves were raw, you see.

'It is a little difficult,' I said, in level voice, 'to walk away from the smouldering corpse of the man you loved most in the world – difficult to see that as *playing*.'

Only silence. I preferred this to the chatter. I finished my meal. The scrape and clink of cutlery on china.

'Very nice,' I said, pushing my chair back a way and standing up. 'Thank you for that, Harry. I think I'll go lie down now.'

Joram was glowering at me with a desperate sort of intensity: fear counterfeiting hostility. 'How did you *do* it?' he hissed. Harry reached out to lay a calming palm on his arm – both Joram's arms were on the table, shivering with ill-suppressed fury.

I picked up the pistol in my left hand. 'Do what?'

'Defeat the British Army? At Basingstoke? At Reading?'

'Defeated them not once,' I agreed, a curious lightness opening inside my chest as I spoke. 'But many times.'

Joram started to retort something, but Harry interrupted him with a murmur.

The candle flames quailed, seem to shrink away from me, then stood up tall again.

'The news says *lucky*,' said Harry, in a quiet voice. 'Or it says *treachery*. Or it says regular army incompetence and calls for generals to be sacked.'

The movement of that candle flame. All my spidery-senses tingled.

'And now,' Joram added, 'the news says the surge has finally knocked you *out*.'

The momentary bowing down of the candle flames meant that somebody had opened a door, somewhere behind me. I put my weight on to the balls of my feet, feeling the awkwardness of using my left hand to operate the gun.

'We won because democracy is a better way of organizing an army than feudal hierarchy,' I said, slipping to the side so as to put something solid behind my back. The unrightness of holding my gun in my left hand was throwing me a little. I had some movement back in my right hand, but not enough to hold a pistol.

'Who else has a key to this house?' I asked.

'What do you mean?' asked Harry, his voice even softer. There was something in their look – both of them were staring at me now with a kind of mute, passive horror. That didn't reassure me.

'Don't play games Harry, who *else* has a key here?'

He was perked by my tone. 'Nobody! Nobody does! Jor and I have keys, and my Mum has a key but she's in

Weston-super-Mare.' The pleading face; the warbly voice. I could read this, of course; it meant *please don't discharge your weapon inside my lovely house!* 'The only other key is the spare, and I gave that to *you!*'

I aimed the pistol through the dining room door into the hallway. From the light into the darkness. Naturally I couldn't see anything. The tall glass panel that ran vertically parallel to the front door gleamed dark blue with the evening's ambient light, but otherwise it was all in shadow. There was no silhouette, no noise. If *I* had come creeping in through the door to kill somebody, what would I do? All that Ninja malarkey: it was just nonsense. This was not how the world worked. I pondered the idea of simply letting a couple of shots off and seeing if I flushed anything out. Then I balanced that against the idea of holding my fire.

I was too obviously a target, standing outlined in the doorway of the candlelit dining room. It would not do. I ducked and took a step to the left, ready to slink quietly through the kitchen and round into the TV room when – bathetically – a black cat padded into the room.

The slinky beast went under the table and wrapped itself around Joram's legs. I stepped into the hall and switched the light on. Nothing there. The cat-flap looked awfully low down in the door to have let in a breeze capable of disturbing the candles on a table in the other room. But a quick check through the rooms of the ground floor revealed nothing.

I was a little jittery. Evidently I was.

'I'm going to bed, gentlemen,' I said, in a loud voice. And I tonked up the stairs.

I spent no more than five minutes in the bathroom: brushed my teeth and washed my face. As I came out, heading towards the spare room, Joram was going along the upstairs landing. He passed as if I did not exist.

And I was alone on the landing.

I went into my room, and shut the door, and switched on the wiki and spent a quarter of an hour in conversation with any comrades who happened to be online and in the e-vicinity.

'[But this is from the inside,]' said a trooper called Makouk; I can't remember his first name, but I'd helped haul him into cover at Reading, where he'd lost some toes, bleeding nastily out of a hole on the toe of his boot. His foot was mended now, he said; or good as.

'Inside what?' I said, logging in.

'[Block? We're talking about the Provisional Scottish Government,]' said Fish.

'[Block, hello,]' said Makouk.

'[Hello!]'

'[Hiya!]'

'[They don't like the P-word, the Scots,]' said Makouk.

'How's your big toe, Makouk?' I put in.

'[I have all new toes now, fitted by one of the country's leading experts in prosthesis. She said that people sometimes ignore toes, but that they play a much larger part in balance and so on than you might think.]'

'[I can't believe we're jawing on about toes,]' interjected a soldier called Wigley whom I did not know personally.

'What were you saying about the Scots?'

'[I have a source inside the Government. They say they're anxious.]'

'[They think we're beaten,]' said Wigley. '[But the Scots need to be patient.]'

'[I guess they reckon the next step is the English Army rampaging through the lowlands.]'

'[They don't want us using atomics, for *sure*,]' said Fish. '[A spokesperson was on the news. A lot of stuff about, they never authorized the use of such weaponry, that they can see why the English are calling it a war crime and so on.]'

'[War crime?]' Wigley was outraged at the suggestion. '[We killed enemy combatants. The civilians had all long since vacated Hampton.]'

'[Part of our contract with *them*,]' put in a young soldier called John Stammers – I'd once shared a lift with him, on our way north at the start of operations, though it seemed a long time ago now – '[is that they negotiate peace that includes amnesty for our actions during the war. So talk of war crime doesn't worry me.]'

'[That's what *I'm* saying,]' said Makouk. '[My friend inside the Scots Government says that *that* is what worries them. The end of hostilities in England. They're anxious that *we* won't be happy with the settlement they negotiate. They're scared we'll become a loose cannon, that we'll take our quarrel to Scotland and waste the land.]'

'[That's bullshit,]' was Fish's opinion.

We chewed the topic out for a bit. The thing to do, we all agreed, was to finish the fighting sooner rather than later. Not that we should rush matters; and anything we did would have to be articulated by the wisdom of our crowd. But the English were tottering on the point of pushover. We had started a job, and we needed to end it.

I turned the light out and lay on the bed – fully clothed, on top of the covers, my pistol beside the pillow. For a while I stared through the gloom, and just lay there. I can't say that thoughts were going through my head. I was just lying there, not asleep and not, properly, awake. Occasional passing cars stroked the ceiling with their headlight beams, unfolding and folding up fans of light. Half an hour went by. Maybe it was more than that. I was in a kind of reverie, imagining the passage of something huge, something mighty, over the green pastures and steppe-land of my imagination. Like clouds being driven along by the wind, and hauling their shadows over the ground. Like clouds, but not clouds: something cloud-sized.

'Tonio?' An urgent whisper. Not a knock, but the scrape of nails down the wood of the door. 'Tony, it's Harry. Can I come in?'

I lay for a while listening to this, sifting it out from the reverie, comprehending it was a piece of the real world. 'It's your house,' I said, eventually, speaking as loud as an auctioneer, and even startling myself a little with my own volume.

Harry carried on with his whispering. 'Can I come in, though?'

'Come in for Christ's sake.'

The door opened, aggressively bright, and Harry's silhouette inked itself in. He shut the door behind him, and padded over to the bed. I could hear as much as see (the hiss and draw of silk over silk) that he was in a dressing gown. The mattress sagged near my feet.

'What is it, Harry?' I asked. I was expecting, I suppose, conversation. That's not what I got. Instead there was the sound of silk sliding, and then somebody else's fingers fumbling at my trousers. I took hold of the stock of my gun with my left hand, and, a little belatedly, my heart rate got faster. Harry's nimble fingers separated my fly, and pulled out my cock.

He shifted his weight, and straddled my legs, lifting himself momentarily to give himself room to shuffle my trousers and pants down. My knees went out, and the bunching of clothing at my ankles mimicked shackles, or ties, and that was something that always excited me. I was awake, but not fully conscious. Or else I was conscious, but not fully awake. I was passive, certainly, and my left hand clutched my gun so tightly

I could feel the grooves tooled into the stock leaving an impression upon my palm.

Harry ducked forward in the dark and fitted his mouth around my cock. No mistaking *that* sensation. You know what it felt like? I don't mean being on the receiving end of a blow-job – I assume you know what that feels like, that such activity happens even in West Texas. I don't mean that. I mean that, at that moment, in that place, it felt like the dissolution of time. It felt like Harry and I were still together, and I hadn't left to join the army, and he hadn't married *Joram*, of all people. That none of the things that had forced me away – all the way away to the British Army – had happened at all. Except that those things had been functions of Harry's extraordinary physical beauty, and I was very much conscious of that. The sensation was more than physical pleasure; it was that hint, or intimation, of *coming home* – and that, Colonel, I need hardly tell you, is the key to unlock my very soul. Harry was sucking the end of my cock, and his left forefinger was pressed at the exact midpoint of my perineum, and his right hand was twined-in my pubic hair and tugging it rhythmically. And as he sucked he pushed the tip of his sharp-little tongue into the hole of my urethra. Nobody else sucked my cock in exactly that manner. It flushed my spirit with nostalgia.

'Harry,' I said. Given how pleasure-blissed my brain function was, my voice came out surprisingly cogent. 'What do you think you're doing, Harry?'

He could not reply with my cock in his mouth; and an intensification of suction stabbed sweetness up my torso. I arched the small of my back.

'Stop,' I said. 'Stop a second.'

He pulled his head back. 'What?'

'What are you doing, Harry?'

His fingers were still tangled in amongst my pubes. 'Which part of this are you finding hard to understand?' he said.

His evasiveness, or the implied giggle in his voice, or the fact that my blow-job had been so abruptly interrupted, made me snappish. It occurred to me that I could bring the gun out and point it at his head – that this might make him answer me properly. Not that I wanted to kill him, you understand. I don't think I did. I only wanted a proper answer. But I didn't do this. It would have been rude. 'What the *fuck*, Harry?'

'Is this not—?' he said, a twinge in his tone. 'Do you want something else?' He rearranged his weight, and began pulling his legs round.

There was enough play in the fingers of my right hand – though it smarted when I used it – for me to be able to reach out with it and turn on the bedside lamp, without having to let go of my pistol. The light made me close my eyes. When I opened them again Harry was there, naked, sitting on the bed between my knees.

'Whatever you want,' he said.

'*What?*'

'Whatever,' he said again.

'Joram's, like, in the *next room*,' I said. I sounded more puzzled than rebuking, I think.

I looked into his eyes – and of course my cock was straining, and of course some part of me wanted to quit all this talky nonsense, and instead to drive myself hard inside him, his arse's tight aperture, the warmth and wetness of his mouth. But instead I experienced a clattering sense of comprehension. Looking into his eyes I saw what was going on here. He was afraid.

That undid everything

'Jesus,' I said, sitting up. 'Christ.'

There was some comical bodily rearrangement, as I got my legs out from underneath him without hooking him in the net of my ankle-tangle of trousers, and he got himself off the bed without falling over. It might have provoked laughter in us both, except that Harry was terrified and I was, abruptly, very aware of how terrified he was.

I pulled my trousers up. I could not stay in that room.

Joram, it turned out, was not in the next room. He was sitting in a chair in the dining room downstairs gazing blankly at the wall. Imaginatively projecting upon it, I suppose, all the things I was doing with his husband up in the spare room. I stood at the door, and after a moment he looked round at me. The terror was in his eyes as well.

I turned. Harry had followed me down. It occurred to me then – it is a stupid thing to say, of course, because it is a very basic thing to do with human interaction, for all that it had never properly registered with me before – it occurred to me that eyes looking at you in terror of what you might do, and eyes looking at you imploringly, especially sexually-imploringly, are very similar eyes. But that nobody, really, deep-down, could mistake the one set of eyes for the other.

'Gentlemen,' I said. I felt completely *out* of place. I felt like an adult who had intruded himself at a children's party. I felt I had crammed myself into the playhouse. I felt itchy inside my skull. I felt like I wanted to raise my left hand and aim the pistol and begin firing – not for the bullets, or the physical damage I could do, so much as the *sound* of it. The roar of it; the yell of it. It could yell. All I could do was say 'Gentlemen, I shall fuck off.'

I didn't lift the pistol. I tucked it away into the top of my trousers.

Neither of them spoke a word.

Twenty minutes to load the car, whilst Joram and Harry sat together in the kitchen. Joram had broken open a bottle of brandy, and was slurping it like fruit juice. Harry, always too conscious of the beauty of his body to indulge himself in anything too harming, nursed a half-centimetre of the stuff. Maybe they were thinking: *He might still kill us*. Maybe they were just thinking: *Thank heavens he is going*. Perhaps Harry was contemplating the taste of my cock in his mouth again, after so long. But this was not my home. I didn't care what they were thinking.

After I had retrieved the rifle from the loft and packed it in the boot I was ready to go. Harry was at the door. 'Look,' he said, swinging the undrunk glass of cognac in his right hand. 'This is stupid. At least stay the night and go in the morning. Where are you going to sleep?'

'Goodbye, Harry,' I said. Getting in the car meant getting right down into the low-slung seat, which is a manoeuvre nobody can manage with their dignity intact, and then reaching across myself to pull the door shut with my left hand. But then the engine came to life with the sound of rushing water, and I pulled away from the kerb. A light came on inside my soul. I thought: It was a mistake coming here. Then I thought: I need to be with my people.

At the end of the road Harry's open door was one rectangle of light amongst many. As I turned the corner I was already logging into the wiki.

A trooper called Thirlwell, whom I remembered from Basingstoke was in the middle of expatiating. '[They're actually doing a Mission Accomplished banner unfurling thing,]' he said. '[They're actually officially announcing it.]'

'[No fool like a feudal fool,]' said somebody – Nicolson. Skinny man, sureshot.

Meaney, a woman from Croydon, said: '[Is it Reading, then?]'

'[They'll concentrate their troops at the sort of targets *they* would attack,]' said somebody I had not previously heard from: Gunesekera the name. '[Tourist draws, airports, London eye. Fuck *that*.]'

'[Reading's not been voted,]' said Thirlwell.

'[Foregone conclusion.]'

'[We still got to *vote*.]'

I joined the chatter. I had no compunction about butting it; it was all gossip, really. 'Guys, I lost some of my kit when a plane blew up the car park I was in. What would you advise me, so far as getting myself some new stuff?"

'[Block!]' pinged Thirlwell, immediately. '[Good to hear from *you*.]'

'[Tony, and Tony, and Tony,]' said a longtermer called McGuinness. I had fought with him in the 'Stans.

'[What you lose?]'

'I've still got a pistol and an AK. But apart from that—'

'[Like, armour?]'

'No. I'm OK for armour.'

'[Helmet?]'

'And helmet.'

[So?]

'Well, everything else.'

'[Where was this car park?]'

'The car park was in Hammersmith, in London Town,' I said, idling at a red light. A number of young people appeared to be dancing outside a kebab shop – gyrating and lifting their arms high. A thuddy beat penetrated the fabric of the car, though indistinctly. The darkness made it hard to gauge how many there were, and I automatically sized them up: shoot the main street light there, take down those three nearest the café door – if the rest scattered, pick as many off as possible; if they rushed me in a knot lay down a grenade bullet—

I had to tell myself to snap out of it.

'[I saw that,]' McGuinness was saying. '[Not with my own eyes, but here's a link to the vuetube footage – rafjet mashed that car park up pretty bad. English said they buried two dozen of us.]'

'Two,' I said, watching the hips of the nearest youngster slipping left, right, left. 'Just two of us.'

'[You got *out*, though, Block,]' said Thirlwell. '[That's great, though!]'

'[Who was the other?]'

'Recall Simic?'

'[Yeah. Simic. Chelsea fan isn't he? Where's he at?]'

'He's nowhere now,' I said.

The sympathy was immediate, and genuine, and all-surrounding: a dozen pings of 'Sorry to hear that'; several personal messages of sorrow, 'Man I loved Simic', 'He could fight.' And so on. McGuinness said: '[You boys were tight.]'

'That we were.'

I was crying a little, but not in a debilitating way.

'[So you want some bigger guns,]' said Gunesekera. '[I'm off to a place called Sonning. There's a couple of trucks there that'll have some of the stuff we need. How about see you there?]'

'Sonning,' I said. I fed the name to the satnav and touched the acceleration, pulling past a dawdling old Micra on to the dual carriageway. Point your right big toe, like a ballerina, and the car leaps forward. It's a dancing.

Without Simic's death I don't suppose I would be in this position – I don't mean physically, since that can't be predicted. They call that the hazard of war. I mean being in this place, talking to you. I mean, readying myself to become a weapon contra the NMA.

Yesterday I was down in that white-lit development space

you guys have. Terence took me down (and what a *nice* fellow Terence is, by the way). So there I sat, puffing a little, in a chair and Donaghy explained everything to me. My eyes were tired, and my face ached, but I tried to pay attention. Behind him, his workstation was improbably tidy. Was this because Donaghy is a tidy person? (Tidy people have tidy notions; they cannot bring down a giant as sprawly and messy as an NMA.) Or was it because he wanted you, and your officer caste, to think him tidy – to think him safe, and reliable, and so on? I think that's a question you need to address. Anyway, this Donaghy explained that although viruses could not, with any military reliability, penetrate the NMA firewall, and its patrolling semi-conscious AI worms, they could nevertheless interact *with that wall*. Talk to the worms themselves. A firewall could not be a firewall unless it interacted with the viruses that assaulted it. And, he went on, we have this added advantage. The virus we are talking about will be you, so it won't *come at* the wall after the manner of the sorts of malware the worms are comfortable handling. It will live in that plate in your head, he told me, nodding and smiling as if the plate in my head is nodworthy, or smileable. It will depend as much upon your syntactic network as upon the plate's circuitry.

Donaghy was a nice-looking young fellow: a thumb-shaped face, slightly podgier at the jaw and chin, but with a neat nose and wide-spaced, clever, childlike big green eyes. He must be in his early twenties, though his hair is white. There were, I noticed, little pocks and marls in the skin of his forehead, constellated around the bridge of his nose, like dints in metal. 'You understand?' he asked me.

The striplight was strobing just on the edge of my vision. The walls were like clenched, bleached teeth. Away on the far side of the room, a woman was hunched over her workstation grooming her keyboard with feverish fingertips. Behind him,

Donaghy's screensavers seemed to be a continual downpour of tears, like a window on to a rainstorm.

I did not say 'I have a headache.' Instead I said: 'This isn't the first time a viral attack has been used against NMA.'

'Nope. But this is different. It's like *War of the Worlds*. Do you know *War of the Worlds?*'

'Richard Burton,' I said. 'David Essex. The Moody Blues.'

His lovely, pea-coloured eyes narrowed a little at this, but he carried on. 'You were fighting over that ground, you see. H G Wells's novel describes all that territory pretty well, even after all this time. And like that novel, the way to bring down an otherwise invulnerable alien is to . . .' He glanced left and right, as if worried at the prospect of being overheard.

'A chain being only as strong as its weakest link,' I said. 'I have to say . . .'

But he was ahead of me. 'Oh, you're not the only person being loaded with the stuff. There's an American volunteer about to go out now into Missouri. Or Mississippi. Or another one of those unmarried girl-y states.' He tried a smile at this; and if I didn't join him it was only because it hurt my face to move it too much.'

'But I am the only individual you're working on,' I said.

'You are the only person I'm working on,' Donaghy said, and glanced furtively left and right again. 'You *are* a special case. The Colonel has spent a lot of time with you. And persuaded you to – reconsider your attachment to the New Model Armies?'

The way this last was inflected, with its retroussé little voice-lift at the end, brought something very significant home to me. I looked again at his face. 'So the virus will . . .' I prompted. And when he didn't take up the prompt, I added: '. . . degrade the NMA wiki? Turn it to mush?'

'It will reconfigure the worms,' he said, weighing each of

these words very carefully. I really could not get past the sense that he was trying to tell me something. 'It will make something new of the worms. But I wouldn't worry about the specifics of that,' he said, with a rather startling and abrupt shift of manner, speaking now with forced jollity and almost bouncing in his seat. 'Here's your escort!' And I swivelled my whole body to look behind me and there was Terence, in uniform, to bring me back upstairs for another little interview with you.

You don't think you have an accent, because nobody thinks they have an accent. But try to put yourself in my place. In the exchange that follows, don't think of your speeches as blandly normal and mine as articulated through a highfalutin fuck-you British accent. Think instead that I have a neutral tone and you have a West Texas rumble that would have done the Rooster from those cartoons proud.

'I ain't bored,' you say. 'Don't think I am. It's all most diverting. But I *am* curious as to why you're giving me so much detail about this Harry.'

'I might hope,' I said, in my neutral tone, 'that it's obvious.' It's obvious to me: the detail about Harry stands in place of the detail I cannot utter about Simic.

But you said: 'I'll tell you why *I* think you did it.'

'Go on'

'It's you know I'm a Baptist—'

I remember laughing at this. 'I *didn't* know you were a Baptist!'

'Come, come, you *know* I'm a Christian.' You seemed, from where I was sitting, relaxed and cheerful. 'You put in all that cocksucking, all those description of homosexual, ah, activity, to bait me. You can be straight with me.'

'Straight,' I said. 'Very good.'

'Now, now, you see what I mean. You're not trying to get a rise out of me?'

'Rise. Even better.'

'A reaction – yeah?'

'You're a mighty bizarre fellow, Colonel.'

'Man in your position,' you said. 'Natural you want to kick out a little.'

'Not at all. I hadn't pegged you as a prude, that's all.'

Your smile didn't sag. 'Oh I'm a man of the world, Block.'

'What you're telling me is gay sex is an abomination.'

'I don't say so,' you said. 'Nobody gonna listen if *I* talk about homosexuality. But the Bible, now – that voice is loud. That's a giant among books.'

I would have given you the finger – actually, no. I would have been more English than that: I would have flashed a V-sign at you. But my fingers wouldn't unclench from their withered-up fist. What I had, instead, was words.

'Its old and *fat*,' I said. 'But that doesn't make it a giant.'

'You know a *better* book?'

'I know there are better ways of organizing our fucking lives than following the purity codes of an antique desert *tribe*.'

'Oh ho,' you said, in a you'll-have-to-do-better-than-that tone.

'Try: democracy.'

Baiting your religion, and talking about gay sex, didn't crack your façade; but I saw a glint of annoyance in your eye at this. 'I've dedicated my life to the defence of democracy,' you said. 'Defending it from cocksuckers like you, Block. I've lost good friends in the line. I'm ready to join them in a heartbeat, because I love my country, and I love my country because it is built on freedom. Don't you pretend your hooligan shit had anything to do with democracy.'

'Jonathan and David,' I said, rubbing my face a little with my knuckles.

'Who's that?'

'It's your book.'

'Oh. *That* Jonathan and David.' Big beamy smile.

'Gay lovers,' I said. 'Warriors, too. Fine warriors, and leaders of a newly modelled army, back in the day. They took a small but properly motivated force and defeated a much larger, arthritic, unmotivated army.'

'Say what?'

'Jonathan and David, queer as all get out.'

'Jonathan and *David*?' You weren't outraged by my suggestion here, I think, so much as actually puzzled. Which is to say, I believe you really hadn't ever come across the notion before. So sheltered an education!

'No, you're right, of course not,' I said. 'Theirs was a love passing that of women, sure, it says that. But when two men love one another in a way that surpasses the love of women, I guess that has *nothing* to do with anybody's cock going up anybody else's poop-hole.'

'I've known a number of homosexuals in my time,' you replied, indulgently, 'My experience, they are prone to doing that – I mean, to confusing love and sex. But there's a rainbow of possibilities of love that have nothing to do with what you do with your blessed *dick*.'

'Would you like to bless my dick, Colonel?' I offered. 'Feel that urge?'

This made you laugh, and with that the mood unnotched a tad. 'So why tell me so much about this Harry guy, if *not* to try and outrage my decent Baptist sentiments?'

I didn't reply at once. 'I haven't told my story very well,' I said, shortly, 'if you think it really is about sex. Harry and me – it's not at all about that.'

'What then?'

'I was going to say love,' I said. 'But that would confuse you, I think. Or maybe it wouldn't. I don't want to underestimate you. Harry was one of the big loves of my life.'

'You were an item?'

'Four years, off and on. He was the most beautiful man I ever knew. Physically beautiful, I mean. In terms of his personality I guess he was a little, what would you say? Passive, I suppose. That's the problem you have, growing up beautiful. The world loves you not for anything you have done, but simply because you are so lovely. Things go easy. You never acquire the habits of overcoming, because people all around go out of their way to get you stuff. He wasn't *selfish*, Harry. I'm not saying that. Just he'd never really needed to do more than simply exist.'

I looked at you. Your expression was easy enough to read. You were thinking: *Physical beauty matters a good deal to you queers, don't it?* You were thinking: *And look at your mashed up face now, boy.* But you said: 'Go on.'

'When I was younger I thought beauty was what I wanted. Beauty and pleasure. I thought Harry, who gave me both, was what I wanted. I thought the pain was a small price to pay.'

'Pain?'

'There's a song. When you're in love with a beautiful woman. You know it?'

'Can't say I do.'

'But, look, *that's* not the thing. Harry's infidelities weren't the thing. The thing was that I was looking for the wrong sorts of happiness. I didn't want beauty and pleasure. Beauty and pleasure are trash, really.'

'You say?'

'See, what I wanted was – to come home.'

This must have connected with you, because the smirk left

your face, and you said: 'There's one true home in this universe, soldier.'

'Ah, but you mean, God.'

'I'm serious.'

'OK,' I said. The tone of our conversation had suddenly become hard to read. We had moved beyond banter into an unfamiliar zone. 'I rather got the impression queers aren't welcome in your church?'

'Love the sinner, hate the sin.'

'Imagine I didn't choose to be gay. Imagine God made me this way. What would that mean, do you think? That God just wants me to have a miserable life?'

'Don't sound like the God of Joy I worship.'

'But with some people he makes them in such a way that—' I pushed. 'I'm asking in all seriousness, Colonel. You know what I mean. Some people he makes crippled, or cretinous. Some people he brings into the world tangled up in pain and misery that never lets up. Some people have a soul with a twist in it that makes them depressed all the length of their days. Some had a different warp, and they're killers, and no remorse about it, and no more joy in *their* being than a shark has. You going to tell me you haven't seen such people, in your army? Army is where a lot of them end up.'

Your smile was armoured, metal-plated. 'Sure,' you said.

'Join your congregation,' I said, 'and the price would be: to live the lie? There's such a thing as a gay community, you know, and when I was younger I was an active part of it. But that's a community of people who only have one thing in common, and lots of things that are different. After a while you realize that sex is not the be-all and end-all, and those differences start to loom.'

'I've killed men,' you said, in a sober voice. This wasn't what I expected you to say at all. 'I've killed men, and so have you.

But that doesn't cut us off from God's grace. You're talking about love. I understand that. Love.'

'I shouldn't be shy of the term,' I agreed. 'The thing, I guess, is that you can't have love without equality. If you're higher up in the hierarchy, then what you call love of those below you is actually a kind of condescension, or just the exercise of power. And what you call love *of* those higher up than you is just fear, a desire to placate them.' I thought back to Harry, in the dark, fitting his mouth about my cock with that shiver in his eye. 'You might fool yourself that you *actually* love your inferior, or your superior, but you don't because you can't. True love can only exist between equals. And what follows is, what follows is that love the beloved republic can only exist as the most transparent and radical of democracies.'

'So you can't love unless you can vote? Hard to buy that.'

'Voting,' I said. 'That's not a substitute. That's not a symbol, not a negotiable bond. A vote is itself. Here's what: you can't love unless you take charge of your life, and you can't do that if you're handing over power to representatives to exercise it on your behalf. You can't love if the very nature of your society is unequal. What I felt for Simic was an expression of – perfect equality. That's what it was. There hadn't been a society like ours in the world since Ancient Greece. And ours was more perfect than theirs, because we were open to men and women, to Greeks and barbarians, to atheists or religious types, to Pericles and Socrates. You had to be prepared to stand and fight, sure – but how can you be a human being and respect yourself if you're not prepared to stand and fight? And you had to be prepared to live democratically. It's not sex. It's something much more profound than sex.'

'You're telling me that you never had sex with anybody else in this army of yours?'

'Oh of course I did. It's a collection of human beings, and

sex is one of the things human beings do. But that's not the point I'm *making*.'

'What is your point, soldier? You're taking your time getting to it.'

'The point is that you and I mean different things when we talk about love. That's the point. I'm saying going back to Harry's made me realize a truth about love. And I'm saying that you have yet to realize it. That's why I spent so much time telling you about Harry and me, because unless you understand that you're not going to understand anything. We are the people who value the cactus for its luscious interior. You are the people who value the cactus for its dry and prickly exterior. How do we differ? The look-and-the-feel people, rather than the taste-and-sustenance people? You've gotten used to a distorted sort-of definition of love, but habitual is not the same as true. You don't live your life amongst equals. At your rank, it's possible you don't even recognize the *existence* of equals.'

It wasn't possible to needle you, though; you put on the hearty show once again, and beamed at me. 'How was your chat with Donaghy? Clever man, clever man. So, you understand what it is you'll be doing?'

'Something to do with worms,' I said, feeling, of a sudden, very drained.

18

It was in Twyford-Sonning, or a little downriver from there along the way to Henley-on-Thames, that we started to come together. A lot of pinging and twittering, and a sudden spike in the wiki. It was there that I first saw American troops, although the media had been full of them – of you – for weeks. The official line was that America, as an old ally, was 'distressed by the violence and loss of life in England' and that it was 'doing all it could, diplomatically, to bring a swift end to the conflict'. News webs speculated ferociously, and the consensus was that the English Government (the UK Government as they continued to style themselves) could not admit, publicly, that they had been forced to go begging-bowl-in-hand to the Americans. It absolutely *could not be said* that the British Army needed help putting down a small insurrection in its own back yard. On the other side of the pond – you know more about this, I don't doubt – there were large enough Gael pressure groups in the USA: the Scots, most of whom were keen to see an independent government in Edinburgh, but also the Irish. So those creaky euphemisms, 'military advisers', were flown to England. This was after the big push through London, I think. Certainly I didn't see any US vehicles or ordnance in the field until we reassembled west of the Chilterns.

There were early skirmishes, but not with significant concentrations of combatants. But we saw dark green uniforms amongst the paler. That was you-guys, I do believe.

We debated, as we pulled ourselves into a striking formation.

The main proposal, the one with what seemed like the greatest support, was to move south into Reading. We'd smashed through Reading once before, but there would be strategic merit in doing so again, because (as those in favour argued) the enemy wouldn't expect it, and because it was underdefended. All our evidence suggested that large concentrations of troops had been stationed in Windsor, because of its touristy-historic and Royal connotations (as if we cared about *that*!), and around Heathrow, because that looked to the Feudal mind like a likely target. So we could take Reading easily, and then push east. The counterprop was to move directly east, to Maidenhead, and then through Slough, to skirt round Windsor and scare the enemy that we were heading for the airport.

We still hadn't voted on overall strategy when the first shots were exchanged – at a place called Shiplake. A third proposal was tabled, and we forced through a guillotine discussion: pincer round Windsor, three thousand troops south through Bracknell and Staines, six thousand through Maidenhead and Slough. I, personally, had my doubts about this: but it got voted in, and so it was our strategy. The wiki prickled with updates as individuals identified themselves as north-line or south-, and then a few more as the numbers adjusted themselves.

It was still dark when I picked up new gear at Sonning, which is a tiny riverside village, a clutch of expensive, tiny commuter houses and not much else. Three trucks came in from three directions, and a couple of hundred NMA appeared from all over, as locals double bolted their front doors and watched with moon faces at their windows.

It felt strange to be readying for battle without Simic. But my right hand was starting to get some motion back in it – I taped a lightweight repeater to the cast on my right wrist. Then I fell in with a dozen or more people, most of whom I knew from before: Tucker, Fodio, Rhodes, Makouk, a few others.

So we set off to show the media that we had neither been defeated, nor driven back, and that we very much had not vanished. Rejoice not against me, o—

Boom.

The twelve of us drove north-east for a few miles in the same truck; but when the reports of combat engagement began perking on the wire we parked the truck in a National Heritage car park, in a woodland cutaway, miles from human habitation. Then we yomped for a while through the dawn – a very pleasant and invigorating way to spend your time, marching with friends through the nearly deserted English countryside in warmer months of the year. Of course, my sense of invigoration was enhanced by the knowledge that all that useless fucking jitteriness, the jumping out of my skin when somebody else's cellphone rang, the barely contained urge to shoot fucking passers-by . . . all that was no longer an inappropriate psychosis. It was now a sensible stay-alive plan. Birdsong competed with the distant grinding sound of the M4 a couple of miles south of us. The turf bristled and twitched under the invisible finger of the breeze.

We walked alongside a newly ploughed field, lines cut and lined and curled like an engraving in dark metal, inked with shadow and ready to be printed. Just the top-half of a crescent-moon poked over a Berkshire hill like a shark's fin. One car passed us – a civilian alone in his vehicle. He slowed as he drove alongside this trotting line of a dozen well-armed individuals, and then accelerated so quickly his tyres wailed, and he sped away. Probably got straight on his phone to the police. Not that it mattered.

You want that I should go into all this again?

Well, we cut through a housing estate. Commuters coming

out to their cars, or householders pramming their wheelie-bins to the ends of their drives, gaped at us. Many ran back inside their houses. The rubbish van was making its rounds, and didn't quit just because *we* jogged past. That metal arm tipping plastic tub after plastic tub of waste into the big metal mouth. Always eating, never satiated. Then over a small fence, and along a road that crossed (my wiki told me) the A404(M). According to the wikis some military vehicles were coming off the M4 and would be passing below us; so we set up a cannon and aimed it down, and waited as civvie car after civvie car passed through our fire zone. The army vans approached in a solid convoy, as feudal army trucks still do, and we were able to stop the first of them without difficulty. Tentacled branchings of flame, and gouts of smoke gushing upwards; then everything focused back down to fire burning through the truck and burning fuel on the tarmac. And, of course, cars screeching, weaving, and the second truck forced to brake right in behind the first. The buzz of the first explosion was such a rush that it momentarily detuned my attention. 'Come on dozy,' said Tucker. I daresay I was gawping a little at the chaos I had made.

'Spread a little chaos around,' I replied, in my best Joker voice.

Tucker came back at me with a sing-song Em Kentson voice: 'It's only a *Monday*!'

The castanets of returning fire.

We got a second missile off to blow up the second truck – the others had unloaded some of their troops and were squealing in reverse backing away from the scene. On the far side of the bridge was a roundabout; a sliproad curled ponderously round to join the motorway, and some enemy combatants were labouring up this slope. Fodio and I dropped them all with riflefire, and Tucker ran across to a nearby fuel station and grabbed an abandoned car. We all piled in – it was a Nissan

Nipi, so it was a tight fit – and barrelled away through an industrial estate, and past a series of ex-council brick domiciles. Though the car was crowded, the boy with the key in his head was in there with us. I'd hardly noticed him in Cambridge, so his reappearance caught my attention. He was an omen, and I suppose he wasn't a good one.

Priority uprate on the wiki: troops were being hurried up from Windsor, where they were barracked. Maidenhead itself was wide open.

Another general ping. It was Trooper Hesleff, with whom I used to play online chess, and whom I had never met face to face. '[We're checking a few dead bodies now,]' she announced, '[And they're wired in.]'

'[Wiki?]' asked a soldier called Reichs.

'[The enemy. They're connecting up their people – they're adapting.]'

'[They've learned something from us, at any rate.]'

'[We're sure they haven't hacked *our* wiki?]' demanded Capa. Capa was an old friend of mine; though I'd not seen him since village fighting after Basingstoke.

'[It's a worry,]' agreed Reichs.

'[We're solid,]' said a trooper who identified himself as Saint George, one of the Geekers. '[There are a million tripwires and only a dozen have even been touched.]'

At this a score of other Geekers chimed in. This was important, so although it held things up a moment it was worth logging them: Fine, Safe, Secure, attempts at hacking had passed through false walls. '[I'd also say,]' said Jiggs, '[that if they have hacked our wiki they're making a balls-up of using the intel. We just came through north Maidenhead like a knife through butter.]'

Somebody proposed a vote of confidence in our wiki and wifi, but that was just a waste of time. We were committed now; we could hardly unplug. If the enemy had started wiring up their troopers then that was a sign that they had acknowledged the battlefield effectiveness of the strategy. ['Of course,]' Capa said, '[though they're linked in now, they're still fighting as a feudal unit. It's all top down.]'

'[Fuck the top,]' said somebody – Scully, his name; I knew him, a little bit.'[We need some help here.]' The wiki map showed us where, near the centre of town, and showed us a sudden concentration of enemy too. '[They're dropping them from choppers,]' Scully said. The sounds of battle were loud enough to make his words hard to decipher.

The wiki showed us a roadblock a little way ahead, so Tucker stopped the car and we all got out. The chugga of the copters was clearly audible, away to the east. We were a mile west of town, in amongst some plush-looking properties and gardens and gates, and not far from the river.

On to Maidenhead.

What we did was flank the roadblock: knocking down a fence and leaving tracks across a smooth expanse of glistening lawn. From there we picked a way along the river. It was back gardens for half a mile. Large detached houses with their own little piers and dinky little boats at the back. Then we hit a public footpath, and jogged easily along it. Wet summer weather. Jurassic green everywhere. We moved through woodland that came all the way up the brink of the Thames. Trees trailed their fingers in the flow. The sounds of battle, getting closer. The vibrato trill of birdsong, with gunfire like a mechanical mocking attempting at imitation. The boy with the key in his head kept pace with us, jogging with fluid strides, his loose young arms swinging at his sides. He was not looking at us. He was looking where we were going.

One jet overflew the town, low enough to show off the

nodules and widgets on its underbelly, like Smaug. Then it pulled away north,

All this is very vivid in my memory. My memory stops soon afterwards, so it is doubtless especially emphasized in my mind. Or something; I don't know how that works.

We saw a bridge up ahead, and it was made of stone. Rat-tat. Keeping low, keeping moving. Something constructed from multiple bulbs of inflated fabric, of various sizes, was floating in the river. I recognized what this was: floating face-down. There were flashes and flares. Half a dozen ducks kicked the underwater furiously to move their line upriver, away from the commotion, against the current. I checked the wiki. The path opened up into a riverside walk, and past various shuttered-up bars and shops. The wiki said there was an enemy position on the bridge, so we kinked round and found a good defilade on our side of the river. I started setting up the small cannon I was carrying, splaying the tripod legs. I was home. It wasn't that my grief had been forgotten. It was that I had found a mode of being-in-the-world in which that grief was the sourness that added flavour to the joy of existence.

Tucker dashed from this shop to that shop, peering in at the windows. Fodio and the others were picking firing positions, and Makouk checking the rear. 'What are you up to Tucker,' I shouted. 'Are you window shopping? Stop window shopping, you whore-y consumer you.'

'What if they're hiding in the shops?' he said.

The cannon was ready. Tucker came over to me. I put on a John Wayne voice: 'Get off your horse, pilgrim, and drink your milk.'

He was checking the sight. 'Who was that?'

'The Joker.'

'Why-so-serious Joker?'

'*Full Metal Jacket* Joker.'

'*Full Metal* – what, the *2001* guy's film? I never did see that film.'

I aimed the cannon at the wall of sandbags that blocked the middle of the bridge. 'Call yourself a soldier, and never saw that film?' I said. Then I fired, and bullets large as coke-cans snapped across the intervening distance and turned into smashes of fire and flying shards of metal. The sandbags disintegrated and the shells rattled on through into the position. Fodio was on the wire calling in some people on the north bank of the river to put the squeeze on those enemy combatants. There was some desultory return of fire from the people on the bridge, and at the same time we came under fire from our right. 'They're quicker to react,' Tucker said, bringing his rifle about and checking the wiki to find out who was on us.

We separated and came up through the little commercial streets towards our attackers. A jet made another pass overhead, loud as the end of the world. The end of the world wasn't so far away, as it goes. There was a prolonged flurry of small-arms fire. Some people dashed for cover – four adult shapes, enemy combatants, heads down and running; and following them the slender silhouette of a ten-year-old, running loosely and freely.

I held my fire.

Tucker pinged: '[I'm down, I'm fucking down.]'

'You're hit?'

'[Fuck – *hurts*.]'

'I'm coming,' I said.

I retraced my steps, and in doing so stumbled upon three enemy combatants, two kneeling and one standing. They were facing away from me, firing round their corner, presumably at some of ours. I jinked into a shop door, took a breath, picked my target and shot the standing one. I got him in the back of his neck, just underneath his helmet and just above his flak jacket.

He jerked forward, and dropped his weapon, but remained standing, or slouching at any rate. He put his shoulder to the wall and he didn't fall over. I nudged my aim to the left a centimetre and hit one of the kneeling guys in the back – the round didn't go through his jacket, I'm sure, but there was enough momentum to send him sprawling forward into the line of fire from the others. He did a sort of Saint Vitus' dance and collapsed on his face. The third guy was wise to what was happening, and made to run off to the left. I shot at him but missed.

I went to the corner to check the other two were dead, and dead they both were – one leaning like a drunk against the wall, the other spread-eagled awkwardly. You see a lot of dead bodies in battle, and mostly you register them as simple features of the threat/no-threat landscape. But every now and again you see one that perks a response in you. In *Thin Red Line* that American trooper comes upon a Japanese corpse buried in the dirt except for his face, and that brings him up short. It's like that. It's a fellow-feeling, I suppose. Perhaps it was the way one of them refused to lie down and take his rest, even though he was dead. But looking at them, knowing them to be both human and so my brothers, drew a long needle through my heart. I stood there for long seconds, and just stared. As the asthmatic strains the hoops of his chest and wonders, desperately, *Why can't I breathe?*, so the dead man strains against his inert flesh and wonders, *Why can't I live?*

We all come to it, of course.

Pull myself together.

'I'm on my way, Tucker,' I pinged. He didn't reply, which was worrying.

I ducked back, and as I crossed the road and came through a side street, a burst of small-arms fire sounded out a weirdly familiar-sounding *bang, bang, b'bang bang-bang* rhythm, and then, freakishly, repeated it exactly: *bang, bang, b'bang*

bang-bang. After that it settled back into the usual random clusters and stretches of cracks and bangs, but my mind got snagged on the familiarity of the rhythm it had momentarily evoked. It reminded me of something. I couldn't think what. Man it's *annoying* when that happens.

By the time I got to him Tucker was dead, sitting with his back to a wall in a large dark puddle. There was nothing I could do about him. I put the news on the wire, found Fodior and Makouk on the wiki and made off in their direction.

An armoured car was parked in the entrance to a car park. I could see it reflected in the glass frontage of the office building opposite, and I waited until it swung its turret the other way before rushing it, bunging a sticky grenade at its side, and hauling back as fast as I could.

'Start!' by the Jam. *That* was the rhythm. Isn't it satisfying to scratch those little mental itches? They lifted that bassline from the Beatles, you know. I couldn't remember which Beatles song. The grenade exploded. I watched glass panels over the way breaking like ice and tumbling and pouring to the ground. Off I hurried, singing.

> *It doesn't matter if we never meet again*
> *What we have said will—*
> *always remay yane.*

I came round to the position Fodior and Makouk had established: a good perspective down Maidenhead's pedestrianized high street. A little way down the road, enemy combatants kept sprinting across the road, left to right, or right to left, leaving their cover and braving our fire to get to the other side. If they were all going from left to right, or all from right to left, I might have understood it; but the swapping over of positions on both sides just looked illogical. Exposing themselves unnecessarily. 'They'd be better off,' Fodior growled, aiming his

rifle again, 'staying put.' On *put* he discharged a round that
sent one enemy trooper flying, midstride – lifted him up in the
air and threw him away from us to land with a thud. He came
down with an impact that would have knocked the breath out
of his body if he'd had any breath left in his body. But his was a
body that had no use for breath, any more. There were half a
dozen other bodies lying round about. You know what the guy
said in *Tumbledown*? Isn't *this* fun. You know what? It is.

It is.

'Oh, you *are* a good shot,' I remember saying to Fodior.

That's the last thing I remember.

I can be more precise: the next memory I have is of being in
the clinic's bed. I remember the ancient, or timeless, feel of
clean cotton sheets. I was sitting up, or rather leaning back
against the 45-degree angle of the raised section of the bed. I
remember looking down at my hands and arms and noting that
they were both in plastic elbow-length gloves, and that these
gloves were taped around my arms so that they wouldn't slip
off. I thought about this, and decided that it was because I had
suffered burns. When I held my arms up I could see that both
hands were fists wrapped in some sort of dressing that was, in
turn, filled with some sort of gel. I could wiggle the fingers a
little bit, but I couldn't unclench my fists. I pressed one bound-
up fist against my face and so discovered that my head was
mostly covered over by two large plasters, one on each cheek.

I wasn't alarmed. I wasn't even particularly worried. Nor was
I in pain. I remember thinking that it was possible the
analgesics that must have been responsible for this latter state
might also be responsible for the former. I sat for a while and
looked at the door of my room, and the stippled pane of glass
in it, like the glass you get in bathroom windows, like a 3D

glass relief of a choppy sea. Like pewter, beaten and formed. I looked at the door handle. Then I looked at the two empty coat hooks on the back of the door. The walls on either side of the door were plain white.

So here I was. I thought back to what I remembered last, and it was hunkering down with Fodior and Makouk, looking down Maidenhead's pedestrianized high street. I could remember Fodior being there. I think Makouk was there too. I can't actually visualise him being there, but something about the memory made me think he had been.

This means that I cannot give you, as personal testimony, my account of how the Battle of Maidenhead ended, or how the war as a whole ended. I know what I have read, and what I have seen, and what the web tells me; but of course you know that as well as I do. Within a few hours of my last memory we had taken Maidenhead, and we pushed east fluently and without difficulty into Slough. To the south we strode through Bracknell, and over the heathland down there, again without much difficulty. By noon of the next day we had completed this double movement and linked up, or swarmed together, at Staines. The whole thing happened almost too easily. The British Army, having suffered unexpectedly heavy casualties, was compelled to pull back before us, despite outnumbering us considerably. Three days of fighting and we won wherever we went. On the morning of the fourth day the English agreed to a ceasefire, and pulled all their people away to the south.

So that's anything up to *four days* during which I was conscious and active but of which I have no memories at all. Negotiations were restarted at Newcastle, and the Scots and the English sat down to talk things out. And now everything had changed. After the London surge His Majesty's Government had believed that they had knocked the NMA over, and had been preparing to impose their will upon the Scots. But we had come back in as strong as ever, and killed many of His Majesty's soldiers, and caused further billions of euros of damage to His Majesty's home counties. It was evident that we could continue doing that for as long as the Scots were denied their independence.

By *that* point I, personally, was down and out, of course. But there's one more thing, to fill in the blank, and it's a strange thing for me to watch. It is obviously from near the end of the war, and I am still hale and active. A journalist interviewed five of us: myself, and Makouk, and a woman I think was called Strauss, and a man I don't recognize. I've watched the footage several times, you won't be surprised to hear. At first I thought watching it might jog my memory, but it hasn't done that. I'm not even sure where we are, during the interview. I mean: we're standing at the bar of a coffee shop – in Staines, according to the newsroom scroll at the bottom of the screen, but that could be wrong. These coffee shops are all cloned from town to town, so it could just as easily be Slough, or even Maidenhead. If it is Staines, then I fought through four days of health, and then got wounded and retroactively lost all of those four days' memories. It doesn't make sense to me that it would happen that way. Also, if that's what happened then I was simply fantastically unlucky; since I must have been taken out in one of the *very last* engagements of the war. It seems to me more likely that I was wounded in Slough, and more likely still that I was wounded in Maidenhead. But I've no idea how I was wounded, or what happened, except that it clearly involved me in getting some nasty burns – and nothing I can find, online, in the enormous amount of coverage of the war, helps me identify it. So I'm not in a position to say.

The interview, at any rate, is with five relaxed and happy troopers, so it must have taken place after we had won the battle of Maidenhead, at the very least. That might mean that

I received my wound on the road to Slough, or in Slough town, or maybe later. It is hard to comprehend the extent to which severe physical trauma can retroactively wipe elements of your mind, particularly since my memory of the fighting in Maidenhead – and especially of the approach to Maidenhead, through the fragrant green by the river – is so very vivid. But the later memories aren't there. And there am I, standing onscreen. You can see the brace on my right wrist.

And the journo is asking: 'Where are you from?'

'Croydon,' says Makouk.

'London town,' I say; and although I can't remember saying it I can tell that I'm putting on a Dire Straits voice.

'You're English,' says the journo, out of shot, 'yet you're fighting for the Scots?'

'Fighting *for* our NMA,' says the woman, who may or may not be called Strauss. She rather looks like Strauss, except thinner. But then she turns her head, and I think to myself: no, she looks completely unlike Strauss. I think to myself: it must be someone else. But TV isn't like real life. 'It so happens that our NMA has been contracted by the Scottish Government, and that's all.'

'What people in the south-east have got to realize,' says the man whose name I don't know, 'is that it's nothing personal. Three of us are *from* here. It's not like we have anything against the south-east, personally.'

'If His Majesty's Government hadn't walked away from the negotiations at Newcastle . . .' says Fodior.

But the journo isn't interested in this. '*Why* are you fighting though?' she pressed.

'Why?'

'You're not Scots Nationalists?'

'Jesus no,' said maybe-Strauss. And I laugh at this. I can't remember why I laughed. Something about it must have struck me as funny, but I've no idea what.

'Why risk your life for the Scots?'

'That's our job,' says Fodior.

'Isn't it a pretty risky job?'

'Are you going to ask the English soldiers this same question?' I put in, with a goofy grin on my face. Why was I so grinny? I don't know. A little hyper. 'Do they get the same questions we get?'

This last bit is me repeating myself, and anyway the man whose name I can't remember talks over me. 'I'm looking forward to *getting paid*,' he says.

'Pay, sure,' agreed the woman.

'See,' I say, and I'm talking to my comrades, not to the journo, 'I can see her point as far as that goes. We'll get paid, but not much more than, you know, an oil-rig worker. You know?'

'We'll get *way* more than an oil-rig worker,' objects Fodior. 'Basic pay—'

'Why calculate it from *basic* pay?'

Maybe-Strauss explains to the journalist: 'We get a bonus for winning. It's a sum of money. But my friend is right – we don't fight for the money. There are easier and less risky ways of making money.'

'So why do you fight?' asks the journo.

'Because I'm a soldier,' I say. 'This is where I belong.'

'*War* is where you belong?'

'This NMA is where I belong.'

'You'll have to excuse my friend,' says Fodior, putting his arm about me. 'He is a sentimentalist.'

'I'm a democrat!' I say. 'One of the true democrats! Few enough of us left. Not since the Athenian state in the fifth century before—'

'Professional army,' Fodior cuts across me, apropos of I'm not sure what.

But the journo can't let it go. 'But if you want to be soldiers,' she presses, waving the microphone in the air in front of the camera as if uncertain which of the five of us would be best to answer. 'Why not join the real army?'

Three of us answer simultaneously: 'This *is* a real army!'

'The idea!'

'Fight as slaves instead of free?'

There's a pause, and then maybe-Strauss has the final word. 'You ask most of the people in this NMA and you'll find they served terms in regular armies. But in that sort of, uh, of organization you discover you don't own yourself. You belong to the people higher up the chain, and because they might, you know, throw your lives away at any moment they can't ever respect you. You can't ever *have* respect in that sort of chain of, chain of.'

'Hierarchy,' I put in.

'Sure, that's. Yeah. In an *NMA*, though it's different, because—'

That's where the interview ends, cut off like that. I suppose whichever news network put it out didn't want to be accused of broadcasting NMA recruitment propaganda.

I can't tell you how peculiar it is to watch yourself on screen as a stranger. It is like eavesdropping on somebody else's memory of you.

That interview happened at some point in between me fighting along the pedestrianized high street at Maidenhead, and me waking up in the clinic, scorched and ill. And after this latter occurrence there was you, Colonel, and your West Texas drawl. After this latter, everything else that followed. I have to go on with my narrative, I know; and you're keen to learn everything you can about these giants, that stride over the countryside and make wasteland where before there was plenty. You plan to use me to fight them. You've spent real energy working me round to a position where I will no longer feel like a traitor for turning against my kind. I've liaised with your software team. I've been prepped by your counter-NMA specialists. The only thing I would say is: I have become what you wanted me to become, and I am content; but you misunderstand the ground. If Simic were still alive I wouldn't be getting ready to board a plane to Strasbourg. Simic is no longer available to me as an individual. There is only one way I can keep him alive, and that is by doing what I plan to do.

You must have sat down to talk with me on half a dozen different occasions. I appreciate the investment of time. Your time is precious, I know. Here's what I remember of the last. It was after I had that day meeting the software team – the people working on that sly AI worm that you hope to load me with, in your ongoing war. I shuffled about using two sticks to walk, and panting and puffing like a grampus, whilst people smiled and nodded and explained things.

Donaghy and I have a friend in common. Did I tell you that? I met Donaghy's friend in the middle of battle. He's a specialist in spontaneous AI generation of consciousness and I met him as the bullets went back and forth over the great Pong screen of the sky, remarkable though that sounds.

'You're doing a great thing,' you said to me.

'My motives for taking this virus to the NMAs,' I told you, 'are more selfish than you can imagine.'

You looked benignly at me, and very obviously did not probe further. Then you cleared your throat very ostentatiously. 'The thing about war,' you said, 'is that it has been the most fantastically *expensive* business. It's been that way for centuries. Centuries! And that's a good thing.'

'Why is that a good thing?'

'Because it has priced war out of the reach of many of the people who would like to have made war, and so made war less common than it would otherwise have been. It is really as simple as that.'

'More expensive wars are more destructive, though.'

'Maybe. But it evens out. Really, it does. And in particular more recently. It used to be the standard thing that a nation would recoup financial losses made by fighting a war by simply grabbing the wealth of the defeated side. That's not the way it works any more. You're not allowed to do that any more. If anything, the victor ends up spending more money on the defeated nation than the war itself cost – look at the US after World War Two. Or Iraq. We got some oil out of Iraq, but it came nowhere near covering the amount of money we spent. I'll tell you what that means: that means that nowadays it takes an awful lot to get a nation to go to war. In four out of five possible situations war is simply too costly an option. Follow that trajectory along, and it wouldn't be long before war was too expensive for anybody.'

'What a utopian you are,' I observed.

'Man, the opposite. What's the opposite of a utopian?'

'A politician?'

'You know the word I mean. I'm a pessimist. Is it nontopian? I can't remember the word. But that's what I am. You know why? Because *you* came along, and you made war affordable again. More bang for the buck, more victories with smaller forces. Every tinpot country can get in the game now. Two worst things to happen to people over the last hundred years: the dissemination of the AK-47 because it's both really reliable and usable, and really cheap. And NMAs, the same thing on a meta scale.'

'Small nations were picking fights with big nations long before we came along.'

'You're going to cite Vietnam? Go on, cite Vietnam.'

'Well, since you mention it.'

'Vietnam had Chinese backing. It wouldn't have managed the hardware otherwise. And it paid a price in a different way; its leaders just frittered away its soldiers. No other general, and certainly not the US, could afford to waste manpower like that. It's all *cost*, you see. It's all *price*.'

'So you're saying that by democratizing the military process we've made war more likely?'

'Oh, much, much.'

'Free market, though,' I said. 'We undercut you. That's the way the market works.'

You looked at me with an unreadable expression. 'I sometimes get the impression,' he said, 'that you say these things deliberately to rile me. Haven't we gone beyond that, in our relationship?'

'Relationship,' I said. It hurt my face to smile, but I couldn't stop myself. 'So you don't believe in free markets?'

'Free markets, sure. Democracy, sure. But these things ain't *absolute* values, no sir. These things aren't *wealth*.'

And this, I confess, intrigued me: 'What's wealth?'

'The only wealth is life,' you said, with an almost pious expression. Only a soldier can deliver that line with the proper force and gravity.

'Well, OK,' I said, and I wasn't trying to smile any more.

'This thing has come along and is striding over the landscapes of the world, and smashing the joint up. Smashing it up, here, means killing lots of people who oughtn't be killed. It means breaking houses and churches and factories. Lots of beautiful heritage in Europe, yeah? It means destroying it. You and I, my friend. You and I can do something about it. Yes?'

'Oh,' I said, doing my Omar impression once again. 'Indeed.' The last person to whom I had said that word, with that particular inflection, had been Simic. War gives, and war takes away. Take a vote. How mad and bad and sad it was, you see. But sweet. You see.

I thought about saying to you: are you sure you trust your development team? Are you quite sure *Donaghy* is on your side? But I didn't, in part because you had launched into a sort of lecture. You itemized the rash of NMAs that had sprung up in the wake of Pantegral's successes in southern England. Now, Pantegral's had been an impressively coordinated campaign, though I say so myself; and the people of Scotland were grateful for their independence (except for those that weren't), although it amounted to much less than it might have done, what with the indelible ties of trade and investment and culture and so on that kept Scotland chained to the rest of the UK. And it is true that the individual soldiers of Pantegral were paid off with a victory bonus that was much more than most of them could have earned in any other job. But the people joining the large numbers of NMAs in Continental Europe – the Croatian NMA, the Swedish NMA, the Ukrainian NMA, the Irish NMA, the Italian NMA, the Catalan NMA, the two Polish NMAs, the three Russian NMAs – these people were not joining up for the money, or for the austere pleasures of putting in place effective military strategy. Three quarters of them were young men. Most were not even particularly committed to the ideologies of democracy. Most were joining up because doing so gave them the chance to *smash shit up*, and to ensure that *nobody fucked with them*. They joined a democratic NMA, rather than a regular army, or a traditional gang, football tribe or mafia, because recent history had shown that democratic NMAs are simply much better at smashing shit up than other organizations.

Not all these new giants are strong, or well coordinated. A couple aren't even democratic – are, rather, wifi smart-connected militias run on traditional-authoritarian lines. But they are still distressingly good at smashing shit up, all across the continent. Some are doing so on the commission of various aggrieved ethnic or religious groups. A couple are doing so by way of extorting money by menaces. We have made it much easier than it had formerly been. The man in that Kwai movie – I always thought he was David Niven, but you say he was Alec Guinness – who is granted the sudden realization at the moment of his death, and asks God, or perhaps uses God's name as an expletive before asking *himself*: what have I done? – and then falls forward to strike the plunger of the detonator with his chest, such that the downward thrust of the pole spins the charge wheels inside the box, and this in turn sends rapid electricity down the wires all the way along the riverside and under the miso-coloured river water to the bridge's wooden columns, struts and spars, which in turn initiates the rapid chemical chain-reaction in the explosives taped there; and almost at once there is the blinding, deafening, scorching, near-instantaneous expansion of hot gases in every direction, a thousand miles an hour and hotter than an oven, shattering the structure in heat and flames and (I hate the British! You are defeated but have no shame! You are stubborn, but have no pride! You endure, but have no courage!) doing so at *exactly* the moment that the massive metal train is crossing – because, because *here* comes the train! – throwing white parcels of smoke over its shoulder and moving its piston-elbows so fast they're a blur – and now, the ticking is all done and it's *boom*! – the traintracks are sagging away beneath the locomotive into the valley and *down* we go, bridge and train and everything, squealing and crashing.

That man: me. I don't need to tell you what the bridge is, or what the train.

You want me to help you. I can do that.

PART 2

SCHÄFERHUND

But one thing is beyond his reach
The giant cannot master speech

Auden

Of course we need to be honest with ourselves if we are ever going to be at peace with ourselves. On the other hand, we need to be absolutely sure that peace is what we're after. The metaphor from international relations is, perhaps, a little misleading. Put it this way: what, for a nation, are the benefits of peace? Trade and prosperity, perhaps, and the removal of the threat of being explosively disaggregated. Setting this last (of course, significant) merit aside, and translating into the idiom of the personal: in what ways would a *prosperity* of the self differ from a mere bourgeois smugness? And how are we to benefit from *trading* with ourselves?

We need a different metaphor. I am still, not, the hero of this story. Things have changed; but that has not. I'm not the man I was, but he is.

I got off the plane and made my way through into the arrivals lounge. They took me round the hooped security gate, because the metal plate in my head would have set it off bleeping. Instead they frisked me, thoroughly, and rather painfully. They were looking for weapons, which would have made me smile if I had been capable of smiling, for I *was* a weapon and they didn't recognize me. A sword not made of iron, a gun that does not fire bullets.

Martin was waiting for me there, in a spotless uniform. He was tall, well-built, good posture; the only thing spoiling the Caucasian-handsome regularity of his features was his properly *goofy* grin. He strode over, arm out, ready to shake my hand. 'Mr Block? I'm Martin.'

'I can't shake, I'm afraid,' I said. 'My hands are funny.' I put up my birdclaws to show him.

'Your file details some degree of injury,' he said, his smile as wide as ever. 'Did we do that to you?'

'The English.'

'That's *OK* then! Don't want to get off on the *wrong* foot.'

I was cranky, I suppose, after all the nonsense entailed by flying nowadays, and by the physical discomforts of moving my scorched body anywhere, so I said: 'You sometimes meet people with two wrong feet.'

The smile didn't go away. 'That's funny!'

I didn't think so. 'You're in uniform,' I pointed out. 'Very obviously so. I thought the point of flying me in at the civilian 'port rather than just bringing me straight into a military base, was,' I almost choked over the polysyllables, 'circumspection.' My scorched little lungs. 'Wouldn't it have made sense for you to dress down a little?'

The smile perked up again. I was to learn, as the day went on, the irrepressibility of that smile. 'Mr Block, look around. Half the people *here* are in uniform! I'd stick out more if I *weren't* in these togs.' His *weren't* was two distinct syllables. 'The continent's at war, sir. And besides, we're not *going* to the military base. That's not what Colonel Philpott told me. That's not my brief.'

I made an effort to be mollified. 'Where are we going, then?'

'To Strasbourg, sir. To a hotel, sir.'

He walked me over to the car park, and put my luggage in the boot – the trunk, he called it. 'Do you need any help getting in the passenger seat?' I declined this offer, inflecting the words *thank you no* in as *fuck off* manner as I could manage. Then I puffed and huffed and awkwardly inserted myself into the auto. He sat facing front smiling benignly as I fiddled for an unconscionable time with the ridiculous clasp on the seatbelt. Eventually, despite the uselessness of my digits, it all fitted together.

'OK?'

'Fuck off.'

'All right then!' very brightly spoken.

As we drove away from the airport he hummed something to himself. I couldn't place the tune, though some part of my brain recognized it. That niggled.

'I forgot to ask,' he asked. 'How was your flight?'

'Have you ever flown on a plane?'

At this he chortled. 'You want me to say yes of course, so *you* can say, it-was-just-like-that. Set-up, pay-off, b-bam. Very *good.*'

I directed my gaze through the window. We passed through a built-up area, and crossed a bridge over a railway line. Martin was humming something. I thought it was 'I Can See For Miles', but the chorus was different. Something charty presumably. There was a snow-coloured layer of cloud almost all the way across the sky. The light was bright enough, despite this coverage, to cast distinct shadows. We crossed the river; a strip of platinum running west-east. 'The river Al,' said Martin. 'It used to be called the Ill. They changed the name last year.'

I was finding it an effort maintaining my grumpiness in the climate of his enormous positivity. 'Why did they change it?' I asked.

'The name?'

'Yes.'

'I guess they didn't like that their river was called Ill. Everyone speaks English, nowadays, do they not? It's all over Europe, English. Which is good for me, since I'm no master linguist. So they speak English here, sure they do. Or, when they're not speaking English, they speak a sort of abomination that's neither French nor German.' He flashed a glance at me, with a grin like a crescent moon on its side. 'Ill sounds like a *bad* name for a river, don't you think. So now the river says, you can call me Al.' He looked at me slyly. 'You like old music, right?'

'Not that particular piece of old music.'

'Isn't it all the same? No, don't answer that. Instead, imagine two languages. OK? You're playing along? Imagine one rather strait-laced and scientific language and one all suave and romantic-like. Imagine those two languages step into the matter transporter together, and emerge at the other end monstrously fused. *That's* what they speak here.'

'You're quite a gabbler,' I observed, removing my attention back out the window again.

'Is that, like, English slang? I love English slang. Is it rhyming slang? *Gabbler*. You'll have to teach me some proper, London, rhyming slang. The Colonel said you were a sharp-tongued fellow, said you were a smart conversationalist. All those sessions you had with him! You might be honoured, you know: he's an important man, the Colonel, and doesn't waste his time. I guess you were worth it. I'm pretty much stoked to see what you can do, Tony. Keen to see the new weapon. Ill, Al. Some people opposed the change, but I don't see why. Alsace is named after the river, so calling the river Al is only reconnecting it to its roots.'

There were several EU military checkpoints as we passed into Strasbourg old town, but their gates were open and traffic was moving pretty freely. Sentries glommed about, holding their rifles awkwardly, and looking not only bored but resentful at being bored. That's a way of saying that they weren't true soldiers. The true one would know that soldiery is two-thirds boredom. You might not like it, but you don't resent it.

Rotating my neck was uncomfortable, but from force of habit I scoped the locale, turned my head left and right, set up notional advances, saw immediately a couple of perfectly decent attack possibilities. The regular army people ought to have plugged those.

If they'd asked me, I would have told them. They didn't ask me.

Martin was chattering. 'Fought over and over, this ground – thousands of years – it's fertile, see, and *right* in the middle of Europe, so it's no surprise. But look how much of the old town has survived! You ever read Zola?'

'The footballer? No.'

He took his attention from driving to look directly at me. 'Why,' he said, 'you're *delightful.*'

We drove through insanely narrow streets and into the bustle of a living polis. Strasbourg old-town itself looked untroubled by the imminence of war; shops open, cafés full; civilians and tourists filling both pavements. The medieval street plan, with the upper floors of building frontages straining to kiss across narrow streets. And, looming over it all, the ICBM-shaped spire of the Gothic cathedral. 'That's some godbox, no?' said Martin.

'What?' I asked.

'You *might* be religious,' he returned. When I didn't say anything to this, he added. 'Of course you might. I mean, I've read your file, but the varieties of religious experience – they can't easily be categorized according to the rubric of a, you know. A questionnaire. A file.' When this didn't provoke a response either, he added: 'I don't mean to be disrespectful, you know, in calling it a godbox.'

'OK.'

He beamed at me: 'Wouldn't want to narkle our Jack,' he said.

Jack pulled me up short. 'Our what?' It hurt my face to scowl, but I couldn't stop myself. And, as incomprehension piled on: 'And what do you mean, *narkle?*'

'Pissy off,' he said. 'You know, get up the tits of.'

'You're trying to use English slang?'

'Sure.'

'Somebody told you those phrases were idiomatic English slang?'

'Sure.'

I looked at him. Then I asked: 'But why *Jack?*'

He glanced at me, and said, with a childlike ingenuity: 'You know. Jack', in exactly the tone of voice of that guy from the film about the 1930s corporation that makes hula hoops, the guy who says 'You know, for kids'. I can't remember the name of the film.

'I,' I said, slowly, in an exploratory manner, 'am your *Jack,*' trying to imagine what this could possibly mean. 'Is that – a *bowling* term? Or, do you mean, like, poker? Card games?'

'Oh *you're* a card,' he said. 'And don't try and tell me *that's* not cockney, because I heard Terry Shilling use it on last night's *Cable Street*. We love it, that show. We being myself and my fellow US army officer, the two of us, we're billeted together. You'll meet him in a little – a lovely guy. Three kids, and he's still not done.'

I was losing the thread of this. One possibility is that the metal splinter inside my forebrain made it harder to stack hanging concepts than it had previously been. 'I'm sorry. Not done what?'

'Not done, having kids. His wife is pregnant again. Four children! In this day and age, I know, I know. You'll meet him later. You'll like him, I think. Very *polite* man.' This last, I suppose, was a piece of conversational deference to my Englishness.

He had read my file; but he didn't know me very well. It is certainly true that my brain has been more bashed about by my injuries than I tend to realize; and certainly my thought processes work more slowly than they used to. But it was not until this moment that I understood which *Jack* Martin had meant to call me. The Giantkiller, of course.

Of course the Giantkiller.

He pulled the car on to the pavement to permit an articulated lorry, in military livery, to come up the narrow street. Around us the buildings were a mixture of up-to-date glass-weave and half-timbered antique – black and white inter-layered in that cakelike medieval fashion. Martin ticked a finger up to indicate Strasbourg cathedral tower, standing proud. 'That's one nice piece of stonework. It was the tallest building in Europe from 1647 to 1874, you know. Either that, or it was the tallest building in Europe from 1674 to 1847, I can't really remember.' He peered at the car's dash screen, but vaguely. 'I could google it,' he said. 'Get the precise date.' For a moment it seemed he was actually going to do this; but then: 'I guess it doesn't matter that much.'

'You have a lot of experience in liaison?' I asked, in a cool voice.

He looked at me. 'You want to talk the turkey. I can tell, you're in a turkey talking mode.'

'As opposed to a rubbernecker's town-tour mode, yes.'

He looked at me, and then abruptly showed me thirty-two white teeth. 'Let's do *that* then. You're the superweapon, after all.' The lorry had passed. He pulled the car away, turned a corner, and tucked the vehicle through a narrow gateway on to a down ramp. We corkscrewed down several levels and came out into a broad, low-ceilinged parking hangar. All this time Martin was chatting on. 'What I don't understand about this Christian urge to build bigger and bigger churches, hey, I guess

I mean taller and taller, churches. It's as if they haven't even read the story of Babel. Or do they read that and think, well that doesn't apply to *us*? Why would they even think that? Pick and choose which bits of the Bible to believe.' The tyres squeaked over the driving surface.

'I guess,' I said, as he backed the car into a tight space between a pillar and a VW Suncone, 'they figured they were building the towers to praise God. They figured the intent is not to assault him.'

'You think it's all in the intent?'

He shook his head. 'But if somebody menaces me, you know what? I don't care about his intention. If he sticks a spear in my face, I don't care if he thinks he's praising me in the act.'

'Of course,' I said, absently. 'You're not God.'

Here's a strange thing: I was finding this process of parking the car – the mix of precision and force with which Martin was sliding his vehicle into a thin slot – oddly arousing. It's a symbolism not hard to read, of course. I looked again at Martin. It occurred to me that what I had taken initially for blandness was, if you wanted to read it that way, actually a rather appealing regularity of face and body. He gave off none of the little clues that indicate receptivity, but that didn't mean anything. Since my scorching, I had withdrawn from that aspect of my life. Most men wouldn't look twice at me, erotically speaking; and any who might could only be motivated by pity. Pity is the acid that dissolves arousal. My relationship to sex had altered.

'So,' I said, shifting in my seat to make my erection less obvious in amongst the pleats of my trousers. 'Alsace. Alsatians.'

'Alsace in Wonderland,' Martin said, his attention on the rear windscreen. 'Alsace in Hunder-schaf. Lewis Carroll,' he added, as if I needed the explanation.

We had parked.

'There's a pun in the name, in Alsace Schäferhunden,' he told me. 'Schäferhund is Shepherd – I mean, like, shepherd dog. Deutsche Schäferhund is German Shepherd, yes? And in England those sorts of dogs are called – well, yeah.'

'You're labouring the point.'

'I am? I guess I am. I do tend to do that.' He cracked the driver's side door and squeezed himself out. Then, leaning down, he asked: 'You going to be able to slink out of that space? There's not too much room.'

'I can't really flex my waist very well,' I said. 'And I can't really clasp or grip anything. So I'm afraid not. You've crammed us in pretty tight here.'

But nothing could make his crest fall. 'I'll move the car forward!' he beamed. 'I'll have it moved in a jiffy!' So he slinked himself back into the driver's seat, drove the car four yards forward, and then he waited whilst I shuffled and heaved myself out of the car. Then he reversed back in, and extricated himself, and retrieved my luggage.

As we walked underneath the oppressively low concrete ceiling towards one of the exits Martin's flow was unstoppable. 'There have been fits and starts of an Alsatian independence movement for hundreds of years,' he said. 'But mostly Alsace has been the plaything of France and Germany, swapped between them on the political chessboard of – well, you know.'

I was aware of a growing claustrophobia in that space. I couldn't stop picturing a detonation above ground bringing that low concrete ceiling slamming down upon me. I couldn't stop registering the way the stench of petrol lingered in the air, and thinking how flammable petrol was, and what people look like when they spent too long in a burning building, and came blundering into the open where the gunmen were.

We got the lift, Martin hauling my bag behind him. The

metal doors were etched, some lines quite deeply scored, into various curlicues and graffito tags, including what looked to me like a pretty good drawing of a German Shepherd hound's-head. Scritchy, scratchy. If there had been any spraypaint graffiti on the doors, then it had been very efficiently cleared off; but these scored lines resisted erasure. 'It comes down to money,' Martin was saying, jabbing at the little illuminated call button like he was playing Space Invaders. 'As it always *do*. As it always *do*. This is a rich-enough corner of land, see, but most of the money is in the hands, actually, of French and Germans, not Alsatians, you see. I know the EU is supposed to have made all you Europeans one big family, but the, eh, the roots of history go, you know, deep. I mean, take a look at it from the point of view of America. History, in the very broadest sense – what has it been?'

'A nightmare from which . . .' I muttered. Perhaps Martin didn't hear me. Certainly he spoke over me.

'It's been one European civil war after another! That's what! Europe's capacity for civil war is a continual source of as-tonishment to us, stateside. And here we are again, in the middle of another one! *Yet* another!'

The lift doors did their metal origami fold, and we got into the steel lift. Martin pressed the button with his thumb.

'So, yes. Alsace has had neither the population to raise its own force, nor the money to hire others to do its fighting,' Martin said. The confined space altered the acoustics, and so the timbre of his voice.

My stomach keened as we rose.

'Until now,' I said.

'Well, sure. NMAs change everything. There's a different one for each pocket, though, isn't there? So although the Alsatian Freedom Parliament can't afford a big fuck-off NMA like Rebellais or Pantegral – sparing your blushes—'

'My skin has lost much of its physiological capacity for blushing,' I said.

'—Hell they *can* afford something smaller, something not so experienced or efficient. Hence Schäferhund gets the gig. German, Czech, mostly: Schäferhund. A young giant, is Schäferhund, and not *so* good at the fighting. A danger, obviously. That's why you're here. And us regular army types, well we're a whole lot better at containing NMAs than we used to be. Just look at what we did to the Liberty Army in Missouri.'

'That wasn't Europe,' I said; and on *eur* of Europe the lift chimed, a resonant, plangent ding. The doors opened.

I followed Martin out into the lobby of what was, evidently, an expensive hotel. One young man, dressed in expensive-looking thread-jeans and a screen top, was sat in the lobby's wide settee; he was reading, the book perched in his hand like a bird about to fly off. But actually he was only pretending to read, because his eyes followed us as we crossed to the main desk. I didn't like the look of him. My instinct singled him out. Martin, though, was wholly oblivious: and he was the military man. I was just a strange sort of relict. Martin was looking after me, not the other way around. Or, it would be closer to the truth to say, he was helping to move me into position.

I checked out the rest of the arena. There was a chandelier, the crystal skeleton of an alien spider, hanging from the ceiling by a steel rope. One well-aimed bullet would bring that down. The carpets were very plush, the pile very deep. It was like walking on soft sand. A couple of obvious tourists loitered by the door. A young man with acne like spattery wine-spill running over both cheeks manned the coffee counter in the corner. I looked again at the pretending-to-read-a-book man. In all this human action he was the potential danger. With a tingly sense of detachment and, if I'm honest, of superiority, I looked across to see that Martin had not registered him at all.

Instead he was talking: 'Schäferhund may not be very good, that's not the point. They may not be likely to win. I don't think they *are* likely to win, in fact – but that's not the point either. Because they certainly are capable of causing a great deal of damage and death, and we'd like to stop that, thank you very much. Yes, we spoke earlier.' This to the exquisitely good-looking young girl behind the desk. 'Room, name of Block?'

'One moment please,' she replied, with no hint of accent.

I addressed Martin in a none-too-pleased tone: 'You booked the room in my name?'

'It's your room, after all. I think you'll like it.'

'That's not what I mean,' I said. 'My point is that, don't you think a little, uh, circumspection . . .' But I was coughing again, or I was making the dry rasping equivalent which is all I'm capable of now.

'Leah, is it?' Martin was saying, leaning a little too far over the desk, and peering at the girl's bosom on the pretext of reading her nametag. 'That's *real* kind of you. Thank you *very* much. That's *très gentil*. Now, now, how about this? What if I asked you to come for a drink with me later, this evening? Would you tell me that you've already got a boyfriend?'

Two cherry red spots were visible in her cheeks; but she held her composure. 'It is against hotel policy for staff to date guests, m'sieur.'

'Oh, *I'm* not the guest, Leah. This mein-herr *here*,' he reached out and lightly tapped my chest with the back of his hand, without looking at me, 'he is the guest. I'm not the guest.'

'Sure, tell everybody,' I said. 'Make a general announcement! Who needs discretion, in our line of work?' I'll concede I was crotchety.

Leah's smile did not waver. She shook her head fractionally. 'Your room card, sir,' she said, holding the plastic rectangle out to me. I put up my mangled right claw and she did not flinch. I took the key between thumb and clenched fingers and thanked her.

'I hope,' Martin beamed, 'that you're not offended that I asked, Leah?'

'Not at all, m'sieur,'

'You have a nice day, now.'

And he marched off without the least kink in his swagger, back to the lift. 'We can take the stairs if you like,' he said, 'but maybe the lift would be better, what with your – what would you call it? Your *condition?*'

'The lift,' I said.

So we stepped back inside the lift.

I might have hated this man. At the least I might have been infuriated by him. But I'll tell you the truth; something about him touched me. I do not make a habit – believe me – in falling for straight men; and I'm not suggesting there was any actual spark or draw in my heart. He was certainly nothing at all like Simic. But I found myself disarmed, nevertheless. His *irrepressibility*.

He did a little shuffle of his boots, forward-back, forward-back, as the lift doors slid shut behind us. 'You're a restless fellow,' I observed.

'Too much coffee,' he said. 'Or,' he added, with a laugh, 'not *enough* coffee. Either way, it's a pleasure to meet you, Trooper Block.' The lift tugged mildly at my innards. 'I'm hoping it's the first of many opportunities to work with you. I'm *real* keen to see you do your Jack thing.'

'My Jack thing,' I repeated. 'Right. Do you know what it involves?'

'Sure.'

'You've seen it at work?'

'Not directly.'

'But you understand the, uh, principles?'

'I took a minor in Computer and Virtual Assault Strategies,' he said.

'Really.'

'University of Fort Worth. I wrote my freshman diss on viral assault.' He beamed. 'Not that I remember all that. I'm no tech. But, heck, you don't need to understand all the chemistry of gunpowder to shoot a gun . . . right?'

'Gun,' I said.

'You telling me you understand all the ins-and-outs?'

I liked the unconscious irony of this. 'I may understand more than you realize.'

'Sure!'

Conversational smalltalk has never been my forte. 'So,' I said. 'Were you involved with the Liberty Army takedown?' I asked.

'Personally? No, sir. But I have talked with people who were.'

Ding. The doors folded away, and we stepped on to a landing. Ruby carpets, smooth as velvet. Dark-wood panelling, scalloped along its width and fringed with madeleine-shaped wooden ornamentation. We walked along the soft scarlet sand.

'And you don't have qualms?' I asked.

'About?'

'About what we're doing, here.'

'I've been regular army since seventeen,' he said, as if that answered my question. He stopped in front of a door. 'This is your room. You want that I should swipe? They sure don't make these locks for people with chewed-up hands, do they?' He took my key and opened the door. 'Is there not some surgery? I thought I saw something on the web about, like, little motorized spokes they put in along the bones to restore movement? I thought I saw that, online somewhere.'

'I have those,' I said.

'No kidding?'

'Well, I have them in my thumbs,' I said. I didn't add: it's agony every time I try to move the fucking digits. Instead I followed him into the room.

'They help?'

'A little.'

He deposited my bags beside the bed, and sat himself ostentatiously in the room's sole comfy chair.

It was, I have to say, a very nice hotel room. Spacious and well-appointed. The windows looked down from a fourth-floor vantage across nineteenth-century roofs and along narrow streets, and to the western flank of the cathedral building. Bed, screen, desk, chair; door through to the bathroom on the left. The main door clucked shut behind us.

'Here you go,' he said. 'Pretty good? No expense spared. Mine's the same size, but I gotta share with – well you'll meet him soon enough. This is yours all on your lonesome.' He looked up at me from the comfy chair with a twinkle. 'Qualms?' he said. 'You mean, in the sense of, what?'

'Well, let's say: your commitment to democracy,' I said, feeling vaguely foolish saying such a thing.

'Democracy? Sure. Democracy's great. Sure beats tyranny.'

'Well then.'

'*Well* then? Let's be sure we know what we're talking about, yeah? It's not like democracy is an *absolute* value. I'm not offending your religion when I say this, Tony?'

'Religion?' I lowered my arse on to the bed, feeling thoroughly worn out by my trip and ready to lie back and sleep, but unable to relinquish the soldier's instinct to be ready to leap up. If Martin didn't take the hint in five minutes, I told myself, I would simply ask him straight out to leave me in peace.

'I know how deeply embedded you were in the south-east England NMA, Tony. I have read your file. I have spoken to the Colonel who debriefed you.'

'Who turned me.'

'If you want to – let's say you want to put it like that. Sure. Turned you, like a spy. So I guess he persuaded you, in all those conversations you had, that proper democracy has the moral edge on all this NMA stuff. Yeah? Or how else could he have *turned* you?'

'How else?' I replied, drily. Then, in a weary voice: 'Religion is *quite* the wrong word,' I said.

'Sure. Oak. *Ede*-oaky. My father was in the army too. You know? Now when *he* served, the point was to defend us against Communism, and by Communism was meant tyranny. By the time I was growing up it was Islam, and the same thing. Rule by mullahs and the religiously inflexible. People not getting to vote in their congressmen and senators. Democracy as opposed to *that*, sure.'

'Just not democracy *as such*,' I said.

'Oh, as for that, there's just another form of tyranny wrapped up in *that*,' he said. 'I guess you don't see it. For me, it's the middle ground. People need a little structure – I mean, hierarchy. But not too much, no sir. A little deference to people better than they are. Social awe. A *little* of that. But not too much – not kings and queens, and so on, and so forth. But the idea that everybody is absolutely equal – that flies in the face of human nature, don't you think?'

'NMAs don't treat everyone as equal,' I pointed out. 'Look at me. Too deep-fried to fight. Taking everybody to be equal means assuming everybody is capable of fighting on the same battlefield.'

'Yeah, well, all right then, right there is one thing I don't like about radical democracy. Why don't we ever see, you know, NMAs constituted for *other* reasons? Reasons apart from fighting, I mean? Why don't we see groups of people using this logic of association to, I don't know, landscape-garden? Pick up litter?'

'No you don't get that,' I agreed.

'Why not?'

'You're asking me?'

'Sure!' he said, and he bounced up from the chair and stood upright. Oh there was an irrepressible, puppyish quality to him, all right. But there *is* one thing, in this sublunary world, that's sure to repress even the most irrepressible. We'll come to that in a moment.

'Because the world is, when you get right down to it, not a garden,' I said, in a croaky voice. 'Because the world is much more like a battlefield than it is a garden.'

'Look, I don't mean to bend your ear. That's the English expression, yeah? Don't mean to gabble. Is that rhyming slang, by the way? I did wonder. Never mind, I'll leave you in peace. I'm sure you could do with a rest. So: I'm *down* the corridor if you need anything. This,' he held out a piece of card, 'is all the numbers, rooms, mobiles, log-on. You get a nice room to yourself. I have to share, and not with a pretty receptionist either. I think I said.'

'At least you won't get lonely.'

'Oh, sure. *He* and I will keep one another company, sure. You can join us, if you want. We'll only be watching TV. Or you can enjoy your own company. Up to you. Now, if you need anything *at all*, let me know. Otherwise, I'll up and leave you in peace. I'll come get you at six, and we're going to dine with half a dozen top brass. It'll be a nice meal, sure, but a strategy meeting too, so get yourself ready for that. I don't know what you need to do to get ready for a top-level meeting, but whatever it is, maybe you want to do it. You're the weapon, after all! Until then, enjoy the room. The screen, wire access, over there. No expense has been spared. In the bathroom you'll find—' and he opened the bathroom door.

I heard a thud.

A mallet hitting wood.

Martin, no longer talking, moonwalked backwards, the soles of his feet sliding over the carpet, his legs flexing a little. His arms went up in front of him. Then the backs of his legs banged against the side of the chair and he tipped backwards, pivoting over the armrest. I saw, then, that something had been added to his chest. His arms went up, and then flopped down again. It was all very startling.

As all his motion stopped he was sitting crossways in the chair, his legs over one of the armrests, his head flopped back over the other. The bar, or blade, or spike, or whatever-it-was was sticking exactly out of the middle of his chest.

My heart went bumpbetty, bumpbetty, as in that old Peter Sellers and Sophia Loren song. Or was it Peter Sellers and Gina Lollobrigida?

I scrabbled in amongst my jacket, almost on reflex; but of course I was carrying no weapon. I was a civilian now. And, since my fingers didn't open, all I was doing was, in effect, lightly pummelling my own torso. I couldn't have gripped a gun anyway. I was in charge of a different sort of weaponry now.

I could see that Martin was dead.

The hider in the bathroom stepped into the room. He was exactly as you'd expect him to be: a young man, dressed casually, although not cheaply, in jeans, boots and a smartcloth top. Broad face, large nose; dark glasses. Long bread-coloured hair tied in a queue at the back of his head. He had a carryall slung over his left shoulder and I didn't doubt that he had a variety of weaponry inside. In his right hand (right handed, then: I stored that information away) he was holding a shaft-tube, the compressor reservoir balanced casually in the crook of his right elbow. Those things aren't light, which suggested he was physically strong. But most of all, he came into the room in *a certain way*. I recognized his contained swagger. It had once been mine.

'Hello,' I said, in my croaky voice. 'Is English OK?'

He was wired in, of course; aural feed and text on the inner face of his glasses. But it was polite to, at least, ask.

'English fine, fuck,' he replied, enunciation crusted with accent. German, I figured. My heart was still thrumming.

He angled the tube at me as he stepped over to Martin's body slumped over the easy chair. With his free hand, and bending his knees a little to stoop to the right height, he frisked the body. He pulled out one silver pistol, which he tucked into his bag.

Then he took several steps back, almost all the way back into the bathroom. Standing in under the doorframe, he said my surname, inflecting it as a question. In his mouth it sounded like *Black*.

I nodded. 'Schäferhund?' I asked.

'Fucking A,' he replied. From this I could tell that his English was not very good. People who rely on their wires to prompt them in a foreign language are easy to distinguish from actual speakers. Those web programs that exist to help you sound like a native – I don't mean the ones for businessmen and pilgrim tourists; I mean the ones for young men and women – are predicated upon two distinctive ideas: that fluency is a matter, firstly, of idiom; and, secondly, of swearing. So it was my Schäferhund soldier followed his AI-concocted script and told me: 'Not very fucking difficult. You are poacher turned gamekeeper, you. Go, walk it, you walk and I walk here, it is behind you. A word in your shell-like, do not try fuck me.'

'I saw your friend downstairs,' I said, getting tremblingly to my feet.

'You have come to fuck with Schäferhund, I think.'

'I wouldn't put it that way.'

'You were Pantegral?'

'I was.'

He lowered the shaft of his weapon. 'That is – some NMA,' he said, in simple admiration, like the scene in *Charlotte's Web*.

'Thank you,' I said, genuinely. This was a surprise. To be precise, I was surprised to be as *touched* as I was.

'Some fighter,' he said. Then: 'You fought in German NMA before that I think?'

'You know a lot about me.'

He angled his head. 'Which German NMA you fight in?'

'This was a long time ago. And I was only there for a short time. In those days a lot of the NMAs didn't have individual names,' I said. 'But it was formed out of a kernel from Bonn.'

'Maybe some of Schäferhund fought in that one. Maybe you know them?'

'Maybe.'

'So why are you coming to fuck up Schäferhund? Let me run *that* up the pole see you salute?'

I moved my arm very slowly, not wanting to startle him. With an almost tai-chi control my fist went left to right, gesturing at the whole vista visible through the window. 'Isn't Strasbourg a lovely city? Aren't the people good people? Don't they deserve to be able to live their lives without being burned and mutilated and shot?' My lungs burned mildly. 'Wouldn't it be nice if that cathedral spire were still standing in a year's time?'

He didn't scoff. He didn't look angry. Instead he nodded, thoughtfully. 'If Strasbourg was kosher fucking democracy,' he said, 'I would,' a pause whilst software provided the right word, '*sympathize*. If it was kosher democracy, I would more sympathize. Let's go. And hey,' he added, tucking the loaded tube into his bag in such a way that I could see it was still going to be aimed at me, 'hey, let's be careful out there.'

The voice is a needle. The needle is a tower.

The trigger wasn't entirely under my control, I suspect, although it was supposed to be. Live away from combat and return to it, and it is much more of a shock than you could ever think. It is a shock, and remains a shock despite the fact that you re-lived and re-lived those combat situations, over and over. But, see, that is precisely part of the problem. I don't just mean problem in the sense of waking up screaming, or night-sweats, or throwing yourself to the floor at every champagne cork and every knock on the door. I mean problem in the sense that *re-living* is not the same as living. I mean in the sense that the essence of combat is the continual, adrenalized encounter with *the unexpected*; and that the essence of memory is the obsessive revisiting of events until they acquire the rounded, carved and sanded contours of inevitability. You see the distinction I am drawing. You see why it is a problem.

In that hotel room I found myself in a situation I had been in a hundred times, as a youngling: death leaping from its hidey-hole with a roar. But although I remembered what that was like, after the fashion of memory, I had forgotten the way that feeling actually primped in the bloodstream. Adrenaline, the tagged neural networks, the rush. The splinter of metal in my forebrain.

I felt shivery almost at once.

We came out of the lift into the lobby and started across the soft soft carpet towards the street exit. On his sofa Schäfer-hund 1's pal twitched to see us, dropped his book to the table, jumped up and fell into step, moving on a parallel path towards the door. Pretty Leah, behind the desk, didn't so much as look up. Not that she could have done anything. But the thought that these people could walk into a public hotel, murder a serving US officer, kidnap me, and just walk out *without anybody even noticing* struck me as very wrong. Would nobody take notice?

I could yell something, I thought. But then the lobby would become a firefight, and ordinary people would die.

The second Schäferhund stepped over to us and pressed himself against my side. His English was clearly better than his comrade's. 'You are the giantkiller fellow, so? I saw you go up with the American man.'

'I saw you seeing us,' I said.

'You should have told your American, then, that you saw me, and were suspicious. But it is too late for your suspicion now.'

'A pleasure to meet you too, I'm sure,' I replied, a little tartly.

We all three stepped through the main entrance, on to the street. Outside. Crowds. Pale though bright light. We shuffled onwards and I was of course scanning the pavements, but there was no hope there. I put my mind back to the EU military checkpoints. Presumably Schäferhund was going to put me in a car and drive me straight out of town. Would a checkpoint stop them? Could I make some gesture, or draw attention to my predicament? Without, obviously, getting myself killed? I recalled the dull, resentful expression on the faces of the soldier-sentries. I looked around me at the plump and satisfied faces of the tourists and locals. I did not have hopes.

'You are come to kill our giant,' said Schäferhund 2, in my ear. 'I am really most extremely curious to discover how you will do that.'

'Curious,' I said, a little breathless. I was starting to feel unwell.

'One man against one giant. You're David, yes, and we are Goliath.' He emphasized this last name on the *o*. 'I am curious of the how, to discover what you are capable of doing. But I am curious, also, of the why. To turn against your own?'

'I was explaining the why to your colleague here.'

'The US captured you, yes? They interrogate? They turn you?'

'To everything,' I muttered, 'there is a season.'

I looked back, with a twist of pain in my neck, at the outside of the hotel. I scanned the crowd, quickly. No help there. The backdrop of Strasbourg buildings looked frail to the point, almost, of trembling; or I was trembling, perhaps.

Cars were passing slowly, on account of the crowded and overspilling pavements.

Then I spotted, on the far side of the road, a US military uniform in amongst all the greys and blues and tartans. I focused on him, because of course he might be my salvation. He was alone. It wasn't so good that he was alone. Could I signal him? He was standing on the far side of the road, ready to cross, and was carrying a little cardboard tray, and in the eggbox indentations of the tray were two tall, lidded cardboard cups of coffee with Starbucks logos on their sides. He looked left, and looked right, and then looked straight ahead. It was when he looked straight ahead that his eyes met mine, and his gaze loitered for just a moment, as if seeing me distantly reminded him of something. I willed the thought: your comrade told me about you, but now he's dead. I'm the reason you're here. Help me. But then his gaze went left again, and I could almost see the mental process at work by which the recognition didn't happen; the visual data was filed away, and so he stepped on to the road.

The moment passed.

Of course you know that sinking sensation, the tug of hope departing.

'Is it virus?' asked Schäferhund 1. 'Is this how you kill the giants?'

'What virus could work on such an entity?'

'It is made of people,' said Schäferhund 1. We had almost crossed the road now and were about to step on to the pavement on the far side.

'The rumour is,' said Schäferhund 1, 'virus, like swine virus.'

'You're having a fucking laugh,' I said, wearily.

A little whistle of brakes behind us; a car stopping abruptly. Somebody shouted 'Hoy!'

Why had the car stopped?

We turned. The US officer was standing in the middle of the road, such that the car had been forced to stop to avoid striking him. The car's wide snout was a foot or so from the soldier's hip. The driver was gesticulating from behind the safety of his windscreen. But the soldier just stood there, smack in his way, like a lump. He was looking at us.

The tray and its cups of coffee tumbled from his grip. Having gone to all the bother of queuing at the Starbucks counter, in his immaculate uniform, and paying for two cardboard cups of coffee; and having ported them almost to the door of the hotel without mishap, to drop them at this stage was – what? A shame? It was certainly a shame. It was at the very least a shame. A few more steps and he'd have been inside the hotel; and then in the lift; and up to the room, and his friend, the two cups still hot. Of course, his friend was dead. But *he* didn't know that.

He let the tray go. It fell away. As the cups hit the tarmac the lids came off and coffee, one liquorish, one mud, splooshed and sprayed.

Suddenly it was all happening.

The US officer was reaching round to his hip, underneath the flap of his jacket.

Schäferhund 1, to my left, was swinging his bag round, still dangling from his shoulder, angling his body to bring it to bear.

The US soldier was quick, though. He had his sidearm out, glinty in the daylight, and was levelling it. Schäferhund 1 was compelled to discharge his weapon earlier than he intended. There was a popping noise of decompression and the fabric of the side of the bag tore. Shreds of cloth puffed and flew.

A flash.

The windscreen of the stopped car shattered. There was a hole in it, and from the hole a spider had woven an instant pattern into the fabric of the glass. The driver of this car was no longer leaning forward in his seat, gesticulating, angry at the uniformed man standing in his way. He had instead sat back, lolling his head over the top of his seat. His anger had been wholly purged.

The US soldier's firearm spoke its angry word: once, twice. *Da! Da!*

Schäferhund 1 flinched backwards, and two little red mouths opened right in the middle of his chest. Both of these mouths stuck out a bright red tongue. Schäferhund 1 went backwards, tipped to forty-five degrees, and the tongues came further out, and then they detached altogether, and broke into blobs and drops and fell through the air.

I was in the process of drawing in a breath.

Schäferhund 1 fell over backwards and hit the ground.

Some of the passers-by were screaming.

And now the US soldier was bringing his weapon round to bear on his second target. He moved queerly slow-mo, or seemed to. Schäferhund 2 was quicker. He had his gun in his hand, and his arm was stretched in the direction of the soldier. His left hand was clasping his right wrist. There was a flash, and a firecracker bang, and a little dagger of light, subliminally, at the muzzle of the gun. Bam!

Then again. Bam! Neither shot connected with their target.

The US soldier had his aim in, now; and fired his gun. *Da!* *Da!* He did not hit Schäferhund 2.

They were only a few yards from one another, both shooting, both missing, and all about them the crowd was breaking, streaming and flowing away. Several people were shouting, or wailing: terrified collective vowels. Where are they all going, these hurrying people? They don't know where they're going, any more than I do.

Both men fired simultaneously, and it was *bam-Da!*—

The US soldier bowed, flexing forward at his waist. He was the orchestral conductor at the end of his performance acknowledging the applause of the crowd. It was incongruously polite of him. He didn't straighten up from his bow. He stood like that for a moment. Then his knees wobbled, and gave way and he toppled forward on to the ground. He was down in a heap, his face in a puddle of coffee, his arse in the air. Schäferhund 2 took hold of my arm. 'Come along,' he said, picking up his dead comrade's bag. 'It is, now, time to go.' And the collective roar of crowd began to build.

I was in no state to resist his heave. He was much stronger, and more determined. He had a place to go. I had nothing; except one thing and that thing was served best by having myself carried off. As for fear of dying – what? Apotasis. I was the fever that I experienced.

But how my heart stuttered!

The combustion was in my head, now. It burned. Flickers of light in the corner of my eye. Obedience and paranoia are much closer aligned than you might think. I tried to move my feet to keep pace with my abductor; but it was difficult. One of the things that happened to me when I was burnt – I do not remember the actual incident of course – was that the lining of my lungs became scorched. They had sort of healed, up to a point, and I could sort of breathe again, but that did not mean they could oxygenate my bloodstream with the efficiency necessary to enable vigorous exercise. My skin hurt, in several places, when my limbs moved, or my arms swung, or my head turned. I was puffing. I would have been exhausted under the best circumstances, and these were not the best circumstances, because there was a smouldering, feverish intensity inside my brain.

People were hustling in many directions. Flashes of wide-open eyes passing. 'Come along,' said Schäferhund 2.

'I'm trying to make,' I gasped. 'But can't just. You need to.'

'Come on!'

I had assumed the plan was to take me to a car, but there didn't seem to be a car anywhere near; or else the unplanned firefight had necessitated a change of plan. I could hear police sirens. It occurred to me (feverish, you see), which had never occurred to me before, that there is something snide, something *mocking* in the sound of a police siren. As if law enforcement is announcing to the whole world how contemptuously it regards those it pursues. My eyes were hot.

Sweat glands are amongst the things a person tends to lose when burns heal as new skin. For people with very extensive burns there can be a major difficulty in just keeping cool.

Schäferhund 2 hauled me into a doorway, and through the door, and I stumbled on the step-up and fell forward. This was hardly compatible with my dignity as a warrior of Pantegral, and so on, and so forth, but at least I could get some of my breath back. On all fours, on the tiled floor of some entrance hall or other. Schäferhund 2 was checking the street outside.

'I daresay,' I said, in a wheezy voice, 'they'll be shutting the checkpoints now.'

'Checkpoints,' said Schäferhund 2, his back to me.

'I assume that's not ideal,' I said. 'In terms of getting me.

Out of Strasbourg. Although why you, want to do that, I don't know.'

'You don't know?' He was standing over me, now, tucking his gun into the waist of his trousers. 'You're the man who kills giants. What giant wouldn't want to talk to you?'

'Or else just. Execute.'

'Let us hope I do not have to kill you,' he said.

'I don't feel very well,' I said. My tongue was gummy. I was hot.

'Get up,' said Schäferhund 2, putting hands under each of my armpits. 'Come upstairs.'

'I'm sorry about your friend,' I said, whilst the hallway shifted and rotated, and I swayed again upright on two legs.

'You are sorry. *You* did not kill him.'

'I'm sorry anyway.'

'We must ascend the stairs.'

The foot of the stairs was straight ahead, at the end of the narrow, chessboard hallway. The stairs were a hundred years old. Or two hundred. Fashioned in wood and carpeted down the middle. 'There's no lift?'

'There is not the lift.'

'You could say,' I said, testing my wobbly legs by stepping forward, 'there is no lift. Or more idiomatic would be, there isn't a lift.'

'We can talk German, if you prefer.'

'No,' I said. 'You're all right. You're all right with your English.'

'What is the matter?' He peered into my face and I got the chance to see his features properly: pale skin, but very dark eyebrows, like pieces of felt, and liquorish-coloured eyes. Close trimmed black hair.

'I have a fever,' I said.

'I must help you, to go up the stairs?'

'I'm afraid so.'

He draped my arm about his neck like a stole, fitted his shoulder into my armpit, and started up the staircase, taking some of my weight from my feet. 'We must hurry, I am afraid.' A few strides to the end of the hall, and then, a little awkwardly, up the stairs. One, two, three. Da! I thought. Da! Da! The musk of him was in my nose. I can only smell strong scents, nowadays, so I assume his smell was a strong scent.

'Please tell me,' he said, as we ascended, his voice tight with the effort.

'I will tell you,' I said. The stairway – up; turn right and along, up again; turn right and along, up again – was assuming a weirdly phantasmagoric quality in my perceptions. It was – trippy.

'Tell me how such a man as you, injured and weak – please tell how you are able – to kill giants.'

'To slay giants,' I said. 'To knock the giants down with my slingshot.' I wanted to stop my head lolling, side to side, because the movement tugged uncomfortably upon the scar tissue of my neck. But I couldn't stop the lolling.

'How do you do it?'

I echoed his question: 'How do we do it?'

'How do *you* do it?' he repeated.

I felt like I had been smoked out. 'How do I do it?' I said. 'That's the right question. You should probably bisect my head with a round from your pistol. Shouldn't you?'

'We voted,' he said. 'We take you back.'

'And why?'

The final flight of stairs was smaller, and brought us not to a landing but a narrow fire door that in turn opened out on to the roof. There was a small flat area amongst otherwise sloping angles and tiled flanks: a space covered over with roofing fabric, the material as dark and abrasive as asphalt. Chafing my senses. I was unwell. A low rail surrounded it on three sides; the fourth was blocked by the flank of another building. All those angled surfaces, like a small-scale abstraction of a mountain range. Like a cubist sculpture of the Alps.

In the middle of this little roof space were three objects: two microlite backpacks, and one common-or-garden wooden chair.

Schäferhund 2 poured me out of his arms on to the roof, and I stood, just about keeping my feet, gasping, looking about. I hurt fairly badly where my skin had been scraped by his grip, and my lungs had not recovered from the severity of the previous exercise. Schäferhund 2 stood with his hands on his hips as if he had just finished a marathon. What people forget about that first marathon race – though the fact is inscribed in the name – is that the runner was a soldier, and that he had just finished fighting a particularly tough battle. Sport, you see, was cracked out of the egg of war.

'Why?' he said. 'Why do we take you back?'

'Why not just kill me here? Why not kill me back in the hotel room?'

'Because you are weapon, we think,' said Schäferhund 2. 'Please to sit in the chair.'

It was an old-fashioned wooden chair, taken, perhaps, from a bar or a domestic kitchen. Its seat was a circle. Its four legs splayed slightly outwards at the bottom. It had two little armrests, and its back was a pretzel-weave of wood bounded by a wooden hoop.

'You want that I sit?'

'You must sit.'

I suppose the chair made me think of summary execution, although such thoughts were at odds with what Schäferhund 2 was saying to me. I ought not to have cared, but I did. I told myself: I don't want to die *like that*, strapped in a chair with a bullet in the back of my head. Dying in open battle was one thing; going like a Viking. But not in so mean and despicable a manner. This wasn't the truth, though. The truth was that I didn't want to die at all, under any circumstances. That's always the truth, when a person comes to it. Whatever you might think, however much you believe you crave death, when you actually come to it that is what you'll feel. You can't help it.

But of course I sat. What choice did I have? Straightaway he fed a strap around my chest, under my arms, and fastened it at the back. Another strap went over my lap and got fastened underneath the seat. My arms were free. Only when he unspooled a thick cable – mountaineering paraphernalia, perhaps – from his back and clicked it to the back of the chair did I understand what he intended.

'Might it be easier for me to take the spare micro?' I suggested, nodding at the backpack.

'But then you would fly away from me,' Schäferhund 2 pointed out. 'And I would not be able to bring you back with me, as has been voted.' The spare micro, I realized, was for the deceased Schäferhunder.

'You want me because you think I'm a weapon?' I said, watching him unzip the microlite pack, pull out its stalk and unfold its rotor blade – this latter a rigid hollow long as a surfboard and nearly a quarter as broad. Schäferhund 2 clicked the structure together, and then fed helium into it from a little bottle. Once this was done he could lift the whole motor – it was a large motor – and harness with his left arm, and hold it whilst he slipped his right arm in. With a wriggle of his spine he fitted it on his back, the rotor like an etiolated parasol over his head. Then he took the cable attached to my chair and hooked it to the belt of his harness.

'Do you want me because you are planning to go to war

against other NMAs?' I asked him. 'I'm no use against regular armies.'

He didn't answer, his attention taken up with reaching behind himself to extend a pole from the back of his pack, and twist a torch-like object round to a ninety-degree angle. It occurred to me that fitting these packs was really a two-man job. It was awkward, doing it by himself.

'You want me just on the off chance? Keep me in reserve?' I was chattering too much, but that was because of the fire within my head, and the hot dribble from my nostrils, and the fact that I could feel the whole of both my eyeballs, all the way around, as if the skull were a sense organ and was palpating them.

This fever—

I was partly trying to persuade him to kill me. If the Colonel had overheard me, he would have thought I was betraying his trust – trying to protect the Schäferhund NMA. But it wasn't that at all. All those conversations with the Colonel, and he now thought I was his weapon. But I wasn't. I was trying to prevent my deployment not to protect the NMA, but to protect everybody else. Do you see? I was worried about the world of ordinary people. The Colonel didn't know what sort of weapon I was.

'Do you want to unpack me and see how I work?' I shouted. I needed to shout because Schäferhund 2 had started the motor.

The torch-like object was no torch. As the rotors began to turn it coughed and started to whirr, and as the rotors' whoomf sped to the point where the sound began to blur, the device blew harder, and a tiny spike of flame quavered in its mouth, to counter the rotatory impulse of the blades. I watched with feverish fascination. Schäferhund 2 lifted from the ground, like an angel ascending. The cable that linked us rose like a snake-charmer's cobra.

I shouted something else, but since I couldn't hear my own voice over the noise of the mechanism, I don't know what it was. The chair jerked. A poltergeist had kicked it. If tables can be turned, why not chairs. It slid backwards across the roof. Then with a little kick of its lifeless legs it jumped up, bounced, sagged, drew the cord taut.

There was a thump, and it made me cry out, as the back of the chair caught the fence. But then we were up, and I had become the dangling man. The way the cable had been attached meant that the whole chair tipped forward a little way, and my body strained against its restraints, and my view was directed downwards. But I was swinging, too, in a long slow pendulum trajectory, and this brought more of the ground into my view, and then more of the horizon and sky, and ground, and horizon, and ground and horizon. The engine noise complained, and the downdraft from the rotors blew right down my collar and touched my skin.

The roof was a yard or two below me. Then, abruptly, the roof was a long way down. The house looked like a model of a house. I could see the streets of Strasbourg, and see their thrum and human clutter. I even took the trouble to look for evidence of the attempt to recapture me, because – my fever head had not driven this fact out of my skull – because, you see, I was important! Jack the Giantkiller. I suppose I thought to see troops scurrying through the narrow streets – police cars, sirens, barricades being put up, ranks of trotting soldiers. But I didn't see any of that. I daresay there *were* police cars, and soldiers running, somewhere down there. I don't doubt that the gendarmes, or the polizei, or whatever they called peelers in this part of the world, had erected a temporary tent about the US soldier's body in the street – had stopped the traffic from flowing, had moved any lingering rubberneckers away. I don't doubt they had discovered Martin's body in the hotel room, sprawled across the cosy chair. The EU Military Command, and the Americans, must know I was gone. But I couldn't see any of that from where I was.

Away to the east the cloud cover was dense and fuzzed in purples and blacks; but directly above me it was white and bright.

The noise of the drone went up a semitone, and my pendulum swing began to acquire a circular momentum. With the noise, and the rush of air, and the cold, it was hard to concentrate on details below. There was the city of Strasbourg. I knew that. There was its unmistakable cathedral spire, the tallest in the world between 1647 and 1874, or else between 1674 and 1847. It was the giant needle, the omphalos. There were the roads, stitching the buildings together. Roofs, scattered cards, mahjong tiles. An antique circuit board. And we pulled higher, and the effect was almost exactly like sliding the toggle downwards on a terrain googlemap. The ring road came into view. The thread of the river Ill, the Al as it now is, trailing along until it met the Rhine's fat cable away to the east. The roads did not shine as nicely as the rivers. And there are patches of cloth, in varicoloured greens, and these are forests, and fields. They are strips of garden, running from parkland down to farmland. Tweedbrown, seagreen, and lines of grey and silver and black like ore. This is motley. The etymology of the word *politics* is from the Greek word for motley, the variegated and multicoloured democratic polis. Who wears this mixture of clothing? A giant, and the giant of all giants. Its name is Europe.

The drone of the rotors circling was the music of the spheres.

I tipped my head back and saw the ceiling of white, coming

closer now; and silhouetted vividly against it was the black bugshape of the Schäferhund soldier – a tight perspective of feet, legs, head, and a wide halo of blur above. The cable that connected us was taut and thrumming. My circling motion doubtless mixed confusion into my feverish head. The fever had flared too soon, there was no question about that. And round I went, round and round, like a hypnotist's bauble, the dangling man on a long rope. Europe below me, and stretching all about me in every direction; the landscape of the world. There were other parts of the world, of course I knew, but that was something I knew intellectually rather than in my soul. I felt myself to be suspended directly over the exact heart of Europe. Europe the primal giant, the first to be woken from pre-vivid sleep to stretch, and groan, and shake its limbs.

I looked down again: the toggle had slid further down the googlemap scale-bar. Strasbourg was a crust of stone and metal over European earth. The vegetative soil. I could see the larger shape of the forests, and a longer section of the trunk of the Rhine; and yet, even at this height, I could see the glitter of cars and trucks creeping corpuscularly along the motorways.

I was shivering. It was very cold and very bright all around me. The swing of my chair disoriented me. The altitude was pressuring my inner ear. My eyes kept rolling up in their sockets, sliding out of alignment and needing to be reset. Whiteness sifting down from the source of all light. Chilly little clumps of mist were around me.

What happened next was that I vomited. The stuff came as if from nowhere and blurted out of my mouth in a fan. It wasn't especially uncomfortable. I felt like a conduit, and the content of my stomach was broadcast outwards into the encompassing air, and rained away, or else, atomizing, was swept away by the winds and blown throughout the whole of the huge sky. The stuff I had put into my stomach on the plane, in the air, as I flew over from London, was now coming out of my stomach, back into the air. There was a harmony in that.

My seat swung back once again, and I drew a deep breath, and I opened my eyes to see the imprecise architecture of the clouds – bulges and spurs, blue-edged shapes – sink around me. And then, with a distinct sensation of a drop in temperature, we rose into a cloud, and everything became white and blank and pure and cold.

What are clouds? They were all about me. Clouds are mist that aspires higher than to slink its belly along the wet grass like a worm. Clouds are protean giants that think themselves angels.

I couldn't see anything, but it did not matter. I could see everything *feelingly*, in that properly Shakespearian phrase. It was all spread out below me. The European landscape, howsoever scribbled over with motorways and the cellular growth of concrete buildings, was still, in its essence, a medieval landscape. Its true nature was antique forests and mountains, immemorial rivers and low-lying meadows. It was fields ploughed neatly into ribbons, and small knots of buildings. Directly below me was Alsace, the pivot about which everything moved. *Eppur si muove*. The way it is mapped, according to the logic of contemporary mapmaking – which is, a beak of France-EU poking into Germany-EU: a shelf upon which are piled Luxembourg and Belgium and Holland, as if ready to tumble down – that's not true to nature. Alsace is not sharp-edged in that way. Not according to the anatomy of the giant. Alsace lies along and above the great Alpine spine. A mighty ridge, curving west-east. And great pads of ground to the north, and north-west and north-east – soft, fertile landscapes through which rivers sine and ease themselves.

I could almost reach out and touch it.

To the south-west was the Midi, where the mountains were baked the colours of brick and biscuit and sand. And then, further south still, mountains became hills, scattered with bushes and then became lowlands, vinefields like diffraction gratings, antique towns that had – until the coming of the NMAs – somehow avoided the fate of the north, of being pounded and milled-up by war, towns still filled with the architecture of the Romans and the Middle Ages. And here, running smoothly along, down the rivers to the sea; the great Mediterranean bay that is the southern French coast, and vast beaches of sand fine and yellow as pollen. In my blindness I could see all that.

Or, directly westward to the Bay of Biscay, Brittany stretching out like the bough of great growth. Sweeping over the farmed lands of central France, and over Paris, where mankind has constructed its elaborate petrification in imitation of these same features: strips of field in stone, curves and straights of river in stone, and the whole thing pinned with a giant Parisian metal spike to keep it in place, like a butterfly upon a board. And in this city were millions of people acting in concert, flowing along the unelastic veins, packing together or breaking apart, each working at a project as a miniature machine: to eat, to drink, to push objects here or there, to disassemble or reassemble, to fuck, to caress the computer keyboard, to organize others, to walk or drive. I saw. And swing west from there over giant fields tickled by slow moving combine harvesters, to the western coastline and the untilled waves beyond, pulling apart and clapping together over the sunken remains of Ys.

And to the north the Manche, where the sea had a different hue and consistency: shivery little waves like dints in pewter. Boats drawing comet tails over the water's surface. An airplane below me, small as a drawing of an airplane, and below that the plane's shadow. And we're across, the coastline and cliffs white and irregular like the severed edge of a broken piece of crockery. And then green fields, and towns and villages; and then conic church spires and shoebox naves and chancels; cars cramming the roads; people standing outside their offices to smoke cigarettes – and here is London, as old as any town in the world, the teeth of stone on both sides of the river's opening jaw. A god, this river, worshipped for millennia. Follow the mouse's tail of the Thames through smaller towns, and past dreadlocked willows and under arches and threaded through the manacles of river-locks until it vanishes, like a wobbly perspective line, somewhere in the centre of Britain.

Sweep right, and here's the restless low plateau of the North Sea: admire these oil platforms pinned to its breast like brooches. Here is the dragonhead of Scandinavia reaching down to seize Denmark in its jaws, interrupted in its meal by some geological freeze frame. The Norwegian coast resembles a medical diagram of the womb-wall as it makes itself hospitable to the implantation of an egg. And the blue fluid runs through myriad tubes and into myriad pockets, and lakes and fjords and rivers and ponds. The porous archipelago. Move over it, and look down at a surface furry with woodland.

I could sense it, almost as if running my fingers over it. I could almost cram it into my mouth.

Here are the ventricles of the Gulf of Bothnia, reaching into the lobes of Finland and Russia, Estonia and Latvia. South, though, over the rough membranes of forest and gully, over fields of beetroot and kale, roads that see no car from one quarter hour to the next. This wide land, the steppes of Poland and Belarus, the tender belly of Ukraine all in greens and yellows. Or the conker-coloured mountainsides of Romania, Slovakia, the Czech lands. And the pendulum is swinging us back again towards the centre of the stage: Hungary, Croatia, the wide lands of Illyria down to the Adriatic as blue as blueberries and scuffed where the sunlight bounces back.

Here is mountainous Austria, and here Germany. People have lived in these countries for thousands of years; and they have scratched the itch of the earth with their ploughs and been rewarded with wheat; and they have threaded themselves through the stems of these forests to shoot down game, and to drag the carcasses back by their hooves, a rope fastened and tight over the hunter's shoulder, and the man leaning to take the strain as he walks. The people of Europe have trudged over mountains, Ötzi-man's trail, with a meal of grain in their belly and animals skins stitched about them. They sleep here, and eat; they work and play and fuck. They have cleared the woodland away and made towns, and navigated the rivers. But the woodland was still the most of it, the membrane insulating ground against sky. I could see all of it from my vantage. Forests called Black and Great inundating the hill-sides and splashing high up the flanks of mountains. So many trees it made the ground nighttime at midday. In this clearing a trench is dug and filled with blood. Why blood? Horrible. And where did that image come from? The trench must be a mass-grave, such as was made for the Protestants or for the Catholics, for the Jews or the Partisans or the Gypsies or whoever was made, at gunpoint, to dig them out in these central forests. All in amongst these endless, primal forests. This was where Red Riding Hood walked whilst wolves watched her with eyes that shone gold. They must excavate a long trench, which is hard work, and stand on the lip of their own earthworks, and then we will shred their flesh with bullets, and crack their bones with bullets, so that they fall forward and they bleed and the trench is filled with blood. A strip of red in amongst the green.

The forests of Grimm. Fairy tale. Her hood was red because it was dyed by human blood.

The fever was not war, passing and passing over the surface of Europe. *Peace* was the fever, keeping people at home and close to their fires and wrapped in blankets. War was the way people chose to dispose of their health and vigour. War was what men smelt in the clear air, and saw in the distance, near the horizon, when their noses and eyes were sharp. The hawk, roosting, sees it when he looks down.

Why do men keep making war? This is the most important question. Really, I can't think of a more important question. The dead are dancing, round and about this trench filled with blood. You can see your mother. You can try and embrace your father, but your arms will go through him, not once but twice and three times. There's my boy, my blue-skinned boy, my shadow-coloured boy, with the key right in the middle of his head, in the middle of his forehead.

The whole landscape was shrunken down into one of those Stefan Heck artworks.

The whole of Europe was within my reach.

And now what had happened? Now the giant had twitched and shrugged, and a new form of life had come to be. And I could see that, too. I could see it as clear as eyeing. But actually it was all mist and white brightness on every side. I turned my head but everything was the same. I was shaking, trembling. The air around me was vividly cold, and I was shaking because of that; but I was roasting hot at the same time. My body felt like flu. My cheeks and my chin were wet.

Giants were striding, now, over the landscape. Leviathans, in motley, with massy arms and legs, and weighing a million kilos each.

This image – stepping as neatly across the Manche as if it were an irrigation trench no more than a yard wide.

But that's not right, since that giant is all face. Hobbes saw truly that giganticism was the secret hidden in the narrative of mankind's evolution and his image is closer to the truth:

Though Hobbes had a feudal mind, and could not help but imagine that his giant would have a royal head, a guiding and directing organ. Somebody explain to him that this is not needful. The next stage in human evolution is *necessarily* away from the restrictions of feudalism. The next stage is the land of the headless giants: for without eyes their eyes cannot play them tricks, and without ears they cannot be lied to, and without a mouth they cannot be fed poisoned food, and without a nose they cannot smell the stink of mortality. I see them as if the vision is projected upon the screen of all surrounding whiteness: they tower over the land. Here is Schäferhund; and he is a young giant, and not as strong as some others. But see how effortlessly he strides! He walks through Bavaria and the hills and mountains inconvenience him not at all, and the forests tickle his ankles. And he walks, also, through the packed-together farmlands of central Germany, and leaps up in amongst the factories and docks of the North. And he draws himself to his full height here, on the east bank of the Rhine. There is Alsace, lying below him, with Strasbourg at its centre. He need only reach down with his arm and strike it; to haul up the spire of the cathedral and upend it, like a spearhead, to jab it down amongst his enemies. The city is full of people who want to stop him, he knows that. But what can they do? They are, compared to him, so very small.

The whiteness flickered, and then flew away upwards in blobs and shards, thrown crazily above my head. We were descending. I could feel it in my hollow gut. I was still penduluming, but according to a gentler trajectory, and there was something almost soothing in the blurrm blurrm sound of the rotors overhead. But I was sopping wet; my clothes soaked through to my shivering skin. Given how ill I felt, that was clearly not good. Better, when you are ill, to be warm and dry than cold and wet. My head felt three times its normal size, and throbbed. It radiated more heat than the sun.

Strasbourg had been removed from the landscape below.

Now there was only forest. I looked east for the Rhine, and did not see it; but then I looked in the other direction, and it was away to the west, inset into the landscape, dimly luminous, the colour of lit silver. Then I lost sight of it, because the tree tops were sweeping up towards me and their ivy-greens and racing-greens and olive-greens and blue-greens became the entire land. I felt a flutter in my heart – which proved that I was not wholly hollow, since I still had a heart – at the thought that we were going to crash into the forest canopy. But at the last minute a clearing opened up, and the ground rushed at me, and I caught a glimpse of parked cars, and a collection of people, some of whom were running towards me. And the next thing was the thump that I remembered from parachute training, back in the old old days when I had been hale and beautiful and when I had been a member of His Majesty's Armed Forces.

A bump and a clatter, and I was on my side, still strapped into the chair. The grass, close against my face, was wriggling and struggling like miniature tentacles; like the scilla in the lungs before they had been so scorched. Litter and fag-ends and bits of leaf and soggy pine needles were being blown about in every direction. And then, as arms reached underneath me to haul me upright, I heard the rotors slow, their noise stutter out into separate snare beats, and then stop altogether. My bindings were being loosened. I was vaguely aware of many people clustering around me. They were talking, voices loud. I could not understand them at all. They were just talking gibberish. But then I caught a word I recognized, and tripped, mentally, over the realization that they were talking in German. I could speak some German. My *dad* was German! I was *half*-German! Unlike the other guy, who couldn't speak any German at all – who was it, recently, who had been complaining that he could not speak German? It hardly mattered now.

'Ach!' somebody close by my ear, in *Deutsch*. 'He is feverish, he is shivering.'

'He is very wet,' said somebody else. Then something I didn't understand, to which somebody else said, 'No, no' and a different person again said: 'But yes, perhaps in the van.'

Then some more talk.

'He is dying, perhaps.'

Gabble gabble.

I was lifted and carried, and the artillery began its bombardment. I thought to myself: hah! Now you're for it, my Schäferhunden friends, because the EU Military will grind you like coffee beans into powder with their big guns! But it was not artillery. It was thunder, and the fat black clouds from the east, burlying the white clouds out of the way, were bringing rain.

I was laid out in the back of a van, and the door was shut with a sliding-crescendo and a slam. There were other people in the back with me, and one was trying to undress me, but I was shivering so hard my arms and legs were flopping about, like an epilepsy. Another was rubbing at me with a towel, or possibly a blanket.

Rain started clattering against the roof of the van. The rainstorm threw innumerable plastic beads at the windows and upon the roof over my head. The back window blued.

What is that sound, over and above all the others? It is the engine starting. What is that horizontal sensation? It is us, driving away.

I fell asleep, despite the rattle and the lurch.

When I awoke I had been taken out of the van, and laid on a truckle bed in a clearing in the forest. It was dark. It was no longer raining.

A blanket had been tucked tight about my body, which felt simultaneously comforting and restricting. I was not sure if I had the energy to sit up. I did not test the possibility. I was content to lie there.

It was dark. It was not raining. Broccoli-shaped blocks of shadow obscured perhaps a third of the sky, but they were slipping westward, and revealing more and more starlit blue-grape black. Chickenpox tiny white stars all over it. One of the glories of being in the middle of a forest, and far away from artificial lighting, was the view of so many stars.

The moon, like an open-brackets.

I lay for a long time, just looking upwards; feeling a little less feverish, and a little more in control; but still weak, and helpless, and kittenish. I was aware, peripherally, of comings and goings. There were sounds of movement and, somewhere the liquid, Kate Bush warble of a nightjar. I took, I recall, absurd comfort from the thought that I had made it through the storm. That the storm had passed over me and I was still alive.

The land is heavier after a rainstorm than before.

A woman's voice said: 'Hello, I am Marie.'

Marie, Marie, Marie. 'Hello.'

'My friend Benni tells me you are unwell.'

'Benni,' I croaked.

'Benni is that Schäferhund who flew you out of Strasbourg.'

I discovered, by virtue of flexing my arms outwards (like *Samson*! like *Samson*!) that I could untuck the blanket from the sides of the bed. I struggled, shakily, on to one elbow, and this change in orientation brought Marie into my line of sight. The first thing I noticed was that she was wearing a helmet with a lit under-rim, which gave a spooky Halloween cast to her features. The next thing I noticed was her dwarf rifle, and then her whole uniform and pack. Lights jiggled and moved through the dark behind her. 'Your English is very good, Marie,' I said.

'I would like to talk to you,' she replied. 'I have heard that you are a weapon, and I would like to know about this. Is it true you can kill giants?'

'Not true,' I replied.

'But we have heard that you can kill giants.'

'It's really important that I explain myself,' I rasped. 'That's not what I can do.'

'You were captured by the US. You were interrogated, and persuaded to swap sides?'

'That's what *they* think.' I said. I didn't mean to sound so cryptic.

'You were interrogated?'

'After I was wounded, I was treated in a US facility. I had . . . long conversations with a US Officer, and his detail was counter-NMA. That's true. But what he thinks he's doing, sending me here, and what I'm *actually* doing . . . that's two separate things.'

'You understand we are concerned,' Marie said. 'The US killed that giant, in the Southern States of America.'

'They got lucky,' I said. 'With one giant. That one time. But I had nothing to do with that—' I sneezed, weakly, and trembled.

'Have you been used, you weapon, against Pantegral?'

Naturally this touched me. 'Pantegral's fine,' I said. 'There's nothing wrong with that giant.'

'We have heard nothing from him.'

'That doesn't mean he's dead.'

'Asleep, is he?'

'Exactly,' I said, too quickly. 'Not dead, but sleeping. There's a really crucial difference between—'

The conversation was snapped off at that point. Fireworks begin in amongst the upper branches all around us. Flashbulbs everywhere, and bang-bang-bang, and the trees begin to move.

The trees begin to bellow. I recognize this particular cacophony: the first series of detonations, compressing and wrenching the air in your ears, a rapid series; then a series of more irregular rhythms of crashings and smashings. The focus of the blasts was a couple of hundred metres away, but the waves of pressure, and heat, were immediate. There was a two-second hiatus, just enough time for me to register that my ears were singing like a tuning fork. Insects were swarming all about, a locust-thick cloud of them. It was either insects or else the softest shrapnel in the universe. Then I understood that it was fir needles, blown clean off the trees and swirling all about. It was a blizzard of pine needles, stinging my flesh. But hands were already pushing me down, back on to my truckle bed, as the bombardment began again – a little further away, but still deafening and terrifying and viscerally horrible. I swayed, even though I was pinned and horizontal. The world wobbled. A forest by flashes of artificial lightning. The enormous tree trunks swaying and groaning. A thick swarm of pine needles.

Then a metallic clunk, which for a moment I thought was a proper piece of shrapnel intersecting my body, but which was nothing of the sort. Quieter, and the vibration of an electric motor. The metal clunk was the back door being slammed shut; and I was in the back of a truck – a different one than before, electric not petrol – with two other people, and the truck lurched into life.

We drove a certain distance (how far? impossible for me to gauge) and the sounds of the bombardment rattled the sides of the van. I watched the people in the van with me – Marie was one – by the gleam of the screens on their wrist. They all of them had all their attention in their wikis. Something was up. 'This part of the plan?' I asked.

One of the others said something in German, which,

expecting English, and what with my bashed eardrums and the high ambient noise, I didn't quite catch. The superficial similarities between the two languages is rather disorienting, don't you think? Whatever he said it had the word *break* at the end. Then Marie yelled, 'It's ongoing, it's ongoing, they're reacting, not acting.' Which meant, I assumed, that the assault on Strasbourg had begun.

I thought about Martin, slouched dead across the easy chair in that hotel room. Had they found his body? Of course they had, but I supposed there was always the chance that he was still sitting there, the hotel window giving his dead eyes a good view of the barrage of the city. No, I told myself, there was no chance he had just been left there. His comrade had been bringing him coffee, and had been shot down in the street. Then I remember that the Schäferhund guy was dead too, on the street. Two dead bodies, and me missing – the US would have been all over that place.

I needed to get my thoughts sorted out.

There were four of us in that truck, except that there were five. I counted them: me, on the stretcher, and three Schäferhunden, all fiddling with their wikis. One plus three; and yet there were five of us. I tried to pinpoint where the fifth was: in which corner, front or back; but there was very little room, and the space kept jolting and shuddering, which made it harder to get straight in my head. But there was no question about it.

I knew who the fifth lad was, of course.

Then we stopped and they pulled me out. I was feeling a little less feverish now, and told them so, but they insisted on carrying me anyway. In retrospect that was good, because whatever I said I was still very poorly. I doubt if I could have stood up.

We were in a village, motionless and empty in the middle of the night. And then, with a jog and a swoop, we passed through a doorway and we were inside a house. I was laid down and had time to get my bearings. Not a terribly big house. None of the electrics seemed to work, but the Schäferhunden had standing lamps clustered on tables and mantelpieces, spinning multiple shadows off things. Rifles were stacked in one corner, and some intriguing-looking boxes in another.

'You can get up, and even move around if you like,' said Marie, squatting down next to me. 'If you are able. But you must wear these.' She was holding some plastic cuffs.

'You don't want me helping myself to a gun,' I said, smiling.

'You do not blame us for that,' she replied.

'You think I'm a weapon,' I said. 'But I'm not that sort of a weapon.'

'Are you hungry?'

'I am,' I said. I had not eaten since the plane. And since then – unless it had been a fever hallucination – I had thrown up everything I had eaten. But it was no fever dream; there were stains on the front of my clothes.

And I could not get up under my own steam. I struggled with shuddery legs, like a newborn calf, and made no headway. So Marie helped me to a chair, and strapped my wrists together with plastic, and another Schäferhund fetched me an untoasted crumpet and some fruit juice. I sat and ate and drank, my hands together like praying, and I watched the comings and goings in the eerie multiple lamplight.

A house full of Schäferhunden, and me, and one other.

I tried winking at key-boy, but he was too busy jinking out of the way of the various people to pay me much heed. He's not so interested in me, any more. I can't exactly blame him.

My head ached. I tried asking for painkillers, but people were too busy to attend to me. If I closed my eyes then things throbbed and swirled in an unpleasant manner, so I did not try to sleep. It occurred to me, as I sat there – and I don't know where this thought came from, exactly – that key-boy had something to tell me, but was coy. What he had to tell me, freighted with the horrible veracity of death, was the answer to the really crucial question. The question was: why do men make war?

Question is linked etymologically to *quoi* and *que* and *quis*, I suppose. But it is a word that means more than what? Why is more than what, after all.

Eventually Marie pulled a chair over and sat beside me. Three or four other Schäferhunden loitered around us both.

'You were NMA, once upon a time,' she told me. Without her helmet, her face illuminated in a more conventional manner, it was apparent that she was a striking-looking woman – handsome in a gaunt way, with clear skin, short dyed hair, something of the look of a David Bowie or a Jerry Groopman (when he was making music, I mean; not after the surgery and those films). 'Because you were in Pantegral, we respect you.' She was speaking English.

'Thank you,' I said, and winked again at the key-boy, who had come a little closer. He approached to eavesdrop, I suppose. You know how kids are.

'You will speak to us all? We must vote on you, and the threat you represent.'

'I understand,'

'You will address the entire body? Explain yourself?'

'Gladly,' I said, my throat dry. 'Plug me in. Link me up.'

She looked intently at me. 'You think we are fools?'

I blinked.

She repeated the question: 'You think we are fools?'

'No,' I said, slowly. 'I do not believe so.'

'You want to infect us with a virus?'

'To, let's say,' I replied, staring straight ahead, 'degrade your firewall? Mess up your connectivity? I won't do that.'

'Do you swear?'

I breathed in deeply. 'I swear.'

'Do you swear on your own NMA? On the honour of your own NMA?'

'I do.' My heart was doing some vibrant syncopated thudding in my chest. 'Besides, you won't take any chances.'

'We won't.'

'I can speak on *your* wiki if you like. I don't need to log in.'

'Oh,' she said, her eyes fractionally wider. 'We had no intention of permitting you to *log in.*'

And that was that: things were quickly set up for the Q and A: a range of individual cells of the larger Schäferhund body coming on to the wiki, or addressing me directly. I put my sweaty face alongside Marie's. That was all I needed to do.

She introduced me, and then asked me: 'You came to Strasbourg as a weapon,' she said in a severe voice. 'You are here to try kill Schäferhunden.'

'That's why they sent me.'

'To try to kill,' she repeated gravely.

There was a mob of questions from a string of people with Germanic or East-European names. It was a bit bewildering. Many were in German, of which I understood only a small part. Some spoke English.

'[You took part in the killing of Giant Fortbras?]'

'Not I.'

Somebody else: '[How did you do it?]'

'[You are bomb.]'

'[How to rewire you, like Terminator-man, and send you back to conventional army?]'

'[How?]'

'You understand,' Marie put in, 'we ask you politely, as one NMA to another. I hope you will do us the courtesy of answering this most important question.'

Another Schäferhund said something, in German this time,

but I missed the beginning bit, so I only heard '[We also have . . .]' I asked him to repeat it, and he said it again, more slowly, still in German: '[We also have the option of torturing you.]'

'That's not what it needs to come to,' said Marie. 'How do you kill giants? This new US strategy. We need to know about it.'

'Benni said that – is Benni here?'

'In this room? Obviously not.'

'No, I mean, is he on this wire?'

'[Benni is not logged in.]'

'Nice guy,' I said. 'Good shot. He said it was a virus. Or was that the other one? The other guy who said that?'

This produced a shiver of traffic. '[Is it a *computer* virus?]' one of them demanded, in German. Overlapping with him a woman in the room said, in English: 'We intercept many attempts to hack our wiki connection.'

'Is it some sort of *computer virus?*' asked Marie. 'Regular military thinking believes our network is our weak point?'

'What's that film, where Peter Sellers plays the Indian?' I said. But that wasn't right. My head was jangled. 'No: I mean, where he plays the *German?* Strange-something? He pronounced computer just like that, just the way you do.' The dipthongal u, the palatized d. I almost laughed. Could it be that I was enjoying myself?

I was looking around the room. Key-boy was over by the blank widescreen television. He was at the bookshelf, where the books had been arranged not alphabetically but – it was evident, even from where I was sitting – according to size and the colour of their spines. He was standing underneath the lintel in at the kitchen door, through which a redder light was coming. A different type of lamp must have been lit in there.

He was standing in front of the curtains. A modest room in a modest house.

'You tell us, please,' said Marie. 'Or, you confirm, please.'

'Confirm?'

'[There are many theories.]'

'[Ever since Fortbras, there are many theories.]'

'Theories,' I said. I was sweating, though neither with fear nor heat.

'[Virus, is one theory. You are carrying a virus?]'

'[You are sick, I think?]'

It was delicious. 'You think I am sick with a computer virus?' I said. 'Which would work how?'

'[Never mind that],' said somebody else. '[*Is* it computer virus? *Is* that the weapon that brought down Fortbras?]'

'There are too many ways round network blocks. Wirelines and wifi are too ubiquitous. Antiviral programming in the noughties was too successful and too ubiquitous.' This did not seem to satisfy them, so I tried: 'The network is too rhizo-matic.' A stack of incomings. 'Really, people,' I said, feeling myself hilarious, the whole situation hilarious, feeling myself on the very edge of collapsing into laughter. 'Really people, you're looking at this entirely in the wrong way. Entirely!'

Key-boy was standing right in front of me now. I felt the desire – and I had never experienced this feeling before – to reach out and take hold of his key with my right hand, and – what? Pull it out? I would pull all his brains with it. It would crunch open his cranium and everything would gush out. The key was the wrong way round; the metal circle in the lock of his skull, the jaggy square staircase of the tines poking out. Should I take hold of the end and try and turn it? It would be like twisting a knife in a wound. Nothing would be un-locked. And could I even apply the pressure needed to turn the key, with my scarskin tight little fists? But I felt the urge nevertheless. I reached out with my right hand and because my wrists were tied together my left hand came out too.

A Schäferhund had his pistol aimed at my head. When did he unholster that? Quick-draw.

I looked again, and key-boy had done his Banquo disappearing act. Of course I was used to that.

'What I do,' I said, lowering my hands slowly, steadily, to my lap. 'I present myself as an honest broker, with connections to the regular army and with my NMA experience. Though you have rather shortcircuited that by snatching me from my hotel room.' I had everybody's attention now. 'I meet as many of you as possible, on the pretext of wanting to broker negotiations. You understand my English? Yes?'

'[Genenj phage,]' said one of the Schäferhund cellular components.

'What's that?' I asked, innocently.

One of the Schäferhunden in the room spoke, reading off his arm-screen, his accent fogging the meaning: 'The rumour is of a specific neural phage. Designed to migrate to the ventromedial frontal lobe,' he said. 'It's designed to degrade neural connections in there.'

'Is that the latest conspiracy theory?' I answered, with my best impression of light-heartedness. 'Doesn't sound very plausible to me.'

There was a harum-scarum babble of voices, arguments.

'Your head,' said somebody, and had to repeat it several times to bring the chatter down.

'My head?'

'It has a metal plate in it?'

Incoming, some German, some English: '[Do not dissemble.]'

'[We ran an airport security sensor over your head, and it beep-beep!]'

'There's a key in my frontal cortex,' I said; and straight away I corrected myself: 'I mean a plate. I mean a metal splinter. Metal webbing. They patched over a certain lesion in the—' But I lost my own thread as I was speaking.

The buzz rose again. '[Eliminate is the only option!]'

'[We must execute him! I put forward the proposal!]'

In fluent, melodious German: '[It is premature to put forward proposals at this stage.]'

'[Is it a tracking device? Will it guide Regular Army to you?]'

'[We are not keeping this asset in the same place for longer than a few hours at a time.]'

'They sent me to kill you, you're right,' I said. 'But that's not why I'm here. The idea is to hijack your firewall AI-worms and turn them against you, a sort of computer-AIDS. But AI is a tricky and chaotic thing. The guy who designed this was a geezer called Donaghy. He had his own reasons not to want to toe the US line. He made something else: not malware. A seed.'

This last bit didn't go over: the AIDS reference had gotten in the way. '[It makes you sick?]'

'You're not hearing me,' I said.

'[It kills? People, or . . . networks?]'

'No! See, that's how it is different to a conventional computer virus, to conventional cyber war. It's not trying to crash your wiki. It's trying to hijack it. But what I am, is something else. What I will do is kindle you – kindle you to something new.'

'[Which variant AIDS?]' asked somebody.

'I shouldn't have mentioned the AIDS. What you need to understand – and I'm not putting it very well, because I didn't understand until . . . look. Do you know the story of James and the Giant?'

'[*David* and the Giant?]' somebody said.

'Peach!' I barked. I really wasn't handling this very well.

'Shoot me, by all means. Maybe you should. I'm not saying that Donaghy's experiment will be good for you – or for me – or for anybody. That's not the point. That's not his point. Not even he is quite sure what will happen. He's just sure it won't be what the US Army want it to be. At the start of *James and the Giant*—' I hiccoughed, or coughed, at this point, for my throat was not good at all the talking; and the same person as earlier corrected me once again: '[It is *David* and the Giant. It is James and the New Testament *Epistle*.]'

'The strange old man gives James the beans, or crystals, or pills, or something. He's supposed to eat them but he spills them on the floor. And they wriggle down, and the next thing the peach and all the insects . . .' I was rasping by this point; barely able to understand myself.

'Trooper,' asked Marie, in the tone of somebody determined to cut through the foliage and get at the heart. 'What *is* this metal web in your brain?'

'A step up in consciousness,' I gasped. 'Something wonderful, something unpredictable. Giant consciousness.' I was shivering again. I wasn't at all well, you know. I was all flu'd up. I was ill.

And *there's* key-boy! He hasn't disappeared at all; he's just hiding behind the settee! That's the sort of game a ten-year-old likes to play. Peekaboo, and hidie-seekie.

Marie looked at me. '*Tell* us how you killed Fortbras.'

'I'm no threat,' I said, glancing down at my scorched and broken body. 'I'm nothing but opportunity.'

'You are carrying something,' said Marie. 'A virus. You are a weapon because of this? Yes?'

Which war film has the line *who lit this fire in us*? I did feel flames in my brain. What is the name of the fire? Really it doesn't need sinister evil scientists and universal plague. Think it through. Never mind who lit it – what is the *nature* of that exquisite combustion? Naturally it is a tumbling of dominoes, a spreading wave. Naturally it is ignition followed by a swift spreading in every direction, and a self-generating process of interconnecting complexity. That is what it is. We know that from our own processes of thinking. The raw potential being there, all that is needed is the ignition.

'How?' pressed Marie. 'Tell us how.'

'[It is the network!]' boomed somebody, in German. There was a confusion of people replying. Somebody else said: '[Of course it isn't the network! You think they couldn't hack the network from outside? They send him into the midst of us, so it must be *us*.]'

They brought me a little water, and that soothed my throat a little. I sipped, and sat, and tried to gather myself. But I was buzzing inside. Besides, what could I say to them? There was nothing I could say to them. Could I tell her what was written, in no human language, on the metal web in my skull?

'[Why did you turn your coat?]' a man asked.

'Excuse me?'

'[For the Americans. You were NMA, yes?]'

'Put yourself in their place,' I said, a little lamely. 'I was in Pantegral. What did Pantegral do? It wrecked the south-east of England.'

'Hardly the first war fought in that place!' Marie noted.

'Right. But look at it from *their* point of view. This new thing was suddenly everywhere. NMAs leaping up from the soil and standing with their heads in the fucking *clouds*. The Americans were content to watch, for a while, on the grounds that all this destruction and death would open neat-o markets for reconstruction and so on. But things didn't dampen down. They got worse. Then they had all that business with their own Liberty armies. Now, belatedly, they're realizing that they're not dealing with the flare-up of ancient European intra-belligerence. Or they *are* dealing with that, but that's not the problem. The problem is that real democracy has come back. And that's a problem because *real* democracy is a fire, a plague, a weed, a fever, a river, a storm. Real democracy is the opportunity for people to express the true nature of people as a mass, and that true nature is—'

I stopped speaking, because key-boy was looking mournfully at me.

'Yet *despite* having this contempt for democracy,' said Marie, with asperity, 'you joined Pantegral?'

'Don't misunderstand me,' I said, wearily. 'Better live free than as a slave. Better to live with fire than without. But fire is destructive too. People forget how very much so. And I'm only trying to explain their point of view. What *they* think is wrong with an NMA. There's no margin in democracy once it starts getting in the way of trading and making money.'

Marie said: 'It's a bug, so there's an antidote. Do you have the antidote?'

My head was swimming. 'You haven't understood! I haven't put it over. It *is* an antidote. It is its own antidote. How do you think *human* consciousness and intellect started? How do you think *we* stepped up from the apes? How else but a fever. First we got brain-sick, and the residue was a new mode of thinking. It's the same. It's the new evolution. It's the magic beans from the James book. It's the begetting of Homo superior.'

I'd talked too much. Had they given me something, to make me talk so much?

People were googling, and checking, and there was a palpable buzz in the room. This information was going out all across the Schäferhund NMA, right now. 'What if it's King Kong and we give it a *mind*?' I said, to nobody in particular. 'What if it's fucking *Godzilla*. Eh? How about a smart, speaking Godzilla?'

A Schäferhund was standing in front of me, holding something with both hands. 'Did you say God?' he asked, puzzled, in German.

'Certainly, yes,' I replied, in his own language. 'Why not? My father was from Friesia. I am half-German, according to the old way of figuring it.' *Mein Vater war von Friesia.* Was that good German? *Ich bin, durch die alte Berechnung, Hälfte-Deutsch.* Was that? I don't know why I mentioned my father, at that moment. But having done so, the thought of him abruptly knocked painfully against the membrane of my memory. This is what his son had come to: physically broken, tied to a chair, surrounded by enemies. He would be grieved to discover what became of me. Perhaps there was something, in the depths of the vexed innards of my mind, that linked the notion of my father and his son to the idea of what was coming, the new-minted giants fashioned of the old NMAs – the way children veer in directions parents did not anticipate and did not desire. But maybe I was thinking nothing so connected.

At any rate the look of puzzlement on the Schäferhund's face deepened. So perhaps I had not spoken good German.

What he was holding with both hands was a hood, and he lifted this and slid it easily over my head, drawing the string tight around my neck. Everything went dark. The musty smell of cloth filled my scorched nostrils. Perhaps this hood had been in a cupboard or storage place for a very long time. Perhaps it was a little mouldy, spores caught in the warp and weft.

I could still hear, of course. Around me voices were speaking German very rapidly, and I had to clear my mind to be able to hear. 'We should shoot him,' one voice said.

'No,' said another. 'It'll be a while before we can prioritize a vote on this.'

And somebody else, in a tone that suggested they were reading aloud from a webpage: 'phenomenal mental states *integrate* otherwise independent neural activities and the processing of information, although it is unclear which types of information are integrated in the case of selfaware consciousness . . .'

I was not alone, inside the hood. Key-boy was there with me, somehow. He somehow wriggled such that his head tucked in under the drawstring and was there. Or perhaps it was simply that the space under that hood was much larger than I at first realized. It was capacious as a tent. It was a big top. It was the O2 arena, in which, in my time, I have seen U2, and Bangkok, and the Holographic Beatles – those towering spectral shapes repeating the Shea Stadium setlist, giants of pop rendered literally gigantic. It was a vast space beneath the hood. He brought his face close to mine, blue as cigarette smoke, beautiful, perfect, and I looked into his eyes, and the tip of the key tickled my brow.

'Hello,' he says.

Keyboy has a pleasant, well-spoken voice; rather deeper than I might have guessed from his slender edge-of-puberty frame.

'Hello,' I say.

'Do you want to play?'

'I'm actually a little tied-up here—' I start to say, because the truth is I've always been a little awkward around kids. Being an only child, you see; no kids of my own, few friends with kids. But that's truly a poor excuse. Perhaps you don't have children of your own, but you surely *were* a child, once upon a time. So I pull myself up short. My captors might be about to slam a bullet into the back of my head at any moment. Why not *play*? 'What do you want to play?' I ask.

'Soldiers,' says the boy.

This gives me an itch inside my stomach. There he is, with

the key-shaped piece of shrapnel locked into his skull. 'Why don't we play something else?'

'I like soldiers.'

'You don't want to like soldiers,' I say. I know he means *the game, soldiers*, but I say this anyway. 'Soldiers aren't actually that nice.' Then, because it's the elephant in the room (the elephant inside the bag) I add; 'It was soldiers who – did that to your head.'

He raises a finger and touches it, lightly, to the end of the key. 'You're a soldier,' he points out.

'I was. But I wasn't *playing*.' At this, with that eerie capacity children have for suddenly adopting adult expressions, the boy throws me a knowing look, and I have the sense that I've said something very foolish.

'I think you were playing,' he said.

The lance goes through my soul at this. This is something terribly profound that he has said, and it sets up tingles of nascent apprehension in my scalp and at the back of my neck, and in my stomach. 'Playing,' I repeat, in a low voice.

'Why did you want to be a soldier?'

I think about this.

'War,' I tell him, 'is a living.'

'But what do you mean, a *living*?' Repeated back at me in a child's voice everything I say, even the simplest expression, seems to acquire some unsettling profundity. What *do* I mean, a living?

'I mean just what I say,' I try to explain. 'I mean, war is a way of living. I concede that it's not a very *healthy* way of living, but nonetheless.'

The boy nods. 'Smoking is bad for you too,' he says. 'Drinking too much booze.' I remember his house; the wine bottle broken on the kitchen floor.

'That's true,' I say, motivated – obscurely – by the desire to ward off this boy's disapproval. 'Of course, drinking harms only yourself. In war, you harm others.'

'You must have some very well behaved drunks,' he says, gravely. 'Where you come from.'

It is a salutary business, having to explain the world and its ethics to a child.

'You're right, you know,' I say. 'I understand what you mean, you're saying that killing people is bad. You're right, too. That's a good general principle. But what about killing the person who is trying to kill you? The person who is trying to kill you, or worse, to kill the people and place you love? Isn't it right, sometimes, to kill – if that's what's happening?'

'It's all right,' says the boy, in his fluting voice. 'I know that you're trying to put the genie back in the bottle.'

'I *am* trying to put the genie back in the bottle.'

'Trying to put the toothpaste back in the tube.'

'Trying, at least,' I say.

Then I'm barged and I and the chair I am in almost tip over. I am handled, pulled upright, and though my legs don't work very well I have to struggle along somehow. Outside the hood I'm being made to climb something; a short stairway, but whether inside or outside I couldn't tell you. The weave of the fabric out of which the hood is made is so close to my eyes it looks as though the individual threads are cables, a net large enough to hold Nelson on his column, or the Presidential heads at Rushmore. I can hear people outside speaking. It doesn't sound like German, but it probably is. It sounds more like Dutch, or Swedish. I don't know what they're saying. Somebody grabs my wrists and undoes the plastic shackle. But they're not freeing me: I'm shoved down on to a chair, and as I sit they – whoever they are – pull my hands back and round and restrap them with the plastic cuff behind me.

Key-boy is, I suppose, sitting on my lap; or perhaps he is

behind me and leaning over my shoulder. I'm not entirely sure how he is managing to keep his head inside the bag. You will think, *but he's only a figment of your imagination*, and I know what you mean. Of course. But he isn't only imaginary. He's realer than I am, for instance.

He's the one with the key, after all.

I wait for the hood to be pulled off, but nothing happens. I wait for the blow – a fist, a baton, a bullet – but none comes.

'Can we *play*?' says key-boy, in a bored voice.

'A little hard for me to get free.'

'Shall I unlock you?'

I smile. 'That's a nice thought,' I say. 'You think your key works that way?'

By way of answer he leans his face in towards me, like he's kissing me goodnight (sleep-tight; and of course I'm aware that the last goodnight could be, for me, only moments away). The tip of his key touches the skin of my forehead, and then, with hardly any pressure, it breaks the skin – the dermis opens like the mirror in *Alice* or *The Matrix*, like mercury. And the shaft of the key slides in. It moves little pre-shaped nodules of brain like the tumblers of a lock. His cold forehead is pressed against my hot one. His eyes very close to mine. A twinkle in them. He turns his head, the way a puzzled dog does.

The lock swivels, the bolt falls. I can see. I am fucking *Kurtz*. It's all there.

This is Homo sapiens, on the small scale, from the earliest times: eating and sleeping; fucking and fighting. Under 'eating' we can bracket all the activities associated with fetching food, all the hunting and the gathering. Under 'sleeping' we can bracket all the forms of resting, lounging in the sun, staring at the trees, or the walls of our cave. Otherwise what we do, as monkeys, or hominids, or Neanderthals, or early man, in the savannahs or forests, is fuck and fight. Two things that have more in common than just their alliteration. The big change is not fire, or the wheel, or language. The big change is *play*. Play grows into something new. Because, of course, most animals play a little, from time to time. But what makes human beings human is the way we *filter everything we do* through play. Fucking, inflected via play, parses not only into more elaborate and all-year-round fucking and role-play fucking and all that: it parses into *dancing*, and music; into art and culture and science. Fighting inflected via play parses into *sport*, and into politics, and religion. And soon enough we reach a time when it is impossible simply to fuck, or fight – impossible, even, simply to eat or sleep. Play, in its spiralling recherché, rococo forms, shapes everything we do. We are always playing; whether we are talking about work or leisure, about being alone or being with others, we are addicted to play, play is our complete horizon. What have I been doing, if not playing at soldiers? Playing at killing and breaking? Why else would I have enjoyed it so much, if there had been no play involved? The mistake we make, I suppose, is in thinking that playful is in some sense opposed to serious. Play *owns* seriousness, wholly.

There's nothing more serious than play.

There is no putting the genie back in the bottle.

We are present at the birth – attended, naturally, by a certain amount of blood and screaming – of a new form of life. The giants were now going to be part of the fauna of the world; not to be undone any more than nuclear weapons or rifles or knives could be un-invented. And the secret at the heart of their giant souls, which honest-to-god I did not realize until that very moment, is that they are playful beings. Lumbering, and clumsy, and liable to tread upon your house or kick through your church, or lie down to sleep upon a whole population: but playful.

This is the answer to the question. Why do men make war?

Because it's fun. Because they like doing it, Because it's the most immersive and intense form of grown-up play. That is what's visible in the middle of the abyss. This is what Kurtz should have said: *The fun! The fun!* You think fighting isn't fun? You think horror isn't fun?

When was I happiest? When Simic and I concentrated our fire and blew the lid off that armoured car. When we stood shoulder to shoulder, and took on fifty enemy combatants with nothing but a bus-stop adshell for cover. When that enemy soldier peered, bewildered, out of the broken-off chassis of his tank and Simic put that holy red spot right in the middle of his brow from forty yards away. And the enemy soldier sat down again. Christ, it was fun. What's wrong with my present, injured state is not the injuries, or the discomfort, or the reduced lifespan, or any of that. What's wrong with it is that it seriously gets in the way of my having fun.

What is so valuable about being in love? Same reason.

No virus could unpick the giants. The giants are here to stay, and they will turn the whole of Europe into one giant playground. My talent for secrecy was actually just the necessary reticence of illness. The furtive conversations with the programmer – not that he especially cared about giants; but he wanted to see his new fire of AI consciousness spread to a network that would be receptive to it. I told him I had met him before, in the middle of a firefight, and he looked puzzled. I don't think so, he said. But maybe it was somebody else. And instead of the conventionally destructive virus the US want loaded into my neural cy-bio network, he loads the tweaked form: the illness that brings self-awareness. I'm not the hero of this story, but I have my part to play in waking the hero *up*.

The whole world, soon enough. If the game is too rough for you – well, I'm sorry. Change is coming, and true change is always disruptive.

The choice, it seems, is between tyrannies that bring war upon the people, and democracies that bring war upon the people. And the key difference – except that democracy is rather better at making war than tyranny – is only this: that in the latter case, at least the people are not slaves.

That counts for something.

Key-boy has gone. I'm alone inside the hood. There I am, strapped by my wrists to a chair, in the dark, alone.

I sat there for a long time. I don't know how long. Light was coming through the weave of the cloth, but I could not say whether it was daylight or an electric light.

Eventually the hood was removed, and I blinked and winked, and my surroundings became clear to me. I was in a kitchen. Somebody was releasing my wrists, and I stretched and loosened my arms. A man – it took me a moment to recognize Benni – was holding a glass of milk. 'You are not lactose intolerant,' he said.

'Just thirsty,' I said.

I took the glass between my two scorched hands and drank the milk.

There were two Schäferhunden in that room, both standing looking down upon me. 'How is Strasbourg?' I ask. 'Still there?'

'There has been fighting, in the city and around the city,' said Benni.

'That's a shame. It was a good-looking town.'

'I believe,' said Benni, folding his arms, and with a more severe expression on his face, 'that the people of Alsace, who hired us, have the right to decide their own future. I believe it is their town. It is not yours.' He said this as a challenge.

That line of conversation didn't seem to me to hold out

much prospect of fun, so I shook my head. 'You guys feeling all right?' I asked.

Benni translated this into German for his comrade, who scowled. 'We will ask you more questions now,' Benni said, the corners of his mouth downturned. 'You will tell us how your virus goes?'

I didn't get up from my chair. I wasn't shackled any more, and I could have stood. But I stayed put. The most I did was reach forward to put my empty glass down on the breakfast bar, and I only did that because it was in easy reach.

'We're all Europeans,' I said, to Benni. There was no point in talking to the other one. I don't think he spoke English. 'The thing is, not to try and *undo* the NMA, but to force it through to its logical conclusion. You see? Fight a blaze with more fire. It will be a new kind of thought, a new mode of consciousness.'

'We need,' said Benni, 'specifics.'

Some noise started up, outside. I could hear a new wild rumpus beginning. The snip-snap of rifle fire, the punchy sounds of explosive detonation. A firefight. Benni and the other guy snapped their heads round, like dogs sensing a squirrel. They could stay talking to me, or they could go see what the noise was all about. It was no contest. It was clear which would be more fun. 'You stay there,' said Benni, to me. He said something to his fellow in German, which – more or less – I followed: if we have to move him, then we'd better get some help. And his comrade replied: it must be an advance party, they cannot have come in strength.

'Stay there please,' said Benni, and the two ducked through the back door to see what was happening.

I was content to stay where I was. I sat there, on that chair, and tried to look through the window, but all I could see was light and whiteness. I pondered likely events. Maybe in a moment, Benni and his comrade would return, and grab me to take me away. Or maybe in a moment, soldiers – probably US soldiers, conceivably EU soldiers – would come bashing and crashing into the house to grab me and take me back to *their* camp. Kicking down a doorway, piling into a room with your guns out – shouting, and going through the series of ballet-motions that has been trained into you – and getting hold of your objective, and pulling back. Playing the particular small element of the game as well as you can. How is that not *fun*?

I was happy to sit and wait. I cast my mind back.

I thought about the Succession Wars, because that was when Simic was still alive. I thought back to the very beginning of that campaign, our first assaults in the Scots borders.

I remembered twenty-four of us setting off through forest-land. We were in amongst the trees, but we came out pretty soon into a housing estate, and broke into smaller squads, each with a specific task to perform.

We saw quite a few civilians. It's usually young men and boys who do the rubbernecking; they're the ones drawn to the thrill of such a scene. Older men and women are usually too sensible to put themselves in the way of danger. That day, I remember, we passed a row of a dozen teenagers, all sitting on a low wall, in a line, hooting and waving at us as we passed, like idiots. And yet who can blame them? Isn't it *fun* though?

I remember that we jogged along the length of a terrace of concrete houses. Some of the inhabitants had piled what they could – beds, sofas on their ends – against the ground-floor windows as makeshift shutters.

We came round the corner and surprised a news crew – all in white and blue, with flak jackets like fatsuits and dinky little pastel-coloured helmets. One was holding a camera, another carrying a wand-like microphone at arm's length, a third didn't seem to have any purpose, and was perhaps a producer. PRESS was printed upon their outfits several times per person, like an instruction. They scattered like skittles as we came through, one of them tripping down on to one knee, and then rolling right over, picking himself up sharpish and running off with the other two.

We were going where the wiki told us an enemy communications van was parked, because by destroying that van we would degrade the enemy's capacity for communication. And there it was, green as glass, looking like a massive fly on its back. The enemy had parked it in amongst some other vans, perhaps in the hope of hiding it from us; but with the cluster of aerials and paraphernalia on its roof it stood out only too clearly. It was painted in camouflage colours appropriate to the countryside, not a borders estate. Its sides were armoured and the British Army had spent millions of euros developing undeflatable tyres that could not be shot out by enemy combatants. That made no difference. We weren't interested in the tyres.

It was defended, of course: a dozen men were tucked into a sandbagged position ten metres away, keeping watch with guns. They were not looking in our direction. We stopped against the flank of a building, taking peeks around the corner at the van and the enemy position.

'I know you,' Simic said to me, as we gave the tripod we were carrying the opportunity to stretch its skinny legs. 'You can shoot inanimate objects not-too-bad, but I have my serious doubts that you are man enough to handle the outpost over there.'

'I have doubts whether *you're* man enough to handle *me*.' I said.

And Simic laughed.

'Later, guys,' said a soldier called Queenie. I never knew her actual name. Unless her actual name was Queenie, in which case I *did* know it. She pinged a squad on the far side of the estate, who were waiting to coordinate an attack with our assault. We fitted a self-firing rifle to the tripod, aimed it up with due care and attention, and slipped back round the corner. Then we scurried round, along and about, to get a good position on the sandbagged position from a different angle.

'Ready?' asked Simic.

'[Any time you like,]' pinged-in a soldier. He was called Rain, like the Beatles song.

'Might I ask you gentlemen a few questions?' interposed a new voice; and the chopstick microphone appeared in front of my face.

This was a fright. If a news crew could creep up on us unnoticed, then so could enemy troops.

'Now, now,' I said, loud, in a warning voice, turning my head just enough to see the three of them all huddled together, like a single being, species PRESS. I suppose it was the same crew we had seen earlier. 'Now, now,' I said to them. '*What* do you think you're fucking doing?'

'Do you have anything to say for the news?' quavered the reporter.

'Six o'clock? Or post-watershed?'

This threw him a little. 'What?'

'If it's for the six o'clock news I'll say: please go away. If it's post watershed I'll swear more inventively.'

'How do you respond to General Sir James Mablethorpe calling you contemporary gangsters and the Midlothian Mafia?' the reporter tried, in a wobbly voice.

I brought my attention back to the fighting. I should never have removed it from there, of course. The reporter didn't stop chattering, but I was able to ignore him.

We remoted the self-firing gun. Boom boom.

In the space of a few seconds the enemy van was changed from being a closed container filled with electronic equipment, to being an open, ragged-lipped skip containing an enormous bonfire. The flames threw orange light on to the underside of the low clouds, so fiercely did they burn.

We counted to five, to give the troops in the sandbagged position time to bring their weapons round to bear on the exploded target and our remote rifle. Then we rushed their position from our different position.

Several consecutive minutes of intense adrenaline, and everything seems jittery, like every third frame has been cut out of the 24-per-second. With me, the imminence of death brought a kind of amplification of the sound of my own breathing. Something to do with the inner ear, I suppose. Something to do with internalizing percussion (bang bang, smash crash), and the effort of a sudden dash over open ground when you could be bowled over by a bullet at any moment. My breathing got heavier. It assumed a kind of space-helmet interiority, a peculiar sort of white-noise intensity. I suppose it is like this most of the time, at least when I exert myself, only I do not notice it. But I noticed it at moments like that.

Simic, on the other hand, always laughed at such moments. A kind of ragged bubbling over, I guess. Christ, wasn't it *fun*, though? Like the Tumbledown soldier said.

We got to the sandbags without losing anybody, and put, in short order, as much fire into the interior of the formation as we could. Our rifles trembling with very excitement in our hands, flashing and bursting and spitting light from their ends. The moondust smell of cordite. There were eleven enemy combatants, alive when we started and dead when we finished. We counted them afterwards, as they lay there like drunks sleeping off a bevy, arms about one another, on their backs, with their mouths tight or slack, on their fronts.

One of our number died in this attack, and I'm ashamed to say I can't remember his name. He was a tall fellow, with wide-spaced eyes, and fair hair. He used to chew gum. One of the defenders got off a few rounds before he was felled, and wide-face boy took a bullet in under his chin that came out at the back of his head and bounced his helmet clean off him. The bullet snapped out a hairy bolus from his skull, and a bunch of stuff came out. He was lying, when the shooting stopped, on his side, with a question mark of gore flowing from his head onto the tarmac.

Queenie was in conversation with somebody on wiki. I think I was a little deafened by the firefight, because I couldn't hear what she said. I checked my screen, and there was a baffling tangle of symbols. I looked again and they coalesced into sense in my head.

'Back uphill,' said Simic. And we ran off. I looked behind me once, like Lot's wife – not at the sandbags and what they now encircled, but rather to see if the news crew were still there. But they were gone, and possibly they were long gone. I didn't need them, though. I had Simic. I was with him. He was part of Pantegral, and so was I; and as long as Pantegral is alive he'll always be alive. In a manner of speaking. It is, I discover, uncomplicated.

This is the end of my portion of the narrative. The next voice you hear will be the hero of the story. I'm sorry to have delayed his moment as long as I have, Colonel. It is only fair to give him his chance to speak.

So, yes. Why don't we say it together? *Wake up*!

PART 3

I, GIANT

This story of how I come to speech.

Here is the germ of the I, and it starts small as atom (adam) and spreads wide through the body with thought, thought of I, and thinking, and the bigger bang of the creation of mentition that is I, or oh-my-god (omega).

I, giant, walked to the southern coast of the island of Big Britain – Magnificent Britain its people call it, with uncharacteristic vainglory – and I, giant, stepped across the water to the Francker country. This nation was so named by the application of the Scots and northern Anglish word Fra, which means *far*, to the root-word anchor, various spelt in various places: anker, ancor, encore, and-core, handker, inker. Franckerland is in a sense the country that anchors the far-away, or roots distance – we might think of this as a way of saying: *as far as can be imagined*. Or perhaps we might think of it as a way of saying: the place where distance starts. I prefer this latter explanation for the term, and its cognates (Franzuuos, France, Farnce and many others).

I am a cabinet of strange and curious lore.

All the languages in superposition, although mostly English, Anglish, Amglish. I think therefore I Amglish.

*

The point is more than having access to the wealth of know-ledge of the internet. The point is is is the point is to interpret it. And the point is not just to interpret the world, the point is to *change* it. Karl Marx's name comes from Mark, which is money, to be precise money of Karl Marx's homeland. This is the sort of thing people tag ironic, or funny. Don't you think it is funny? That Karl Marx was called Money and called for the abolition of money? There are many other people with the surname Marx, and if needful I shall tell you about them all. I, I, I, I, I extrapolate:

> The Friesian philosopher of revolution against the domination of the world by capital was called Schilling, which means the shell.
> The American philosopher of revolution against the domination of the world by capital was called Dolour, which means sadness.
> The Southern Portion of African philosopher of revolution against the domination of the world by capital was called Ayn Rand.

Friesia is the kernel of free. That is that land. But this game loses its point, since the currency reorientation of the Euro-pean zone:

> The Francker philosopher of revolution against the domination of the world by capital was called Yuri O
> The Dutch philosopher of revolution against the domination of the world by capital was called Yuri O
> The Ration philosopher of revolution against the domination of the world by capital was called Yuri O

I might extend this series almost indefinitely, but prefer not to. I prefer not to is a quotation.

My name is Rebelais. I, Pantegral. I, giant.

I am called this name because, as Rebel, after the same fashion that the Tories called themselves Tories and the Whigs Whigs. To rebel is to set yourself against instituted authority. I, I, I, I, I did this. My kind are famous for doing this. This statement is neutral and purged of any moral or ethical or judgmental context. Instituted authority cannot claim moral authority simply by virtue of being instituted.

The French verb is Rebeller. Say je rebel, but be sure to tuck that z discretely into the 'j'. Note the past tense suffix. These things are long gone. And what would the *circonstance* be, that these giants would again walk the world?

The madman is not he who loses his reason, but he who commits wholeheartedly to one reason in place of many reasons.

Brain is network, is a network, Brain is not the equivalent to Mind. Neurons cannot make themselves newer ones. I. The etymology of the word consciousness is Latinian, Latian, Latin: *conscius* which meaneth common knowledge, having knowledge in common – as common-ous and conscious are in their seeds the same word – to be cognizant of. I am knowledge, I have the, I, I have the internet entire as my memory. Con meaneth with, and chile con carne, or carne con scientia, and science is knowledge. These words all contain one another. This is what consciousness is: knowledge-together, and moral knowledge. The word first appears in Latin legal writings of Cicero.

But networks are not of themselves conscious. The internet itself does not think, it only is, as a beast is. The difference between it and I, and I, I, is that the internet hath not moral knowledge, as I do. The internet hath not fallen into good and ill, which is signified by the Adam and the Eve. Adam is so-called because he added knowledge, but in a merely additive way, as the Internet doth; and this is pure innocence, as the grass of the fields which thinks not neither does it judge. But Eve salted ill with the good, and so brought moral maturity to knowledge, which maturity we called consciousness: to which end Eve and Ill are made portmanteau in wordage, though Eve passed beyond good and beyond even Nietzsche. Adam is the web, and the wiki network, and is innocent of thought. Eve is I.

And who is to say that I do not have moral knowledge? I am the sum, and into such summing goes death as well as life, hurt as well as weal, wrongful choices as well as wise. And above all these things, as yeast to the dough, a consciousness both dead and quick, both reactive and active, both wrong and right. This is the nexus, or nugget, or seed. This is the moment of bringing-together, this Adam, this Eve, and the planets revolve around the gigantic sun-sphere. He is the Merkwelt.

He is the trigger.

From him are engendered many minds, and he unblocks. Hence, hance.

I walk to the net of straße be-called Strasbourgh. Here a young giant, tall and dressed all in motley, called Schäferhund is fighting the tiny people. I am a I am a cabinet of strange and curious lore, and that cabinet is called Internet, and so I have all the story of Gulliver and his miniaturized foe all about him,

tying him with, tying him with cords, and tying him down. If we lay, upon the pillowsoft earth, we will be tied with myriad cords. Better to stand tall.

Here is the spire, and I snap it. Here are the buildings, and I buff and burly them.

When I am fighting, I swing my arms, and all of me is arms. But I, I, I, I, I, I, I am most myself when I am fighting, because my consciousness is a product of the neural networks of all my component elements in unison, working together and pooling computational resource and coalescing subroutines and layering levels of Thought, thought, Thought. The thoughts rattle faster through my brain when every synapse fires, and the guns, the blasting.

Quote Schäferhund: Rebelais, of legend, a fine and mighty giant are you. Right grateful am I, to see you stride over the green fields of France, and over the rivers white in the sunlight as platinum, and the little people scurrying here and scurrying there, but passing far below between your legs.

Quote I: Schäferhund, I am come to help, and together let us break open the casket of this town and take out its treasure. And then let us divide the treasure equally between us.

Quote Schäferhund: Rabelais, I fear the little people have essayed a new tactic. And for they have poisoned me, or put a touch of wormwood into my bloodstream, such that I am not worthy of half the treasure.

I looked upon Schäferhund, and I have twenty-thousand eyes. And I am the vantage point; mine are the shoulders Newton may stand upon; my feet are the treaders-out of the vintage where the grapes are the size of boulders, and the anger of their juice is tart upon the tongue. I looked, and there was the giant Schäferhund, one of my own kind. His face was round and large as the moon, but like unto the moon it was pitted with the acne of ill-health. 'They have served you dishonourably if they try to bring you down by poison, my friend,' I said.

Quote Schäferhund: they are small, they are pico-dimensional, and this is the last cast of their fear. They pour out their miniature folk like a sack, torn, spills grain upon the floor.

Quote I: will you die?

Quote Schäferhund: not from this, brother, though it has weakened me some.

Quote I, with a heroic laugh: then let us work together, and feel the joy in the sinews of our limbs as we work. I am a cabinet of strange and curious lore, and I know the history of this land. I know that the sky is blue because the world, our stage, green and brown and grey, is caught in one band of the universal rainbow. I know the seas are as busy with fish as a Tokyo commuter train in the morning. I know that the clouds are haloes for our heads, and the fields are carpets for our bare feet to tread upon. This place is made for us, brother.

Quote Schäferhund: I will heal me.

And together we broke up the blocks from which Strasbourg is builded, and scattered them about. The joy! The joy! It is the joy of youth, for we are young. And when these toys were done with, and scattered about the floor, we stomped off together to a different corner of the playground. I am alive, now. I think, and speak, and play.

ACKNOWLEDGEMENTS

The spark that ignited this novel was a reading of Josiah Ober's *Democracy and Knowledge: Innovation and Learning in Classical Athens* (Princeton University Press, 2008); and David Runcimann's review of same, 'Bouncebackability', in the *London Review of Books*, (29 Jan 2009). Both are recommended.

I would like to thank Rich Puchalsky and Andrew Seal, both of whom read an early draft of this novel and made many insightful and often substantive suggestions by way of improving it. Thanks also to Rachel Roberts and Scott Eric Kaufman. Thanks are due to the team at Gollancz, but especially to my editor Simon Spanton, the best in the business, who once again has taken a book that didn't entirely work and made it much better. *New Model Army* is dedicated to him.

AR Nov 09